TOO TEMPTING TO RESIST

Lily came with him willingly, when she should have been bolting in the other direction. When Alex faced her under the tree, he understood why. He recognized the longing in her eyes, the emotion that made her lips tremble. Her innate sensuality coupled with her physical beauty intoxicated him. He'd never imagined a woman so perfectly built for love.

"If you're concerned with your reputation, as you should be, you ought to leave this instant." Despite the harsh truth of his words, his voice vibrated with passion.

"I am concerned, of course," she murmured. "But I'm also where I want to be."

With him. She didn't have to elaborate.

Sliding his hands along her satiny arms, he lowered his lips to hers. She couldn't miss his intention. Yet rather than move away, she lifted her face to his in anticipation.

Still he delayed the moment, gave her yet one more opportunity to say no. "Have you ever been kissed by a man?"

She gazed up at him, unblinking, for a long heartbeat. Then, to his shocked delight, she slipped her hand along the back of his head, making his nape tingle with pleasure.

"Not until now," she breathed . . .

Dear Romance Reader,

In July of 1999, we launched the Ballad line with four new series, and each month we present both new and continuing stories set everywhere from medieval England to the American West—the kind of passionate, romantic stories you love best, written by the most gifted authors. At the back of each book, we tell you when you can find subsequent books in the series that have captured your heart.

This month, rising star Cheryl Bolen offers the third installment of her atmospheric *Brides of Bath* series. What will happen when a man driven by honor loses his heart to **A Fallen Woman**? Next, the always talented Tracy Cozzens explores **A Dangerous Fancy** in the next entry of her *American Heiresses* series as a proper young woman, who has caught the eye of the Prince of Wales himself, discovers that a roguish nobleman might be her unlikely savior—and the kind of man who could win her love.

The fabulous Pat Pritchard continues her *Gamblers* series with the second of her incredibly sexy heroes. A U.S. Marshal posing as a hardened card player has no time for romance—until he meets a woman who makes him feel like the **King of Hearts.** Finally, promising newcomer Kate Silver whisks us back to the glittering French court of Louis XIV in her brand-new series . . . *And One for All*. When a Musketeer in the King's Guard learns that his comrade may not be all "he" seems, he must promise to keep her secret, **On My Lady's Honor**—unless passion sweeps them both away. Enjoy!

Kate Duffy
Editorial Director

American Heiresses

A DANGEROUS FANCY

Tracy Cozzens

ZEBRA BOOKS
Kensington Publishing Corp.
http://www.kensingtonbooks.com

ZEBRA BOOKS are published by

Kensington Publishing Corp.
850 Third Avenue
New York, NY 10022

All Kensington titles, imprints and distributed lines are available at special quantity discounts for bulk purchases for sales promotion, premiums, fund-raising, educational or institutional use.

Special book excerpts or customized printings can also be created to fit specific needs. For details, write or phone the office of the Kensington Special Sales Manager: Kensington Publishing Corp., 850 Third Avenue, New York, NY 10022. Attn. Special Sales Department. Phone: 1-800-221-2647.

Zebra and the Z logo Reg. U.S. Pat. & TM Off.

First Printing: August 2002
10 9 8 7 6 5 4 3 2 1

Printed in the United States of America

One

"How can a man enjoy a young lady's charms without ruining her reputation?"

Prince Edward's voice instantly made Alexander Drake feel he'd returned home. As he entered the private room, a servant closed the door behind him, then locked it.

He gazed about the mahogany-paneled interior, breathing in the almost forgotten scents of cigar and pipe smoke blended with a hint of opium and fine port. In the right half of the room, several gentlemen gambled over faro. Before him, a half-dozen men encircled a marble-topped table presided over by the Prince of Wales.

Nearby, Richard Walford, the duke of Inderby, reclined on a chaise longue by the fireplace, his lanky frame cradled by silken pillows. He puffed desultorily on his bubbling opium hookah, his dark eyes half closed in pleasure. His sallow face contrasted starkly with his black pencil-thin moustache and slicked-back hair.

Everything is the same, as if no time at all has passed. Alex took satisfaction from that thought. He had every intention of enjoying a life of pleasure during his London stay. After all, he had no idea how long he'd remain in the world's most sophisticated city. At any time, the queen and her advisers could send him to yet another distant land to gather intelligence.

Only a handful of gentlemen, embodying London's most elite society, ever set foot in the back room of the Marlborough Club. Here, away from prying eyes, the men engaged in honest discussion about politics, business, and world affairs. They also engaged in dishonest vices, such as gambling and imbibing forbidden substances. No women were allowed; but exploits involving women were a primary fascination, encouraged by the prince's own recreational pursuits.

Alex was the only man present without a title, but his service to the Crown and Prince Edward's favor gave him easy access to the prince's inner circle.

Leaning back in his Louis the Sixteenth chair, the prince noticed him standing near the door. "Alexander Drake! Welcome back. When did you return to our glorious homeland?" He waved to the chair beside his. Taking the hint, Baron von Fusterburg vacated it without question or hesitation.

Alex strode over and sat down. "Yesterday, Your Royal Highness. It's good to be home, for a while at least."

The prince dismissed his comment with a wave. "No need for formalities here, Drake. You know that."

Alex chuckled. "Too long mingling with diplomats, I fear. Hello again, John." He nodded to his longtime friend, Lord Jonathan Moseby, who sat across from the prince. He'd shared dinner with the young marquess a few hours ago and managed to catch up on some of the gossip. During his stay in Baghdad, reports he'd received from London had focused on politics and economics, enabling him to work to protect Britain's commercial interests in the war-torn land. But he had no idea who was in town for the Season, who had gone bankrupt or made a fortune, who had seduced whom.

Tonight, in the company of these good gentlemen, he'd rectify that.

He greeted each of the men in turn, then leaned back and locked his fingers across his stomach.

To Alex's eye, Bertie, as his friends called him, appeared even more corpulent than when he last saw him. Apparently the forty-eight-year-old prince still indulged in ten-course meals five times a day. The cigar tucked between his fingers was probably his twelfth of the day. And, yet again, the prince was obsessed with a lady not his wife.

Bertie stroked his beard, which Alex noticed was now touched with gray. "You've arrived just in time, Drake. I've posed a question, and I have yet to hear an adequate answer." He looked around at those gathered. "I ask again: How can a man enjoy a debutante's charms without destroying her prospects?"

"Well, if no one finds out, have you truly ruined it?" Moseby asked.

The prince considered a moment, then shook his head. "No. Far too risky. People are bound to find out. My movements are difficult to keep secret."

So the prince wasn't posing a hypothetical question after all. He had his eye on some woman—again. He had no compunction about dallying with other men's wives. When Alex was last in London, Bertie had been recovering from a scandal involving Lady Blandford.

Apparently, this time the woman was unmarried, inexperienced, and virginal, which posed a near insurmountable obstacle for the romantically inclined prince. His reputation would never survive if he seduced a chit barely out of the schoolroom. "Are you sharing who this young lady is?" Alex asked.

"Certainly. She's Miss Lily Carrington, from the United States. The most gorgeous creature ever to grace London society with her presence. Ever since I saw her riding in the Row, I decided she must be mine." Rotten Row was an oddly named area of Hyde Park where the social elite drove their open-air broughams for the sole purpose of seeing and being seen.

"I'm not familiar with her," Alex said. Not surprising, considering he'd been out of the country for more than a year.

"More pity you," said Moseby. "You must get up to speed as soon as possible, Drake, or you'll be quite useless in our intrigues."

Alex found this particular intrigue only mildly interesting. "Well, then, find her a husband," he said with a shrug. "If she's as lovely as you say, that can't be too difficult to accomplish."

"Ah, there's the rub!" The prince held up a sausage-shaped finger. "I am not keen on sharing this spirited jewel, not even with a husband. Ah, certainly most American girls are delightful—lively, flirtatious, good card players, good storytellers, and they wear the most stylish frocks. But Miss Lily Carrington . . ." His voice softened. "She's of another world."

"I don't know what all the fuss is about. One woman is certainly as good as another." The duke's dry voice drifted over along with smoke from his hookah.

Alex agreed with the duke, but hardly for the same reason. To him, each woman had unique appeal, be it the way she arched her neck, the curve of her soft bottom, the grace of her hands, the flush of her skin. He considered himself a connoisseur when it came to appreciating women's charms. Still, he was far too accustomed to the prince's obsessions to believe this Lily was as captivating as the prince seemed to think. "I've never heard of her."

"She's the younger sister of Countess Sheffield," Moseby supplied.

"Countess Sheffield? Benjamin Ramsey is married?" Alex asked. This was news. He'd thought the earl to be too involved with his balloons and science experiments ever to take a wife.

"We must deal with the problem at hand," Bertie said, slapping the tabletop. "Now, assuming Miss Lily did marry as Alex suggests, how can we keep my . . . involvement . . . from causing an inconvenient divorce?" Several of the prince's affairs with married women had resulted in scandalous divorces, upsetting Queen Victoria and filling the papers with gossip. Still, Bertie was never deterred from enjoying his pleasures.

He continued, "The marriage must be foolproof. Lily would gain every benefit of the married state, yet her heart. . . . Ah, her lovely heart in that soft white breast . . . *That* would belong to me."

Alex arched an eyebrow. "And you don't think her husband would have something to say about that? Or the girl, for that matter? Not many men would fail to be intimate with their own wives." He glanced around the table and caught a few men nodding.

His gaze skimmed over the duke on his chaise, and a thought occurred to him. The duke appeared to be asleep except for the puffing motion of his cheeks on his opium pipe. "Unless the fellow had a preference for Greek love, of course."

Bertie's eyes lit up. "So, you're saying—"

"Marry her to the duke," Alex said. "She becomes a duchess, something any American chit ought to relish. The duke gets a wife, something we all know his mother would relish." The men laughed. For years, the duke's mother—unaware of his true nature—had been pressuring him to marry and produce heirs.

"And—" Bertie prompted.

"And she's yours." He meant his remark as a joke, but the prince's eyes glowed with excitement. Alex began to regret his offhand suggestion.

"That's a wonderful idea!" Bertie slapped him on the shoulder. "Why, even if she becomes with child, what's the harm? The get would be of royal blood!"

The duke removed the hookah from his mouth only long enough for a wry response. "I would have no complaint about that. It would get my dear mother off my back."

The prince turned to the duke and gave him a pointed stare. "So, you'll do it? You'll pursue her as a wife?"

At that, the duke's eyes snapped open. "Is that a royal command?"

Prince Edward turned back around, his face creased in irritation. "Did I say as much? I think not."

"One might be persuaded." Again the duke returned his attention to his hookah, as if the prospect of marrying the girl mattered not a whit to him.

"I should think so," Bertie said. "In fact, the more I think about it, the more this idea intrigues me. What do you think, Alex?"

Alex lifted both his hands, palms up. "I'm only an observer. I haven't even laid eyes on the girl in question, much less determined whether she could succumb to the duke's charms." Granted, the duke wasn't bad looking. He had the requisite charm. As long as his vices remained secret . . .

Alex shook his head in irritation. He had no stake in the situation. While he found the intrigue mildly amusing, he refused to become involved. He had his own concerns, chief among them advancement in his career despite his lack of a title. He intended to spend this time between overseas assignments securing a high-level position with the Foreign Office, such as an important post in India or even an ambassadorship.

He himself never used subterfuge when wooing women, perhaps because he'd never been that desperate for a particular woman. And he certainly never planned to be.

"Why, you'll have the opportunity to see Miss Lily tomorrow," Moseby said enthusiastically. "I do believe she's being presented to the queen."

"Ah, yes. I enjoy looking over the new crop of ladies at the start of each Season," Bertie said.

Alex sighed. Tomorrow was the first Drawing Room of the Season, a ceremonial reception presided over by Her Majesty during which debutantes and other ladies were officially presented. Members of the diplomatic corps were expected to attend. Since he'd already planned to be at court to report to the queen's advisers, he'd be unable to avoid Miss Lily Carrington.

To Pauline, Clara, and Meryl Carrington
New York, New York

My dear little sisters,

I'm so thrilled by my news, I simply must share it immediately. Even if you won't be receiving this until after it happens. Tomorrow, your darling eldest sister Hannah (also known as the illustrious countess of Sheffield) will be escorting me to the Queen's Court. I'm going to be presented to Queen Victoria herself!

Mother has spent all afternoon drilling me on proper decorum. I've also been practicing my curtsy. One must bow very low indeed before a queen. I know Miss Beckindale would think it silly, being so excited about meeting royalty. After all, she always taught us that we Americans "threw off the yoke of the monarchy." (Please give our governess my fondest regards. I miss her dearly, too.) Yet I can't help it. There's something about royalty . . .

Perhaps I'll figure it out after I actually visit Buckingham Palace and meet the queen! (No, she hasn't invited me for tea, as in the song.) I do know that once I've been presented, I will be able to attend official court balls and concerts. Doesn't that sound exciting?

I shall write again tomorrow.
Your loving sister,
Lily

Lily sighed and adjusted the three ostrich plumes at the back of her head. Accenting a headpiece with carefully selected feathers was one thing. These foot-long plumes made her feel like a strutting peacock. Following royal protocol, all the ladies being presented at court were required to wear them so the queen could easily identify them.

By court ruling, her white gown had a low neckline, short sleeves, and a train exactly three yards long. Though her arms were dressed in elbow-length white gloves, her neck and shoulders were bare. Yet, unlike the other ladies' gowns, hers had no bustle. The French designer Charles Worth had assured her she had the right figure to introduce this latest style to London society. Lily knew she looked good, and adored sporting a new fashion. If only she could show it off, instead of cooling her heels in this dreary, stuffy antechamber!

"I didn't expect being presented to the queen to be quite so tedious," Lily whispered to Hannah, not wanting any of the other ladies in the chamber to hear.

Hannah smiled. "True, but you only have to do it once."

They'd awoken early, spent the morning dressing, then spent more than two hours in Hannah's phaeton traveling along the Mall toward Buckingham Palace. Two hours in a carriage! Lily had never seen such traffic, so many carriages heading toward the palace and the Drawing Room which began at three. She only hoped she would still have energy for the ball that would follow.

Finally, a gentleman-in-waiting gestured Hannah and Lily toward a door leading to the audience chamber. Lily's heart jumped. The presentation was almost here. Now that the time had come, her excitement returned in a rush.

She adjusted her train over her arm, hoping she wouldn't drop it or trip on it.

"Take a breath, Lily," Hannah suggested. "You don't want to pass out."

Lily caught her older sister's teasing smile and nodded. Together, they were directed into yet another anteroom.

Finally, their turn came. At a gesture from a gentleman-in-waiting, Hannah entered the audience chamber with her usual unconcerned gait, as if she were walking to market. Despite becoming a titled noblewoman the previous summer, she had remained unaffected and delightfully relaxed. For Hannah, attending court was more a favor to Lily than anything she personally enjoyed. As the one making the presentation, Hannah remained on the side of the royal gathering, but Lily was expected to advance to the queen.

A lord-in-waiting took her train from her arm and spread it out behind her.

Lily sucked in her breath, suddenly conscious of how naked she felt. Not until her coming out last year had she worn such revealing gowns. She felt every pair of eyes on her, and there were so many strangers here! In the vast chamber, dozens of officials and visitors formed a circle before a podium bedecked in gold velvet. Upon the podium sat the queen. She wore a black silk dress, a train trimmed with crepe and net, and a cap with a long white veil ornamented with large diamonds. Beside her stood a rather short, pudgy man, whom Lily recognized from the papers as Prince Edward Albert. He wore a red-and-black uniform decorated with medals. His wife and the queen's daughters wore white dresses in the fashion of her own, with the addition of tiaras on their heads.

As regally as she could, Lily began the twenty paces needed to reach the royal family, keeping her back straight and her eyes on the queen.

Halfway to the podium, Lily felt an intense gaze on her, coming from someone in the group to her right. Instinctively, she sought the source of the feeling. She found herself gazing into the cobalt eyes of a tall, bronzed man with sun-streaked chestnut hair. His strong brow, aquiline nose, and square, clean-shaven jaw gave him an unusually rugged air for a gentleman. A shiver danced up her spine, and her step faltered. Her foot caught on the hem of her dress and she stumbled forward.

A strong hand encircled her bare upper arm, giving her just enough support to steady herself. Again she found herself looking into the stranger's eyes, rimmed with thick lashes. Without a word, he released her and stepped back. Lily paused a moment, awash in embarrassment and confusion.

The man's commanding touch had set her skin on fire. She could still feel the imprint of his callused palm, still feel his eyes on her. He had behaved with proper decorum, yet she couldn't help feeling he was only playing the part of a gentleman. She dared not look at him again. "Thank you," she murmured, then advanced once more toward the queen.

Despite her stumble, both the queen and her son smiled at her indulgently. Perhaps she hadn't committed the worst *faux pas* imaginable. Nevertheless, she was mortified. She'd practiced so long at this! She'd wanted desperately to make a good impression and not embarrass her family or her country.

The card bearing her name was handed to the lord chamberlain, who read it to the queen. "Lily Carrington, sister of Hannah Ramsey, the countess of Sheffield." Just as she'd practiced, she dipped into a deep curtsy, so far down the tips of her feathers brushed the floor. She was grateful for the excuse to hide her face, even for a few moments. But she couldn't stay in such an awkward position forever, unfortunately. She straightened and faced the queen.

"Lovely. Simply lovely," the queen murmured.

"Indeed," the prince replied.

Lily's gaze flicked to him, and her stomach tightened at the oddly intense look in his eyes.

"Please excuse my clumsiness, Your Majesties," she blurted out, determined to apologize. "I'm so honored to be here. And I practiced so much!"

"You have done well." The queen gave her an indulgent smile, and Lily saw Prince Edward's lips twitch.

"Welcome to court," the prince said, his eyes sparkling.

Lily sighed in relief. "Thank you, Your Majesties."

She curtsied once more to the prince and the other royals, as she'd been instructed. That accomplished, she extended her arm so that another lord-in-waiting could drape her train over it. She began backing out of the room as she was supposed to, conscious that she was once again passing the man who'd caught her. Who'd touched her.

This time, she showed greater restraint and kept her eyes firmly forward. Nevertheless, she felt his gaze on her until she slipped out door.

She and Hannah were directed to the Green Room, then back to their carriages. It was over.

"Did I make an awful fool of myself?" she asked Hannah.

"What do you mean? I didn't notice anything."

Hannah wasn't as attuned to the nuances of social interactions. "I nearly tripped and fell! The queen didn't seem to mind, but if that gentleman hadn't caught me—"

"Oh, that." She waved her hand dismissively. "You were fine."

Lily felt a little better. "Who was he?"

"Who?"

"The man who caught me."

"Oh. I have no idea. I've don't believe I've ever seen him before. Or if I have, I don't recall it. Honestly, I didn't even get a good look at him. I doubt I'd recognize him again if I *did* see him."

Not recognize the gentleman? Lily shook her head, amazed. She would never forget him. How could Hannah be so blind? He was the most dynamic male she'd ever seen, and that included hundreds of young men in London, Paris, and New York.

She sighed in exasperation. Hannah had no eyes for any man but her husband Benjamin, the earl of Sheffield.

For filling her in on gossip or telling her who was who at court, Hannah was a disaster. She preferred to shut herself away at home with her husband, tinkering with their science experiments.

Lily adored her sister, but she found it hard to understand her. Obviously the true adventure lay out here, in the sparkling, lively city. Tonight they would attend their first official court function, a ball heralding the opening of the Season. As usual, the queen wouldn't attend, but the prince would. Everyone who was anyone would be there.

Now that she'd received the queen's blessing, like magic a new life opened before Lily. Last year when she first came to London for the season, she'd merely been a foreign visitor. Oh, she'd received her share of attention, paid visits to school friends and gone to the opera and the ballet. With Hannah and Benjamin, she'd even attended the duke of Marlborough's ball at Blenheim Palace, the most exciting event she'd ever experienced—until today.

I've met the queen. And the prince. Even spoken to them. A giddy sense of unreality filled her. London was nothing like staid, dull New York, ruled over by the staid and dull Astors and Rockefellers. The prince and his Marlborough Set ruled London society. After today, she might actually be invited to some of their elaborate functions. She would be introduced to barons and earls and even dukes.

She planned to meet as many eligible men as she could. Talk to them; dance with them. She'd decided that young men were a lot like various dishes one could choose for dinner. Each of them had fascinating qualities of one sort or another. Some were humorous. Some paid her decidedly worshipful attention. Some could recite poetry and sing. But so far none of them had managed to hold her lasting interest.

A man must be able to do that, else why marry him? Marriage would be for a long time, after all. No, her future husband had to be perfect. Why not? There were so many beaux to choose from. Not only would he be handsome—like the man who'd helped her today—he'd be clever, funny, and captivating in every way. Above all, he'd have a title. She'd help fulfill her mother's dream of seeing her daughters married to the cream of English society.

Did the stranger have a title? Was he married already? She prayed not. If he met both requirements, he was already the front-runner in her race to make a brilliant match.

Suddenly, Hannah grasped her hand. "Lily, you know how we always teased each other, about me being all head, and you all heart?"

Lily slowly nodded.

"I know you long to follow your heart," Hannah said with uncharacteristic concern. "But please, be careful."

Lily smiled and patted Hannah's hand. "Of course I'll be careful. You needn't worry about me. I promise."

Two

Alex felt as if he'd inhaled the duke's heady opium smoke.

Even now, three hours after the Drawing Room had ended, he could not reclaim his usual detachment. Worse, he'd barely been able to focus during his afternoon meeting with the director of the Foreign Office, a meeting in which he'd intended to shine. Instead, the director had asked if he were taking ill, of all things!

Now, standing in the glittering ballroom at St. James Palace, the air filled with chamber music, the scent of roses, and the conversations of several hundred guests, he struggled even harder to orient himself.

He longed to blame this extraordinary feeling on being too long away from London's social scene. He couldn't. He'd been overseas too often, for even longer periods, for mere distance and time to be the cause.

In truth, he knew the cause perfectly well, though it mystified him.

Bertie had commented that "his Lily" would be attending this first royal ball of the season. Alex had already searched for her lissome figure among the guests who'd been announced, to no avail.

Soon she'd be here, in this room, he found himself thinking for the thousandth time. He shouldn't care.

But he did.

When she'd appeared in the audience chamber, he felt as if he'd been punched in the gut. At first he'd thought it a trick of the light. But the closer she came, the more lovely she appeared. That swanlike neck! That face—oval, with finely molded features perfectly in accord, except for larger-than-usual eyes. No bustle had obscured the hourglass curves God had given her, a courageous step for a girl so new to society. She'd worn the latest fashion with the poise of a princess. Nevertheless, by her innocent demeanor, he doubted she fully understood the power she could wield over men.

Queen Victoria's edict that all ladies attending the drawing room show décolletage . . . My God, when she curtsied so low, how the prince must have relished the sight of her ivory bosom swelling above her low-cut gown. Any man would. Any man, except—

He glanced around the room for the duke. Sure enough, the man stood beside the prince, deep in conversation. No doubt they were planning how the duke would court the girl, when she arrived here tonight.

And once she did arrive, he would realize his mind had played tricks on him. *I'll see her again, see that she's no more remarkable than any debutante, and the spell will be broken,* he assured himself. *Everything will return to normal.*

"Didn't I tell you she was fabulous?" John approached him and passed him a brandy.

Alex feigned ignorance. "Who?"

"The girl! The one Bertie wants. The one you kept from falling on her face." He chuckled. "Wish it had been me."

She lost her balance when she looked at me. Alex

fought a warm feeling at the thought, and told himself to read nothing into it. He'd startled her, is all. Every woman being presented to the queen walked on rubbery legs, they were so afraid of doing something improper in the royal presence.

"She's fair enough," he said, staring into his brandy as he swirled the amber liquid in the crystal glass. "I'm sure she has some flaw or other. Every woman has a flaw."

"I have yet to find it," John said.

"No doubt she hasn't a brain in that pretty head of hers," Alex continued, determined to convince himself more than John. "Probably tedious to talk to. Young girls don't have enough life experience to say anything of consequence." He preferred worldly women, by far, ones who knew how to please men.

"Why, Alex, that's bloody unfair. You wouldn't want her talking policy or philosophy or anything of that nature. I say, that would be dreadfully dull."

Alex sighed. Although politics was his career, he preferred to separate business from pleasure. A lovely woman who could discuss a range of topics, that would be ideal. Perhaps this American chit *had* been trained in the art of conversation. That was no reason to heap such attention upon her. This worship of a girl barely out of the schoolroom—and from another country, to boot!—was downright ludicrous.

Schoolroom? With a figure like that? A vision appeared before him of Lily Carrington's lush form straining against a girl's pinafore. He bit down on his smile at the ridiculous notion, until he began to imagine removing said pinafore. His humor dissolved, replaced by much more dangerous thoughts. What might she look like wearing only what God gave her? He shook his head to rid himself of the too-pleasant thought. Now wasn't the time or place. And Miss Carrington definitely wasn't the woman.

John continued, "She captivates those lucky enough to receive her attention. I'm quite happy to say that included me. She danced with me twice at the duke of Marlborough's ball last summer."

"You're not in love with the chit, are you?"

John frowned. "I don't believe so. I would pursue her, perhaps, but with Bertie being determined . . ."

"He may change his mind. You know how fickle he can be when it comes to women. I can't imagine the duke will ever really propose to the girl, anyway."

"I do hope you're right. Then I might have a chance." His face lit up. "Look. She's here."

Alex followed John's gaze. At the entrance to the ballroom, the footman had just called out her name, along with that of her sister and husband, the earl and countess of Sheffield.

Alex looked past them to Miss Carrington. As she strolled in, she glanced about with a bright smile, her countenance revealing a passionate fascination with her surroundings. As custom demanded, she wore the same luxurious yet virginal white gown she had worn at her presentation. But she'd relaxed, her posture and movements fluid with natural grace.

He swallowed hard in a suddenly dry throat. The spell she'd cast over him remained intact. If anything, he was becoming even more mesmerized. How could that be? He'd never been the type to fall for a particular woman. Not even Sikara, much as she'd come to mean to him, had ever obsessed him in this way. The whole thing irritated him to no end. He'd always thought himself above such foolish emotions.

He was forced to admitted the truth—though only to himself. Lily Carrington was the most captivating creature he'd ever laid eyes on.

And she was destined to belong to the prince. Already the duke had approached her. Bowing low before her, he smiled broadly, then swept her onto the dance floor. A sick feeling swelled in Alex's gut as he considered the royal intrigue about to surround the girl. Did she have any idea what was transpiring?

Perhaps she didn't care. Perhaps she would welcome becoming the prince's latest mistress. Some women would think it a great honor, despite their lack of worldly experience. He almost wished she would turn out to be a conniving little minx without a heart. If she longed only for titles and social status, he could easily wash his hands of her, for she would receive exactly that.

If, however, she had romantic notions of marriage, what the duke and prince planned for her would crush her spirit and break her heart. And he could only blame himself.

By God, he'd not only witnessed the scheming, he'd aided and abetted it! *He'd* suggested the girl marry the duke. He may be a self-interested cad in some people's eyes, but even he had a sense of honor, one this situation was sorely testing.

Don't get involved, his common sense countered. *Don't get involved. It's none of your affair.* His work for the government had taught him not to become emotionally attached to people, no matter what his heart told him. Why should this particular lady be any different?

Why, indeed?

"Thank you so much for inviting me to this ball, Your Highness," Lily told the prince as they waltzed across the polished floor. "I've never enjoyed myself so much."

"I'm pleased to hear that." The prince smiled at her. He was barely her own height, a portly, graying man. His hand felt clammy even through her long white glove, and his breath smelled of strong tobacco and alcohol.

Still, he was terribly polite. Besides, he was the *prince*. Someday she could tell her grandchildren how she'd danced with the future king.

Lily knew being selected to dance with him was a great honor. At least three hundred ladies were present, yet he'd chosen her. She could hardly wait to write her sisters in New York about her adventure.

Being officially recognized by the queen had worked wonders for her socially. She hadn't had a chance to rest since she'd walked into the ballroom. *That's why you're here. To meet men. To meet your future husband.* Perhaps he was here tonight. Perhaps . . . Her gaze drifted to the north wall, where he'd been standing since she arrived an hour ago.

All evening, as she'd passed by in the arms of other men, she'd found her gaze drawn to him. He stood with feet spread, hands clasped behind his back, in an almost military posture. His rugged, square-jawed face remained motionless, yet his cobalt eyes seemed to follow her every step, as if on guard for danger despite the frivolous atmosphere surrounding him.

"I'd heard the American debutante was a lovely creature, but she's more striking than I expected.

Alex followed Lady Brighton's gaze to Lily Carrington in the prince's arms. As soon as Bertie had claimed his dance with Lily, Alex had sought out Anna, a lush redhead and his former mistress, and joined them on the ballroom floor.

Despite the prince's apparent good manners toward

his partner, Alex knew exactly what the man was thinking. How could he not become lost in carnal thoughts, holding that soft, sensual body in his arms? Her generous cleavage swelled against the low neckline of her satin bodice. Her rib cage tapered to an unusually tiny waist. She reminded him of a fairy-tale, a true Snow White with red lips, raven tresses, and ivory skin . . .

Annoyed at his uncharacteristic flight of fancy, he jerked his attention back to his partner.

Luckily, Anna was still studying the girl, too, and didn't notice Alex's keen interest. "Such a full figure, yet she's remarkably slender. And she has the face of an angel. She certainly wears the latest fashions better than I ever could. Even without a bustle, her figure draws the eye. Rumor has it that Worth himself created new designs especially to fit *her*. Every woman here will be demanding similar gowns within the week. And I can guess what the men are imagining. Goodness, Alex, I fear I'm growing jealous."

Determined not to stare at Lily, Alex swung his partner in another direction. "Nonsense, Anna. You're the most beautiful woman here."

She chuckled in a knowing way. "You haven't lost your charm, despite spending months among godless natives. I admit I've longed for your return—along with your other paramours, no doubt. My husband is as dreadfully dull as ever, and absent just as much, no doubt occupied with that dancer he's taken up with. Have you heard?"

"Ah, no, Anna, I haven't. I'm sorry to hear it."

"Nonsense. It frees me to pursue pleasure in my own fashion, you know that." Lifting her gloved hand, she trailed her fingers along his jaw.

Alex gazed down into her face, studied her round cheeks, delicately freckled skin, and Cupid's-bow mouth. He'd spent many an evening of unbridled passion in this woman's arms. Yet, holding her now, he felt no more than a simple fondness, a nostalgia for good memories. He could dredge up no sense of excitement, no desire to pursue further pleasure in her bed.

Yet as recently as last week, during his ocean voyage, he'd enjoyed a French woman's charms. What was wrong with him?

"Well, Alex? Am I not speaking plainly enough for you?" Anna chided.

Alex smiled but knew he had to put her off. "Sweetheart, I've barely returned to town. I still need to settle in, learn the lay of the land."

She gave him a skeptical look. "Oh, come now, Alex darling. You can be straight with me. If you're otherwise occupied, simply say so and I'll stay out of your way." She pouted delicately. "Regretfully so, but I'll make do."

He sighed in relief. "Very well, then, my sweet. We had marvelous times. But I'm feeling rather . . . out of sorts."

"I'm sorry to hear that," she murmured.

Alex looked past her, and again found Lily in his sights. As if aware of his nearness, she lifted her gaze to his. His heart tightened at the unguarded, curious expression on her face. Unfortunately, her distraction gave the prince an opportunity to study her bosom, his own expression one of pure lust.

A surprising surge of rage raced through Alex's blood, and he accepted the truth. If he didn't act to save this girl now, he'd never forgive himself.

But how? He couldn't simply reveal the prince's plot. Doing so would ensure an end to his career, and he lacked a name to fall back on.

To begin with, he needed to know the girl's nature,

her assumptions about the high society she'd entered. Perhaps she was capable of taking care of herself. He'd have to speak with her. That should be a simple matter. John could provide an introduction.

But then what? Would they stand here in this hot crowded, ballroom and discuss her love life? No, that wouldn't suit. He needed to see her alone.

"You're somewhere else, Alex. Perhaps we'd be wise to end this now."

Alex jerked his attention back to Anna. "Excuse me?"

Though the waltz hadn't ended, Anna stopped dancing and led him off the floor. Turning to him, she took his hands in hers. "I wish you the best, Alex, in whatever you do. It's clear to me now that we belong in the past, and I accept that. Good luck." Rising on her toes, she bussed his cheek, then strolled away.

Alex stared after her, alarmed that his adroitness at romancing women was being affected by this quandary over a girl he hadn't even been introduced to. *After you solve this problem, things will fall back into place,* he assured himself. *After you rescue the American chit from her own damn charms.*

John strolled over to him. "She's promised me the next dance," he said with a broad smile. Alex didn't have to ask to whom he referred.

Pulling his friend behind a nearby set of potted ferns, he lowered his voice. "John, I need you to do me a favor."

Looking past the prince, Lily spotted the stranger dancing with an elegant redhead in green velvet. Despite the allure of his sophisticated partner, he was looking right at Lily. For the briefest of moments, their gazes locked, sending a secret thrill through her. A moment later, he vanished in the crowd.

She tried hard to forget about the stranger, to think only about dancing with the prince. After all, the stranger hadn't asked to be introduced to her. If he was as taken with her as she was with him, surely he'd want to meet her. She fought down her disappointment. The evening was still young. Perhaps he didn't want to appear too forward.

Perhaps he had no interest in her. Perhaps he was already married.

She could no longer stand the suspense. "Excuse me. Who . . ." Ask the prince? Actually gossip with him? Oh, Lord, what was she thinking? She was losing her head over this stranger!

"Yes, dear?" the prince prompted.

"I was wondering who"—Lily scrambled to complete her question with something innocuous—"who your wife's tailor is. She wore such a lovely gown today at the Drawing Room." She breathed a sigh of relief. The prince's interest in sartorial matters was well known. He himself was a fashion trendsetter.

"Worth, I believe. One of the few tailors worthy of dressing a royal personage."

"Thank you, Your Highness."

He smiled warmly at her. "I noticed your own lovely gown this afternoon at court. A new style for a brand-new decade. I've heard that Monsieur Worth designed the new style especially for you."

"You heard that? About me, Your Highness?" How had he known such a thing? True, the diminutive designer had been excited to clothe her, because she'd was lucky enough to have a well-proportioned figure. But to think the prince himself knew such a thing! Lily felt her face heat. "I didn't realize you knew who I was."

"Very few gentlemen here aren't aware of the fashionable young lady who has come across the sea to grace us with her presence," he said, his eyes twinkling.

"I'm flattered." Lily's head began to swim with his praise. He couldn't possibly mean it. Why should the prince pay attention to her? She was merely one in a parade of debutantes, both English and American. He must say such things to every young lady. Of course he did.

But what about her stranger? Had *he* noticed her?

She had to stop this. She had to stop worrying about what one single man thought of her. She had to shake this terrible hold he had on her. And she still didn't know who he was!

Lord Moseby, a marquess she'd met the previous season, shifted impatiently nearby, waiting for the prince to release her. When he finally did, Moseby stepped forward and gave a short bow. "I believe this next dance is mine."

He took her into his arms, and once again she was dancing. Lily found it almost impossible to focus on the steps. She longed to rest, just for a moment. She felt completely overwhelmed, and desperately needed to put things in perspective. "Lord Moseby, if you don't mind, I'm growing fatigued and would appreciate a respite."

"A capital idea. In fact, I was going to suggest we take a turn about the palace." He stopped dancing and escorted her to the edge of the dance floor. "I know just the thing. Have you seen the palace's display of historic portraiture? It's along the hallway, just there." He gestured to an archway that led to a vast gallery fronting the ballroom. Several couples were strolling there.

Lily smiled. What an excuse. Obviously the man

merely wanted to walk with her, to stroll with her in surroundings more amenable to conversation. She'd been flirted with enough to recognize the moves, the tactics young men and women employed to be alone yet keep their reputations intact.

"No, I haven't. This is my first time at St. James." At least leaving the ballroom for a few minutes would give her a chance to catch her breath.

"Then, if you'd like, I can show you the best pieces. I know a little about art."

"That's a marvelous idea, Lord Moseby. You have quite read my mind." She smiled at him, and his ruddy face turned even more pink.

They strolled down the gallery, Moseby stopping before various portraits to give her a detailed account of the art and the artist. She enjoyed art, up to a point. But his discussion of brush strokes and lighting made her restless.

Listening with only half an ear, she found herself studying her companion. He was fairly handsome, with thick blond hair, a shock of which seemed determined to fall out of place across his forehead. His pale skin showed every blush—so unlike her stranger's bronze tan. A thick moustache kept his face from seeming too round. Yet it was a kind face. He had a thoughtful, serious demeanor as he went on about technique and method and oil paint. He had good manners, a sunny disposition. What would it be like to marry a man like him?

Of course, they'd have to find something more than art to talk about . . .

Lily adored meeting new people. She found she could read most personalities upon a very short acquaintance. She quickly became attuned to them, and almost always found something interesting to discuss.

Yet right now, she wasn't inclined to entertain Lord

Moseby with scintillating conversation. She burned for answers. She wanted to talk about his friend. She'd seen Lord Moseby talking to the attractive, mysterious stranger more than once. With any luck, that meant the stranger also was a nobleman, someone she could marry and still please her family.

Marry? What nonsense, having designs on a man she hadn't even met. She ought to be giving Lord Moseby her full attention. After all, right now, he was her partner. But she felt so terribly restless! She toyed with the fan looped around her wrist, partially opening it and flicking it toward him. The teasing gesture only seemed to make him nervous, so she stopped. "Ought we to return to the ballroom, perhaps?"

Lord Moseby cleared his throat. "Yes, well . . . The finest piece in the collection is on display just over here," he said, leading her to an open parlor door. Lily peered into a room lushly decorated in blue and gold. No one was inside.

She looked back over her shoulder. They'd strolled well away from the entrance to the ball, and from the other guests. If she went much farther, her reputation could be imperiled. "I'm not sure . . ."

"Please, Miss Carrington, it will only take a moment. You haven't seen all St. James has to offer the art aficionado until you've seen the Henry the Eighth."

His gray eyes pleaded with her, surprising Lily with his intensity. He must truly love art. She did feel comfortable with this man, knew in her heart he wouldn't hurt her. Besides, a pair of palace guards stood at the closest end of the gallery, so they weren't entirely alone. "I suppose, but only for a moment."

Smiling in satisfaction, he nodded and walked briskly into the parlor. Lily followed him to a life-size portrait depicting the hefty monarch in his royal regalia. "I take it this is the painting in question? It's certainly impressive. I can see why you're so interested."

"Yes. Ah, Miss Carrington?" His tone had changed, and Lily turned to face him. "The thing is . . . I'm afraid I've been rather misleading in my purpose."

"What do you mean?"

"The reason I brought you here . . . That is, the reason we're in this room . . ." He opened his mouth again, but nothing came out. He looked like a fish fighting for breath, his mouth opening and closing to no purpose.

"What is it?" Lily asked, amused by the intense yet confused look on his earnest face. Her heart went out to him, he was struggling so.

He gazed over her shoulder as if desperate for help. "Well, what I mean to say is—"

Just then, a deep voice spoke from directly behind Lily, sending a shock down her spine. "He's trying to say he brought you here to meet me."

Three

"You!" Lily stared at the stranger, amazed and thrilled despite her better sense. He'd sought her out. He'd noticed her, even gone so far as to arrange a secret meeting. She was barely aware of the door closing softly as Lord Moseby exited.

Without a word, the stranger strode past her to the door, his posture commanding and sure, then swung it closed. The hasp slid into place with a soft click. A shiver ran up Lily's spine. While she trusted Lord Moseby, she knew nothing of this stranger. Now he'd taken the indecent liberty of being alone with her.

"This is hardly appropriate, sir. I don't know what Lord Moseby was thinking, leaving me alone with . . ."

He turned back around, his blue gaze burning with secret intent. He wore no moustache as most men did, so she plainly saw the corners of his mouth lift in a smile. She'd never realized a man's lips could be so intriguing to watch. She forced herself to finish her sentence. "You."

"Forgive my unorthodox means of introducing myself. You must trust that I have my reasons."

"Do you, indeed? Whatever they are, I can't imagine they supplant good manners and proper etiquette. I'm here with a chaperon who will no doubt be anxious for my return to the ballroom."

"Lord and Lady Ramsey left for a walk in the garden a half hour ago. They seemed preoccupied well enough with each other."

Lily knew he spoke the truth. Her sister and her husband had eyes for no one but each other. In truth, Hannah wasn't the best chaperon. But she trusted Lily to behave with proper decorum. *Of course, she trusts me. How else would I behave?*

Yet here she was, alone in a room with an incredibly suave, attractive man. Though she kept a careful expression of haughty disdain on her face, secretly she absorbed every aspect of him—broad back, long legs, elegant hands as tan as his face, evidence, perhaps, of long months spent in sunnier climes. Under his tuxedo, would the rest of him appear as golden? Mortified by the direction of her thoughts, she reminded herself sternly that she was a well-bred lady. "I demand that you open that door and allow me to leave."

"I mean you no ill will. Quite the opposite. I'm concerned about your well being."

"This is a strange way to show it."

"Miss Carrington." He planted his hands on his hips under his tailored jacket, giving Lily a much better view of his athletic torso, clad in an elegant dove gray vest. His confident posture only made him more attractive. He gazed closely at her. "Are you aware of what men will do when driven by their passions?"

Their passions . . . Oh, Lord. Did he feel passion toward her, as she did toward him? Was he warning her about himself? "Excuse me?"

"I apologize. That was rather poorly put. I think you should be aware that not every man has your best interests at heart."

"I am quite able to discern a true gentleman, which you, sir, obviously are not."

He grinned ruefully. "You wouldn't be alone in that assessment."

"I still have no idea who you are."

"Forgive me. Alexander Drake, at your service." He gave a quick bow at the waist.

"And are you . . ." Lily prompted.

"You look puzzled. As a debutante seeking the best match possible, no doubt you're wondering what my title might be. That is your ambition, isn't it? To marry well?"

"I never said—"

"I have no title."

"Oh." No title? He wasn't of the nobility? She tried not to feel disappointed. "Then what—"

"What am I doing here, at the prince's ball?"

Lily found it disconcerting, the way he kept taking the words right out of her mouth. This time, she didn't reply.

"I am a liaison with the Foreign Office. I suppose one would call me a high official in the government, but you won't find me behind a desk."

"You're a spy?"

His smile faded, and Lily suspected she'd surmised correctly. "Not in so many words."

"It was only one word. *Spy.*"

He sighed. "Miss Carrington, I didn't bring you here to discuss my profession."

"Apparently not, if it's a secret profession," she said.

His eyes sparked, and she sensed he appreciated her wit. Somehow, he'd moved closer to her. Or had she moved closer to him? She felt drawn to him, as if by a magnetic force. His voice lowered to an intimate timbre. "Do you always flirt so outrageously?"

"Flirt? *Me? You* are the one who closed a young lady in a room without her consent." She reminded herself that she ought not to be here with him, much as she longed to continue their repartee. "Speaking of which—" She moved the three steps to the door and reached for the knob.

"Not yet." Moving as fast as a panther, he thrust his arm across the door and braced his hand on the lintel. Grasping her hand, he gently removed her gloved fingers from the knob, one by one. The warmth of his touch sent tingles up her arm. She longed for the touching to continue, but she only had five fingers. When he had completely freed her hand from the knob, he released it.

He gazed down at her, his look so intense, she feared—hoped?—he intended to kiss her. She backed up a pace and found herself trapped between him and the wall. His subtle masculine scent of spices and musk reminded her of the exotic Orient, adding to his mystique. He was so worldly and experienced . . . She ought to protest. She ought to scream. She ought to—

"Miss Carrington. In your quest to marry a nobleman, you can't assume those with titles have your best interests at heart."

She lifted her chin. "Do you resent those who *do* have titles?"

"I said nothing of the sort. I'm telling you to be on your guard. Some gentlemen are wolves in sheep's clothing."

"Yes, and I'm looking at one."

He frowned in annoyance. "Not *me*. Damn it, woman, how can I get through to you?" He studied her face for several long heartbeats, and Lily feared he could plainly see her weakness for him. His gaze slid along her neck to her bosom, then even lower, drinking his fill of her figure. Lily had never been gazed at with such impertinence. She should slap him. She would. Except she'd never felt more alive than she did at this moment. No other man had ever made her feel such a delicious, tantalizing awareness of herself as a woman.

Finally, his compelling gaze returned to meet hers. "Tell me. What is it you hope for? What do you see in your future?"

"The same as any young lady entering society. I hope to find a man to love me. One I love in return."

His gaze darkened, and she noticed a crease in his brow that hadn't been there before. "That's it? I assume you want to marry well."

"Of course we would marry, if we love each other."

He smiled, but his expression held little humor. "Such romantic notions!"

"Well, naturally I hope my marriage won't disappoint my family. My mother, especially, believes I can make a brilliant match."

"Brilliant? I should say so. You could have any man out there." His voice thickened. "You must realize that."

Her breath jamming in her throat, Lily watched in a daze as he lifted his hand toward her face. As delicately as a butterfly's wings, his fingertips skimmed her cheekbone, traced her jaw. "You're different from the other debutantes."

"Don't be silly." She couldn't keep her voice from trembling. "I'm just one more girl hoping to find a husband who will love her."

"No. You're unique." His husky voice vibrated along her nerve endings. "You're so much lovelier, so much more alive . . . A brilliant jewel with a warm heart."

He was making love to her . . . Oh, Lord! The most handsome man at the ball wanted her! Lily closed her eyes and took a deep breath, conscious of her breasts pressing against her low-cut gown. He stood so close now, his warm breath danced across her face, and she inhaled faint traces of tobacco and whiskey. Yet unlike the prince, the heady male combination magnified his masculine appeal.

Lifting his finger, he tapped her lips, making them tingle deliciously. "I realize now this jewel has a critical flaw, one that could cause her to shatter." His tone turned harsh. "You're too damned naive for your own good."

Naive! Suddenly, everything clicked into place. The man had nefarious designs on her. He'd hoped to find her ready and willing for his potent seduction!

She shoved his hand away. "Sir, if you had imagined that I would become your mistress, or succumb to your charms, or submit to you for some illicit purpose, then you are *most* correct. I am naive. I am innocent. And it's to my *good* that I will have none of *you!*"

She began to move, but he threw out an arm to block her way. He settled his other arm on her other side, effectively trapping her. Like a horse on a trace, she immediately stilled, dreading yet anticipating what he might try next.

"Look at me, Miss Carrington."

Slowly, she brought her eyes to meet his and found his face only inches from hers.

"If you hear anything I tell you, you must hear this," he said, his voice intense and sharp. "Don't believe what you see."

Lily kept her chin high, trying desperately to maintain her composure. "You make no sense."

Dropping his arms, he instead grasped her gloved hand and lifted it between them. "If you are to survive in English society, you need to see past the surface."

She struggled to think about his words, to determine why he would tell her this. What could he possibly mean? Being so near him made logical thought nearly impossible.

His palm traced a path down the outside of her arm, setting her afire. "See how this glove covers your arm?"

Lily didn't respond, aware that if she moved, this delicious feeling would end and she might never feel it again. His countenance bewitched her; his words seduced her. He'd captivated her as surely as if she'd been placed in chains. She did not protest, even when he thumbed open the buttons and began rolling her lace-topped suede glove down her arm, past her elbow, then off her fingers. She was too shocked, too entranced to protest. Clearly he was experienced at removing ladies' evening gloves.

Tossing her glove over his shoulder, he cradled her bare hand in both of his, his skin warm and familiar on hers. He gave her hand a squeeze to emphasize his words. "This is real, Miss Carrington. This is who you are under the pomp and gentility. The same is true of your suitors. Unless you can peel away the superficial, you will never know who you are dealing with."

"I know I'm dealing with a cad," she bit out, yanking her fingers free. "A proper gentleman would never talk to a lady in such a way."

"Proper gentleman, is it? And I'm not, apparently."

"Apparently. Now, if you will excuse me—" Snatching her glove from his shoulder, she turned toward the door.

With her head held high, she intended to strut from the room like a queen. Unfortunately, the door of the centuries-old palace resisted her pull. She could feel him behind her, no doubt silently laughing, as she yanked harder on the handle. When the door finally sprang free of its frame, she had to fall back a step to catch her balance. With his rich chuckle in her ears, she waltzed from the room with as much dignity as she could muster.

Alex took a deep breath, willing his heart to slow to a more normal rhythm. He'd thought the girl fascinating before. Now that he'd spoken to her, he understood the prince's desire for her—and his own.

He'd enjoyed her company more than he ever expected. Not only had he delighted in her flirtatious banter, their more intense confrontation had sparked passion deep within him. My God, he'd almost kissed her, he'd been so swept away by her charms. She had an innate sensuality he doubted she was aware of, but that called to men like a siren song.

A sweet sensuality the prince intended for himself.

He grimaced. The prince, with his rolls of fat and tobacco-stained hands, would use the innocent young Lily until he grew bored with her. She would have no say in the matter. Her reputation would be dragged through the mud, her illusions shattered as surely as her innocence.

Usually the prince dallied with married, worldly women who enjoyed—or even sought—his royal favor. Women who had taken previous lovers, actresses and jaded socialites. Women nothing like Lily.

This time, Bertie was going too far. He couldn't allow him to ruin Lily. He couldn't. He would have to find a way to prevent it, yet remain in the prince's good graces. He couldn't very well defy him openly, not if he intended to advance in his career. Lily was worth a great deal, there was no doubt of that. But she wasn't worth ruining his life over.

If the girl fell in love with a suitable gentleman, as she imagined doing . . . And married the fellow . . . Why, that could work. If her marriage was strong, not only wouldn't she be vulnerable to the prince's attentions, she'd have a husband to protect her. A husband who, unlike the duke, truly cared about her, rather than serving as a procurer for the prince.

The door swung open and John entered. "Well, what did I tell you? Isn't she fabulous?"

"She's . . . interesting," he said dryly, determined not to allow John to see how the girl had affected him. He studied his friend, an idea starting to form. "You've talked about settling down one of these days, haven't you?"

"Me? Oh, of course. If the right girl comes along. Someone like Lily, for instance." He grinned. "As if I could ever land a girl like that."

"Why not? You're reasonably attractive, aren't you?" His friend was certainly better-looking than the prince. At twenty-eight, he was only a year younger than Alex himself. It was a good age to marry and start a family, if a man was so inclined.

Unlike himself, John had often talked of marrying. Also unlike himself, John would make some woman a decent husband. He was kind-hearted, with no more than the typical vices. Indeed, John usually retired from the gaming tables long before Alex did. Nor did John dally with the ladies as often as he. He couldn't recall the last time John had taken a mistress.

Even better, John had one of those damned titles that debutantes so loved. His chest tightened. Carefully modulating his voice, he said, "You meet every requirement the girl has, I'm sure."

"I wouldn't want to anger the prince," John said slowly.

Alex arched a brow. "Is that all that's keeping you from wooing the girl? I wouldn't worry about that. You know the prince. In a few weeks he'll have moved on to another woman and forgotten all about Miss Carrington. Meanwhile, you will have made great progress courting her."

In truth, he doubted the prince would forget anything. But his cautious friend needed a push in the right direction. If John didn't take the bull by the horns and pursue the girl, he'd ruin Alex's plan to save her.

Putting enthusiasm behind his words, he continued, "You will have to work fast, John. Pour your whole heart into the pursuit. Don't let any other suitor gain the upper hand."

"You truly think I have a chance?"

The hope in John's voice made Alex smile. He clapped John on the shoulder. "I guarantee it."

The more Alex considered it, the stronger his conviction grew. Yes, it could work. It had to work. The best way to save Lily was to marry her off, as soon as possible.

To Lord John Moseby.

Hannah and Benjamin's carriage returned Lily to Mrs. Digby's home on Chapel Street, where she was staying during the London Season. Hannah had invited Lily to stay at her home in Grosvenor Square, but their ever-sensible mother had felt it important for Hannah, still so newly wed, to be left alone with her husband.

Despite the late hour, Lily found Mrs. Digby waiting up for her. The plump widow rose and faced her, a bright smile on her lined but pleasant face. Gray hair jutted from under her ruffled dressing-gown cap.

"Lily, darling. I hope you had an enjoyable time at the ball. You've quite arrived, I daresay, being invited to such a royal event!"

Lily smiled and nodded. She'd had an interesting time, enjoyed dancing with dozens of men. But only one man truly fascinated her. Only one man remained in her thoughts.

"Would you like a spot of tea?" Mrs. Digby asked. "Or perhaps warm milk to help you sleep?"

Lily wasn't keen on discussing the ball in the kind of detail she knew her patron longed to hear. "No, thank you. It's rather late. You needn't have waited up for me. Though it was quite kind of you, I hate to think how I've put you out."

Mrs. Digby settled a pudgy hand on her arm. "Well, dear, I thought you should know. I've found out about that fellow, the one who caught your fancy at the presentation."

"He didn't catch my fancy," Lily lied, then smiled. "Only my balance."

Mrs. Digby chuckled at her remark. "Oh, Lily, you are such a delight."

After returning from court, Lily had asked Mrs. Digby to help her learn the identity of the man who had helped her. She'd promised to ask the ladies at that evening's charity meeting.

Lily continued, "In truth, I was merely curious who he was. But tonight I learned his name, so I'm done wondering." She began to ascend the stairs.

Mrs. Digby called up to her. "Ah. But—did you, perchance, *dance* with this man?"

Lily paused. Not wanting to be rude, she turned around. "No. But I did speak with him."

Mrs. Digby's expression immediately changed, her eyes widening and her mouth drooping in dismay. Lily began to regret asking her about Drake. The matron knew everyone who was anyone, and Lily had hoped for a quick, uncomplicated answer. Hoped to learn he was a suitable beau. Now, the troubled look on Mrs. Digby's face made her uncertain she wanted to hear anything more about the man.

Mrs. Digby continued, "Lady Dawson told me *he* was the one who *touched* you during your presentation at court. If I'd known it was *him*—"

Lily stepped back down the stairs, unable to resist learning more. "Then . . . what?"

Mrs. Digby sighed. "Come into the parlor, Lily. Perhaps we should chat."

Lily followed her across the foyer. In the parlor, a single lantern burned. Here, in her favorite room, Mrs. Digby had no doubt sat up waiting for her return from the ball. Waiting to tell her about Alexander Drake. What could be so critical that she'd spend hours anticipating her return?

Lily sank onto the overstuffed sofa, fighting her trepidation and the oppressive feeling this room always gave her. Dark wood writing desks and half-moon tables filled every available space. Doilies coated the sofa and chairs to protect the fabric from the macassar oil men used on their hair. China cupids and stuffed birds competed for space with numerous postcards, dried flowers, and framed photographs.

"Now, dear." Mrs. Digby settled beside her, shifting the cushions.

Lily could tell by Mrs. Digby's expression that the news wasn't good. Still, she longed to know more about Alexander Drake—everything, in fact. Anything. Lily said softly, "All I know of Alexander Drake is that he serves in the Foreign Office." *And that his touch sets my skin on fire . . .*

"Yes, that's true. Until recently he was stationed overseas. In Persia, I believe, or some other uncivilized, heathen place. Apparently, he's been all over the world. But he's spent enough time in London to gain quite a reputation."

"Oh?"

Mrs. Digby grasped Lily's hand, her face revealing earnest concern. "Dear Lily, he's a terrible rake! Simply terrible. He gambles, he drinks, he stays up until all hours. He's part of the prince's set, you see, and they can be quite wild. You must be on guard for your virtue at all times around such a man."

"Is that it?" Relief filled Lily. Being part of the Marlborough Set hardly made a man disreputable. Nor did drinking and gambling and attending parties, all things she herself enjoyed, at least in moderation.

Mrs. Digby shook her head. "Oh, no. There is much more, unfortunately. Rumors have connected him to women. *Married* women."

"I see." So, he'd had affairs . . . Lily pondered this. Why didn't it make her think less of him? *Because you already know he's a scoundrel, Lily Katherine,* she told herself sternly. *He tried to seduce you as well, this very night!* Still, even though she'd walked out on him in anger, her fascination with him hadn't wavered. She was afraid to analyze it too closely, merely knew she felt a deep attraction toward the man despite his faults.

"Oh, Lily, it's worse," Mrs. Digby said. "At least *those* women were Christian Englishwomen. But you see, he had this . . . *mistress.*"

"Mistress?"

"Major Ruddington told Mrs. Ruddington, who told Lady Crenshaw. He should know, shouldn't he? He was stationed in the East."

The anticipation was killing Lily. "Know what? Please, Mrs. Digby. If you're going to tell me, please do. Otherwise I'll retire."

She sighed. "Very well. I suppose there's nothing for it but to be direct." She leaned in close, her voice lowering confidentially. "The talk is that when Mr. Drake was overseas, he lived openly in sin. And not with just any woman." Her voice dropped to a strained whisper. "With one of those native *colored* women."

"I see." Lily sat back and tried to determine how this affected her impression of this man she scarcely knew. Her head spun from this wealth of new information, triggering all sorts of images in her mind: Alexander at the gaming tables raking in piles of money; the corner of his attractive mouth lifted in wry humor; Alexander visiting with foreign nabobs in golden palaces, reclining on satin and plucking plump dates from a bowl with his elegant fingers; Alexander embracing an exotic dark-skinned woman draped in veils and pearls, their lips meeting in the candlelight . . . The image began to transform. The silk-draped room became the room at the palace, and the woman became herself. He was gazing at her with longing, with heated desire, his fingers sliding along her face once more . . . Lily could almost feel his arms encircling her, his lips lowering, sealing against hers in a deep, sensuous kiss. . . .

An alarming shiver of heat danced through her. She stiffened, desperate to break from its hold.

Mrs. Digby began patting her hand so hard it hurt. "Lily, my dear, are you quite all right? Oh, no. I can see I've shocked you utterly. I'm dreadfully sorry. I know the constitutions of young ladies can be quite delicate. But I felt it was necessary to impress upon you the truth, so that you understand exactly why he isn't someone you could ever consider suitable."

"Of course not," she said softly.

"I promised your mother I would look out for you,

assure that you make a proper match, if not a brilliant one." She squeezed her hand. "We'll find you someone appropriate."

Lily said dryly, "Someone noble?"

"Of course. Otherwise you might as well return to New York and marry some merchant's son, hadn't you?" She fluttered her hand as if ridding the air of such a ludicrous thought. "But we won't let that happen. You'll have the title 'lady' if I have anything to say about it. Look what I did for your sister!"

In truth, Mrs. Digby had very little to do with Hannah marrying Lord Benjamin Ramsey, but Lily wasn't in the mood to set her straight. Instead, she said thanked her as was proper and said good night.

Four

The grandfather clock in the foyer was chiming twelve o'clock when Lily finally came downstairs. She'd slept far later than usual. She'd tried so hard to sleep but had a difficult time fighting her thoughts of the ball—and her fantasies of the dynamic Alexander Drake. She hadn't drifted off until dawn, when the room's black shadows had begun muting into grays.

As soon as she came downstairs into the foyer, she was met by Mrs. Digby. The poor lady looked nearly apoplectic with excitement. She waved a fistful of cards and letters in the air.

"Oh, Lily, I'm *so* glad you're up. I didn't want to rouse you, but I admit it took every ounce of my fortitude to resist the temptation. Just look at all of these!" She gestured to the silver salver on the hall table reserved for correspondence. There, several dozen more cards lay in a heap. "The doorbell's been ringing nonstop with footmen delivering invitations and calling cards."

"Really?" Lily's stared in amazement at the pile of buff, ivory, and white engraved cards and invitations. "Those are addressed to me? I'd expected to receive a few invitations after attending the royal ball, but I never imagined . . ."

She picked up a half-dozen envelopes and began

thumbing through them, noting the names of the senders. *Countess this and Marquess that, Sirs, Lords, Ladies* . . . Her heart surged with excitement. All her childhood dreams were coming true. She'd been the belle of the ball. She knew she'd made a good impression on the prince and his associates, but to be so roundly embraced—why, it exceeded even her dear mother's hopes for her.

And yet, a single question pressed itself on her mind. She riffled through the cards once more, seeking a specific name. Not here. Still, there were a dozen or so more cards to examine.

Mrs. Digby pressed her plump hand to her arm. "I've served as patroness to dozens of young girls, but never—and I do mean this, Lily, truly I do—*never* have I seen such a result from a single ball! You are quite the most popular young lady in the city, I daresay. And to think you're staying here, in my house. Everyone will be talking about it." Her apple cheeks glowed with satisfaction.

Lily smiled at her. "I'm so glad you're pleased. I simply had no idea. I'm stunned, to say the least."

"Why, I should say every drawing room in the city is angling to host you. And the best part is, you'll have your pick of gentlemen suitors." She clasped her hands in glee. "This is going to be the best Season ever!"

Lily lifted another handful of cards. Answering them all would take the rest of the day. With Mrs. Digby's help, she carried the piles into the parlor. Sitting on the sofa, she began to sort through them. The calling cards went in one pile. These had been dropped off by ladies interested in visiting her or having her call on them in the future and by gentlemen seeking permission to court her.

The invitations she placed in another pile, then began sorting them by date of the event. Most of the events were at least two weeks away, since it was customary for invitations to go out a fortnight in advance. A few were for the following week.

But there was nothing from Mr. Drake. Lily fought her disappointment. After all, she oughtn't to be socializing with the man, according to Mrs. Digby. Even if he did send her a card, Mrs. Digby would hardly allow him to court her.

She shouldn't be so selfish. She was already receiving so much attention, why should she long for one more suitor? Yet, all she truly desired from the coming flurry of social activity was to find a single man—the right man.

"Look! Here's one from Duke Walford." Mrs. Digby pressed a card into her hand. "Oh, dear, he would make a brilliant match, positively brilliant! It would be the talk of two continents. He has never shown interest in any of my girls. But you've changed that, Lily. You've caught his eye!"

The duke . . . Lily stared at the name and tried to recall the face that went with it. Was he the tall, slender fellow with the impeccable manners and the heavily oiled hair? She'd met so many people at the ball, been introduced to a plethora of names and titles. Unlike British girls, she was still learning the various ranks and trying to decipher who was related to whom. The hierarchies and protocols were ridiculously confusing. "I suppose being a duke means he's an important person?" she asked, feeling a little silly for not knowing.

Mrs. Digby laughed. "Oh, dear. I forget sometimes you must be taught these things. The ducal rank is second only to that of the royal family itself. There are only seven in all of England. Let's see . . . Three of those are married. The other two are too young, and one is a widower about to leave this world." She furrowed her brow. "The duke of Marlborough's heir would make a wonderful match, of course, but unfortunately, he's already wed. So, that means Richard Walford is, indeed, the greatest catch in all of England!"

Lily smiled politely and nodded. She didn't need to make the greatest match to be happy. She hoped her choice pleased her family, of course. With such interest in her, the chances of that were excellent. She desperately wanted to marry well. But to her, that meant marrying a man she wanted to spend the rest of her life with. An interesting man . . . An attractive man . . . A fascinating man . . .

Once again, her thoughts had betrayed her, circling back to Alexander Drake, a man with no title and, according to Mrs. Digby, a terrible reputation. She would have to get over her infatuation with him. It's not as if he had sent her so much as a calling card.

Her gaze dropped to the floor, and she noticed a letter had fallen there. Reaching down, she retrieved it. There was no return address. Turning it over, she broke the wax seal and unfolded it.

Miss Lily Carrington
34 King Street
London

Dear Miss Carrington,
No doubt you will consider this personal note rather forward of me. I apologize in advance and beg your indulgence. I am writing to invite you to attend a small dinner party. Since the party is planned for two nights hence and I have just returned to London, time did not permit the formality of an engraved invitation. I hope this let-

ter will serve, and that you (accompanied, natu-
rally, by your chaperon) will be able to attend.
The time and the address of my home are below.
Respectfully yours,
Alexander Drake, Esq.

"Who is that one from?" Mrs. Digby leaned toward
Lily, her eyes bright with curiosity.

Trying to appear calm, Lily flipped the letter face-
down. "No one. That is, the event isn't for several
weeks, so I don't need to worry about it yet." She
slid the letter under the stack of invitations, then retrieved one from the top and shoved it into Mrs.
Digby's hands. "What about this event next week?
Do you think it would be appropriate for me to attend
the Royal Ascot with the duchess of Inderby? I can't
recall meeting her, but she's invited me to share her
box."

Mrs. Digby's eyes widened into two round circles.
"Oh, my! Why, Duke Walford truly *has* taken a fancy
to you, dear. He's convinced his *mother* to invite you."
She pressed her plump hand to her breast in an effort
to contain her excitement.

Lily exhaled silently, relieved that she'd success-
fully distracted her from Mr. Drake's letter.

Mrs. Digby pressed her hand to Lily's arm. "This
is so exciting! The Walfords are leaders in the world
of Thoroughbred racing. The dowager duchess is a
veritable icon at Ascot! As a guest of hers, everyone
attending will notice you. Now, what should you
wear? You must be the most well-turned-out lady
there; you simply must. We need to make certain you
have a perfectly lovely hat. All the ladies wear the
most stylish hats at Ascot."

With great flourishes, Mrs. Digby began discussing
the Royal Ascot, the duchess, and her son, the very

eligible duke. Lily nodded and pretended to listen, all the while pondering the much more humble invitation that beckoned to her from the bottom of the pile, and what it might mean.

"Thank you again for escorting me, Hannah," Lily said. She rode with Hannah in her sister's carriage, on their way to dinner with Mr. Alexander Drake. She'd taken longer than usual selecting just the right frock—a tasteful gown of pale green. She ran her palm across her skirt, enjoying the crisp feel of the crepe fabric.

Since it was a dinner, the dress appropriately showed a generous amount of cleavage. Monsieur Worth had been effusive about her décolletage and designed the gown to show off what he considered one of her finest assets. Lily wondered if Mr. Drake—as worldly as he was—had even noticed her figure.

"I love spending time with you, you know that," Hannah said. "Was Mrs. Digby unavailable tonight?"

Lily avoided Hannah's gaze. Mrs. Digby thought her young charge was spending the evening at Hannah's home. Lily hated misleading people, but she also couldn't bear the thought of missing this opportunity to see Mr. Drake. "Mrs. Digby was indisposed."

"I don't know the gentleman," Hannah commented, "but I trust your judgment. I know while you might keep the truth from the oh-so-proper Mrs. Digby, you would *never* lie to me, your dearest sister."

Lily threw up her hands in surrender. "Stop it, Hannah. You're making me feel guilty. All right, I'll tell you the truth. Mrs. Digby said some rather unpleasant things about Alexander Drake, but you and

I both know how these Brits can be about people who lack titles."

Hannah nodded, but her gaze was speculative. "Just tread carefully, Lily. Your Season has just begun, and there's no rush to wed anyone. Don't give your heart to any man until you're ready. I'd hate to see you hurt."

Lily gazed at her archly. "Well, I should truly like to fall in love with a titled nobleman as you did, Hannah—in a single afternoon! And, as I recall, you were wed within the week."

Hannah laughed. "Touché. Well, we're here."

Lily gazed with interest at the brick town house on King Street, a modest yet tasteful structure adorned with crenellated gables and framed by an iron-grill fence. It was neat and tidy, if not ostentatious. Lily liked it at once.

Hannah's driver, Chauncy, helped them from the carriage. They climbed the steps to the stoop. Before they could knock, the door swung inward. A dark-skinned, exotic-looking man in a turban and claret-colored silk pajamas bowed before them. "Welcome to the home of Mister Alexander Drake," he said in cultured English. "Please, come in." Stepping back, he extended his arm.

They entered a foyer decorated in mahogany and tapestries. A marble inlaid table held an oriental vase that displayed ivory-yellow chrysanthemums that matched those woven into the forest green runner under their feet.

The manservant led them into the parlor. Foreign-looking masks and pictures hung on walls paneled in rosy teak and papered in a subtle forest green and gold pattern. The wood shone warmly beneath glowing electric wall sconces. Unlike Mrs. Digby's cluttered rooms, the curios here were few. But these souvenirs of world travels were far more interesting than Mrs. Digby's china cupids. Overall, the room spoke of elegance, taste, sophistication—and a touch of the exotic.

Just like Mr. Drake.

The man in question waited by the black marble fireplace. Lily was barely aware of Lord Moseby rising from a deep green sofa. Barely aware that both men were welcoming them.

Mr. Drake was as compelling as he'd been when she'd first met him. Flickers from the low fire turned his chestnut hair red in places. Along with his white tie and black tails, he had donned an ivory satin vest with alabaster buttons. Her gaze settled on his tie, and she realized she enjoyed the sight of his smooth, tanned neck.

She hoped by the end of the evening she would know his intentions toward her. And know whether she truly wanted his attentions. Perhaps, by becoming better acquainted with him, she would break free of her infatuation with him and be ready to concentrate on titled noblemen. She would have to, if she intended to satisfy her family's ambitions for her.

Caught up in her thoughts, she missed her cue. Hannah had to prompt her to introduce her to the gentlemen. "This is my sister, Countess Ramsey."

"*The* Countess Ramsey? Of ballooning fame? I'm most pleased to make your acquaintance." Lord Moseby barely paused in his gushing long enough to kiss her sister's gloved hand. "I do hope we may talk further about your incredible exploits."

"We certainly may," Hannah said with a smile. She loved to discuss her experiments.

Then it was Mr. Drake's turn to kiss Hannah's hand. He smiled and spoke the usual greeting. "Charmed." A spurt of jealousy filled Lily. He'd never been so gentlemanly toward *her*. Then again, perhaps that's what she liked about the rascal. He wasn't at all awkward around her, as other men seemed to be.

His eyes sparkled as they met hers. "As you've no doubt noticed, my home is still in a disorderly state since I've just returned from overseas."

Lily had seen nothing of the sort. Now she looked about and saw how sparse the furnishings were. Through the door, she glimpsed the dining room, where all but one high-backed walnut chair was still covered in cloth.

"My pantry is unstocked, and I've yet to hire a cook. So, if you're not averse to the idea, I'd like to take you all to the new hotel, the Savoy. The manager, a fellow by the name of Cesar Ritz, has brought a French maître chef with him from Paris. He's determined to make his restaurant as good as those on the Continent, and so far, he's succeeding admirably. I've dined there every evening since returning to London."

"That sounds superb," Lily said. "I love to try new dishes, and visit new places, for that matter. There are so many places to explore here in London, and I've been hearing wonderful things about the Savoy. Didn't it just open?"

He looked pleased at her awareness of London's cultural events. "Yes, indeed. The doors opened just last week. It's a short walk from here, a mere six blocks, and the evening has turned out to be pleasant."

Hannah glanced around. "Is this the extent of our party?"

"Yes, the four of us," Alex said.

Hannah arched a brow at him. "That's it?" She shot Lily a look.

Lily prayed her sister wouldn't read anything into

the situation. At the same time, she secretly rejoiced. He'd only invited *her* to dinner, no one else. Well, except for John. After all, he'd needed a fourth to round out the party.

As they entered the foyer, Hannah commented, "I am curious why you're entertaining so soon after returning to London."

"I enjoy entertaining, whatever the circumstances."

Lily met Alex's gaze and got the strong feeling there was more to it than that. He was a complex man, and he was plotting something. Something involving her. A burst of excitement filled her. She'd never expected her Season to start with such intrigue. This was so much more thrilling than the usual balls and dances.

To her disappointment, on the way to the Savoy, John instead of Alex fell into step beside her.

"It's such a lovely evening, isn't it, Lord Moseby?"

"Ah, it seems to be, yes." He said nothing more.

After a few more steps, Lily said, "I'm looking forward to dinner. Have you dined at the Savoy?"

John nodded. "The first night Alex was in town, he took me there." Again he fell silent.

"And?" she prompted.

"And . . . what?" He looked mystified.

"Did you enjoy it?"

"Enjoy what?"

Hadn't he even been listening to her? It was proper for a gentleman to engage in small talk while with a lady, but discoursing with him was tantamount to pulling teeth. "Did you enjoy the food, the restaurant?"

"Oh, yes. Of course. Then again, I don't have as fine a palate as Alex has. He's always going on about sauces and wine lists and whatnot. I can't tell an expensive meal from one cooked by my grandmother."

"Truly? Then I say your grandmother must have been an excellent cook." She laid her gloved hand on his arm in gentle flirtation. He began to turn an alarming shade of pink.

"Yes. Well . . ." he said, then again fell silent.

Lily dropped her hand. Sighing, she gave up on the conversation. Maybe he'd grow more loquacious later in the evening. She looked ahead to where Mr. Drake was strolling with her sister. They seemed to have no trouble conversing. It sounded like Hannah was asking him about his life overseas. Lily longed to hear every detail, but couldn't very well barge in and insist they let her in on the conversation.

The group strolled down Bedford Street to the Strand, a noisy, congested thoroughfare filled with carriage and foot traffic. Businessmen hurrying home from their offices passed delivery carts laden with crates and boys hawking the evening newspapers. Ahead, the Savoy rose prominently, filling almost an entire block and dominating the waterfront of the Thames.

"Miss Carrington," John burst out. He was practically shouting to be heard over the noise of the street.

Lily looked at him. "Yes?"

"I must apologize. I know you've been thinking ill of me since the ball. Since I tricked you into talking to Alex. I'm not usually so bereft of manners."

Lily's heart filled with sympathy at his distress. "You needn't concern yourself, truly. I didn't mind all that much, though it was a rather strange way to meet someone After all, if I'd been angry, I wouldn't have accepted this invitation, now would I?"

"Well, then," he breathed out, his lips lifting in a smile under his moustache. "I must say you've given me no small measure of relief, Miss Carrington."

"I'm so glad." Lily hoped perhaps now Lord Moseby would be more relaxed around her.

"I'm so glad, too. I was worried I'd utterly ruined . . ." He faltered and looked at his shiny shoes.

"Ruined what?" she asked innocently, though she knew what he'd intended to say. Ruined his chances with her, no doubt. "Surely not my reputation?"

"Oh, heavens, *no*. If I'd thought—That is, I never . . . I meant—ah . . . nothing." Again he looked distressed, his smile gone. Lily sighed. She shouldn't tease him. Some men simply couldn't handle it.

And some men relished it . . .

Her gaze returned to Mr. Drake, now entering the Savoy behind her sister. A doorman held open the door for them, and Lily walked more quickly so as not to keep him waiting. A small smile flitted over the uniformed man's mouth as she passed him, as if her concern for him was unusual.

Inside, electric lights in ornate lamps illuminated the vast lobby, making it bright and cheerful. Plush sofas filled the corners, while the walls were hung with pale-blue brocade tasseled in gold. "Here it is, the talk of London," Mr. Drake said, holding out his arms in an all-encompassing gesture.

Lily gazed in fascination at the deluxe interior. Leaving John behind, she slipped beside Mr. Drake. "It's lovely. Have you ever stayed here?"

"Not— Well, in a way." He seemed disconcerted, and Lily pondered his reaction. If he was the rake Mrs. Digby seemed to think, perhaps he'd had a liaison here. She shivered at the deliciously wicked thought. Despite knowing such behavior was wrong, she did not think less of him.

"In a way . . . You mean you visited someone who

was staying here? Perhaps—" she dropped her voice to a whisper, "a *lady?*"

He shot her a sharp look and spoke low in warning. "Young ladies shouldn't discuss such things."

"And gentlemen shouldn't engage in such activity." She smiled victoriously.

He drew even closer and whispered in her ear, "I never said I was a gentleman." He turned and led them toward the restaurant, leaving Lily with the disconcerting realization that, for once, she'd been bested.

Just inside the grand foyer of the restaurant, itself an immense room, a tuxedoed gentleman warmly greeted them. "Mr. Drake, come this way. Your table is ready as you requested, with the best view in the house."

The party followed him down sweeping stairs into the carmine-carpeted room, where men and women dressed to the nines clustered around delicately carved tea tables. Rose-colored marble pillars lined the walls, supporting an immense vaulted ceiling. Golden chandeliers and triple-branched wall sconces with shell-pink shades gave the foyer a surprisingly mellow atmosphere despite the bright and numerous electric lights.

Lily took note of the clientele, recognizing many faces from the royal ball. Several gentlemen seated at the tables—and a few ladies—greeted Mr. Drake in particular as the garçon led them through to the restaurant.

They were shown to a square table draped in silk-fringed cloth and covered in white linen. Each setting was laid with sterling silver and china edged in gold. Though the restaurant was decorated with gilt-framed mirrors and paintings, Lily's eyes were drawn to the panoramic windows.

The view stole her breath. Past the Embankment Gardens and the Thames, Big Ben rose above the Houses of Parliament, the evening sun glancing off its enormous face.

"Please seat the ladies on this side of the table, so that they might enjoy the view while they dine," Mr. Drake told the garçon.

"Very thoughtful, Mr. Drake," she murmured to him.

"I'm determined, Miss Carrington, that you experience a pleasant evening, in every way." His words caused a strange tingle along her skin. Feeling a little flushed, she was grateful for the chance to sit. Hannah took the chair beside her, also facing the window.

"John—" Mr. Drake gestured to the chair on Lily's other side, but Lord Moseby had already yanked out a chair on her sister's side.

For some reason, Mr. Drake directed a scowl in Moseby's direction, but Lily wouldn't have it any other way. She was delighted to find herself beside Mr. Drake.

Barely a moment passed before a waiter appeared. "Mr. Drake, you are back!" He sounded positively delighted to see them—or at least Alex. "It is a great pleasure to serve you again, and your guests. Monsieur, ma'am'selles," he smiled and nodded at each of them. The manager's French influence had apparently penetrated even to the wait staff.

"It's our pleasure, Hiram," Drake said, then looked at Lily as he said, "You are about to embark on a delightful first experience—what Auguste calls *haute cuisine*. It's exceptionally delicious."

"Mr. Escoffier heard your appeal for an Indian dish," the waiter said. "He has created a special curry sauce that I pray will delight you. It is delightfully spicy, yet so very smooth."

"Thank you, Hiram." With great ease, Alex ordered a seven-course meal for them all, selecting dishes and sauces—including the curry—with the knowledge of a gourmand.

As the waiter departed, Lily leaned toward Mr. Drake and murmured, "You've met the chef?"

He lowered his voice and leaned in close, drawing her into an intimate sphere with his gaze. "Don't look so amazed, Miss Carrington. I'm a diplomat. I've learned it pays to become acquainted with those who are in a position to further one's social goals."

"A chef can do that?"

"Chefs—like hotel managers, butlers, and doormen—have more power than you may realize."

Despite his logical explanation, the fact that Alex received such special attention after a few days' acquaintance spoke volumes about his sophistication and the respect he garnered, even without a title. She realized that he must have money to entertain as he did, not to mention traveling in the prince's circle. Was it family money? Or had he earned it on his own? The mystery surrounding Mr. Drake continued to deepen, and her curiosity burned even hotter.

As the meal was served, she learned at least that Lord Moseby was right—Mr. Drake was a connoisseur of the finer things. As she took her first taste of dessert, the chef's latest creation, Peach Melba, she realized she'd just eaten the best meal she'd ever had.

While the meal couldn't have been better, the conversation was very confusing. Every time she tried to talk to Mr. Drake, he'd direct a question to Lord Moseby. Moseby would give a terse reply, then continue conversing only with Hannah.

She tried yet again to engage him in conversation. "Mr. Drake, thank you for bringing us here. I feel so . . . *sated,* I suppose is the word. You've treated us to a positively decadent meal, and this dessert—it's simply exquisite." She took a last bite of her Peach Melba.

"Satisfying your hunger has been my pleasure," he said, his gaze focused on her mouth.

"Mmmm . . ." She slid out the spoon and returned it to her plate, enjoying the feel of its smoothness against her lips—and glad she finally had his attention.

"Exquisite," he murmured. His heated gaze caused a curious sensation in her stomach.

Then his eyes darkened and he turned his attention to Moseby. "Don't you also enjoy a good meal, John?"

"Me? Well, of course. When one is hungry, one must eat, after all." He turned to Hannah. "You haven't yet told me all the details about your husband's experiments. I understand he broke the altitude barrier in his balloon."

"Yes, he certainly did," Hannah said.

"But I heard you were also in the balloon." He leaned toward her, excitement in his voice. "Tell me, what did it feel like, going up so high?"

Hannah and Lord Moseby were soon analyzing every aspect of her and Benjamin's balloon flight of the previous summer, including arcane scientific theories that bored Lily to no end. Irritated that she'd once again lost Mr. Drake's attention, she studied him when he wasn't looking at her. He was staring at Moseby, a look of confusion on his ruggedly compelling face. A face that had constantly been in her thoughts. What was going on? He couldn't possibly be shy, this man of the world who had so captivated her. No, she knew that wasn't it at all.

"I didn't realize you had such an interest in science," he said to Moseby, his tone cool despite his smile.

Moseby barely looked at him when he replied. "Well, Alex, who wouldn't be interested? Tell me, Countess, what were your findings, after you analyzed the atmospheric samples?"

Hannah began, "To start with—"

Mr. Drake interrupted. "John, weren't you telling me the other day that you'd like to visit America?"

"America?" Moseby appeared at a complete loss. "I say, Alex, I don't know what you're referring to."

"I distinctly recall you saying you thought American girls had a lot to offer us stodgy British gentlemen."

"I suppose so, yes." John shrugged and turned again to Hannah. "About the experiments. You were saying?"

Hannah nodded. "Yes. It helps, first, to consider previous theories about the atmosphere . . ."

Mr. Drake sighed and looked at Lily. Leaning toward her, he said low, "He's not generally so ill-mannered."

"Is it less ill-mannered for you to interrupt a conversation they're both clearly enjoying?" Lily asked with a smile.

His dark brows gathered into a frown and his eyes sparked. Lily was glad she'd gotten such a reaction from him. Finally, he was paying attention to *her*.

"Do you really think we American ladies believe British gentlemen are stodgy?" she asked.

He smiled at that. "I had heard as much, yes."

"I don't think you're stodgy, Mr. Drake. Ill-mannered, yes. But I already knew you were ill-mannered from our first meeting. Is that a result of living overseas?"

"I admit I've seen things most men can only imagine. Or could never imagine." A shadow crossed his face, darkening his eyes to a deep azure.

Lily longed to know what he was thinking, what he'd experienced. He must have experienced something painful, which he found difficult to discuss. Yet he was letting her in, this far. "Tell me, Mr. Drake," she encouraged. "Tell me about yourself."

He seemed oddly reluctant to proceed down this path with her. Was he ashamed of something in his past? Or did he not want her to know the sort of man he truly was? Mrs. Digby's warnings echoed in her head, but the intensity of his compelling gaze stilled her voice.

To encourage him to talk, she laid her hand atop his where it rested beside his plate. "I sincerely want to know."

"Lily . . ."

The sound of her name, spoken so sweetly, warmed her like fine wine. He shouldn't be using her Christian name. Yet somehow it felt right. "Tell me."

A corner of his mouth lifted in an ironic smile. "I would like nothing better. But now isn't the time or place."

"Then we'll have to arrange a better time and place." Lily's impulsive words startled even her. She'd often gotten into trouble for being too spontaneous. But to suggest to a man that they arrange a secret tête-à-tête—she didn't realize until now she was capable of such a thing.

And, even more shocking, she didn't regret it for a moment.

Mr. Drake continued to gaze at her, not in shock as he should be at her bold suggestion, but with delight—perhaps even admiration—shining in his eyes. "You are the damnedest woman—"

"More wine, Mr. Drake?" The waiter appeared at

her shoulder, and Alex moved to a proper distance, taking his hand with him. He appeared composed, yet Lily knew in her heart it was all an act, made possible by years of practice hiding his deeper feelings.

She could reach him, if she had the chance. If they weren't interrupted. If she could somehow be alone with him.

If an opportunity ever presented itself, she decided, she would most definitely take it.

Five

Alex fought the urge to take John's neck between his hands and strangle the life out of him. On the way back to his house, he watched in disbelief as John fell into step beside the countess, walking beside her instead of Lily. Alex heard him ask yet another question about that damned balloon flight.

How could a fellow miss so many cues? He'd done everything he could to help John engage Lily in conversation, to begin to court her. But he'd remained stubbornly blind.

Which had left Alex to entertain Lily. He fell into step beside her, wishing he didn't enjoy her company quite this much. It would do neither of them any good. He'd meant it when he told her dinner wasn't a proper time or place to share himself with her. There *was* no proper time nor place, not for the two of them.

Despite knowing that, he found himself strolling leisurely at her side, lagging behind John and the countess, drawing out this rare moment of privacy. Regularly spaced gaslights pushed back the deepening twilight, and now and then a nightingale's song floated through the air. Even though neither said a word, a summer's eve could hardly be more pleasant. He gazed freely at her, watching the cool evening breeze brush the tendrils of her black hair against her ivory neck. His gaze slid toward the tantalizing globes of her breasts bursting above her gown's neckline, and lower, to her nipped-in waist and rounded hips.

Aware that he was appreciating her figure, she arched her back slightly, a move that lifted her breasts even farther. He bit down on a smile and forced his gaze away. She seemed to have an innate understanding of men, a sophistication beyond her years or experience. Or was it an understanding of him?

Too soon they reached his own block, strolling along a hedge bordering a private garden where jasmine bloomed in intricate tendrils. The flowers' overpowering smell increased his appreciation of Lily's own subtle scent, which had teased his nostrils all through dinner.

"To be honest, I wondered if you would accept my invitation," he finally said. "We didn't exactly part under the best of circumstances."

She shrugged her shoulders, bare under a lacy shawl. Her gaze was bright as she looked at him. "Perhaps that's why I wanted to accept. You must have a reason for tolerating such a *naive* female in your company."

"I don't *mind* your naïveté. In fact, I find it refreshing."

She cocked her head and smiled. "Ah-ha. I see. Then my assumptions about your motives are correct."

He stopped in his tracks. "What?"

She arched a thin brow. "Do you really have to ask? You host a dinner party you're ill-prepared for, on very short notice. You invite only myself—as well as one of your friends to round out the party and make it acceptable. Your friend occupies my sister with boring talk of science, leaving us quite alone." She gestured up the street, to where John and Hannah were almost to the corner, oblivious that they'd left them behind. "It's certainly obvious to me, Mr. Drake. You're courting me."

He opened his mouth, aghast. Her inaccurate—if logical—assessment of the situation flummoxed him, but only for a moment. "You've read things wrong, I'd say."

"I doubt that. It's quite apparent."

My God, such confidence in an untried female! "You're wrong," he said bluntly, determined to convince her—and himself. "I hope I don't hurt your feelings, Miss Carrington. But I have *no* designs toward you. It's for John's sake I invited you. He's quite smitten."

"Lord Moseby? Seriously? He's pleasant enough, I suppose." Furrowing her forehead, she looked down the street toward the gentleman in question. He was just turning the corner with Hannah. A second later, they were out of sight. "So you're trying to make a match between us."

"Absolutely."

"And of course, you have no interest in wooing me yourself."

"Absolutely not."

Rather than hurting her feelings, Lily seemed to take his revelation in stride. She smiled brightly. "You certainly are a terrible matchmaker, Mr. Drake."

Alex realized the absurdity of his claim. Yes, matchmaking had been his intent. But how could she possibly believe that when he was standing here with her, virtually alone? And how he enjoyed the privacy! No chaperons to listen in, or prevent him from saying and doing as he liked with this sweet woman.

A sense of magic enfolded him, and he felt strangely out of time. Despite the occasional carriage that passed on the street, he would have sworn that the only two creatures alive were himself and this gorgeous young lady with the teasing, entrancing smile.

"I know how you long for a title," he said brusquely in an effort to shake the odd feeling that had enfolded him. "In case you've forgotten, I don't happen to have one."

She had the audacity to tap his chest with her finger. "No, but you do have other attributes."

Intrigued, he took a step closer. "Such as?"

Her teasing mien faded, her dark eyes growing serious. "I think it's best if I not put them into words. I have a strong feeling you are already well aware of your effect on women. I've no interest in bloating your self-esteem any farther, to no purpose."

"Who says it would be to no purpose?" he murmured, surprising himself with his honesty. "Perhaps I need as much tender care as the next fellow. Did you consider that possibility?"

Her dark eyes studied him, and he had the queer sensation she could see his soul, see his weaknesses. "I long to believe it's so. You advised me to look below the surface, not to believe only what I can see, do you remember?"

How skillfully she'd turned the tables! "That is my advice, yes."

"Very well." She pressed her hand against his chest, where his heart thudded heavily in wary anticipation. "Then you cannot deny me the right to see the real you."

With that simple statement, he could no longer fight the magic he felt between them. *She longed to give, and he longed to receive what she offered.* Such a simple, elegant arrangement, an irrefutable meeting of minds—and hearts.

He slipped his fingers around her arm, something

he never would have done had they not been alone. Instead of reacting in shock or dismay, she allowed him to pull her closer, slowly closer. They stood in the shadows between streetlights, next to a solid hedge. Across the street, another couple strolled arm in arm. Otherwise, they were still alone in their private universe.

What he wanted from her at this moment . . . His better sense told him to forget it. His sensual nature told him he might never have another chance. She would no doubt marry her titled lord—be it John, the duke, or whoever, and he'd lose his opportunity. He was unaccustomed to magic but knew it had to be rare and precious, for he'd never felt anything like it. He owed it to himself to explore it, with her.

He led her a few feet along the wall to an iron gate. Extracting a key from his pocket, he unlatched the gate and swung it open. Grasping her hand, he pulled her into the private garden that served his house and other houses bordering it on each side of the block. No one was about. A single gaslight illuminated a gravel path through the greenery. He led her off the path onto a grassy rise under a spreading oak tree.

She came with him willingly, when she should have been bolting in the other direction. When he faced her under the tree, he understood why. He recognized the longing in her eyes, the emotion that made her lips tremble. Her innate sensuality coupled with her physical beauty intoxicated him. He'd never imagined a woman so perfectly built for love.

"If you're concerned with your reputation, as you should be, you ought to leave this instant." Despite the harsh truth of his words, his voice vibrated with passion.

"I am concerned, of course," she murmured. "But I'm also where I want to be."

With him. She didn't have to elaborate.

Sliding his hands along her satiny arms, he lowered his lips to hers. She couldn't miss his intention. Yet rather than move away, she lifted her face to his in anticipation.

Still he delayed the moment, gave her yet one more opportunity to say no. "Have you ever been kissed by a man?"

She gazed up at him, unblinking, for a long heartbeat. Then, to his shocked delight, she slipped her hand along the back of his head, making his nape tingle with pleasure.

"Not until now," she breathed. Then she touched her mouth to his.

Six

Lily closed her eyes and fell into a dream. Alex slid his lips over hers gently, leading her slowly into a new world of sensuous pleasure. She'd never felt such longing to explore her feminine nature, and could imagine no other guide except this dynamic man.

The tip of his tongue brushed each of her lips, then teased the corners until she parted them. He pressed her closer as her mouth widened to his, opening to the full brush of his tongue on hers. Languid, heavy heat began flowing through her blood like a drug. She wrapped her arms around his neck and pulled him closer, closer still, until her breasts in their low-cut gown were pressed against his chest. Her breasts tingled and tightened against her satin-lined corset.

Heaven . . . She'd entered heaven in this man's arms.

Angling his head, he kissed her even deeper, his tongue stroking hers in an intimate, heady dance. His fingers burrowed into her chignon, knocking free a lock of hair.

He broke the kiss and pulled back, breathing heavily. "That's enough of that. They're bound to miss us." He stroked her face, fingered the loose lock. "You must fix your hair."

She, too, fought for breath. She said tartly, "That's

it? We'll simply fix my hair and pretend nothing happened?"

"We can't very well keep this up forever."

She smiled. "I rather like that idea." Tightening her arms about him, she kissed him again, immediately rekindling the heat between them. He responded hungrily, desperately, pressing her so hard against him she felt the buttons of his vest through her dress. Still she wasn't satisfied, knew there was more, much more.

A moment later, he'd again set her firmly away from him. Yet he continued to touch her, as if finding it hard to break free. He stroked her bare shoulders, his palms leaving her skin tingling with heat. She realized then her shawl had fallen to the ground.

"You have to stop doing that," he said. "We both do. Your reputation—"

"My sister would never say anything to hurt me. Besides, it's not as if we're going to . . . allow you to ruin me, right here in this garden."

"We're heading in that direction."

"Were we?" Had they really come that close to—to *consummation?* And how glorious would that be, when merely kissing him rocked her very soul?

She'd been taught that only tarts and prostitutes succumbed. She was neither. Was she really supposed to believe that their sensual exploration was wrong? How could she, when it made her feel transcendently alive? When it made her feel so close to this wonderful, fascinating man?

"Come. Let's get back." Reaching down, he grasped her shawl and laid it gently around her shoulders. Using it to pull her forward, he kissed her forehead. "You're a marvel, Lily Carrington. But you know this is wrong."

She caught his gaze in the moonlight, and studied it. "It doesn't feel at all wrong, and you know it."

"It's not that simple. We enjoyed ourselves tonight, but it has to end here."

"No. There's still so much about you I don't know."

"Lily, I can't court you."

"I don't care about courting. I care about you. Can't we meet again, just to talk? Please." She laid her hand on his arm.

"I can't see why . . ."

"Please."

Alex couldn't refuse her. He found himself nodding. After all, if he met her again, if he revealed all his shocking secrets, it would surely destroy that starry-eyed look in her eyes. She would completely lose interest in him. She might even grow to despise him.

The thought made him ill, but he knew it would be best for them both. It had to be better than this painful longing that now plagued him.

Besides, he rationalized, he needed to keep an eye on her. His ploy with John had failed, but the duke and the prince still had plans for her. How better to stay involved than to meet with her? She herself could alert him if she intended to accept the duke's suit.

And then what? Somehow he would have to convince her not to acquiesce, yet maintain the prince's good favor. *Later. I'll deal with those details later.* After all, he was an expert at thinking on his feet in tense, difficult situations. That's why the Crown paid him so well.

"Meet me here, in this garden. I'll send word when." Slipping his hand into his pocket, he removed the gate key and pressed it into her palm.

Taking her arm, he led her out of the garden to the

sidewalk. This time they walked at a brisk pace to his house.

"What were you thinking, John?" Alex demanded. "I did everything I could to build you up in the girl's eyes, to encourage you to talk to her, yet you completely ignored her!"

John merely shrugged. "Well, I'd read about the earl's balloon flight, and I was curious."

As soon as the ladies had departed in their carriage, Alex had wasted no time grilling John about his behavior.

To his relief, John and the countess hadn't seemed to notice that he and Lily had come in well behind them. He'd found them sitting on the sofa, John watching in fascination as the countess sketched a scientific diagram on a sheet of paper, explaining something arcane.

Now, his body still thrumming from his intimacy with Lily, Alex grew even angrier. If John had played his part correctly, Alex never would have tasted the lady's sweet lips. He wouldn't be standing here now, burning from the inside out, fighting to forget how perfect she felt in his arms. Fighting his hopeless desperation for more.

"That's *it*, you were curious about balloons? What about Lily? What about that gorgeous creature you're so infatuated with? How could you *ignore* her? How could any man ignore her? I gave you so many openings, and you did nothing!" He chopped the air with the side of his hand in a characteristic gesture.

"I'm sorry, I just . . . It didn't feel right," John said.

"Didn't feel right? *What* didn't feel right? Everything feels right with Lily Carrington!"

John gave him a queer look. "By God, Alex, you needn't get so twisted out of shape. One would think you were infatuated with her yourself."

Alex caught himself, and realized he was showing far too much outrage. With an effort, he reined himself in. He wasn't about to let John lead him down that very private path. "This isn't about me."

Pausing before the hearth, he crossed his arms and studied John. This time he spoke with moderation. "I just don't understand, John. We had a *plan*. You were to court her and marry her before the duke could. Before the prince could get his hands on her. Explain it to me, in a way that makes sense."

"Lily is . . ." John sighed. "Well, she's perfect. You know that."

"Precisely. Go on."

"She's a . . . a goddess. I suppose I'm too much of a mortal to court her."

The man was intimidated by her. The lovely young chit had him so discombobulated, he couldn't handle it. Couldn't handle *her*.

"I'm not a worldly fellow like you, Alex," John said.

"She's only a nineteen-year-old girl," he protested weakly, knowing his words fell far short of describing Lily.

"I haven't enjoyed the pleasures of the East, or made love to actresses and such," John said. "Oh, I've had my share of liaisons, but they were women I could talk to. Regular women. Women like the countess, not that I have designs on her. I know she's in love with her husband. But you understand, don't you?"

Regular women? Who would want a regular woman when he could have Lily? Of all the women he'd met, here and abroad, he'd never met one like Lily Carrington. Despite her innocent appeal, she exuded sensuality. He squeezed his eyes shut, fighting a wash of physical pleasure at the memory of her eager seductiveness. To take such a woman to bed, to lead her in a full exploration of her voluptuous nature . . .

"Damn." Filled with frustrated energy, he began to pace. "Damn, damn, damn! We have to do something."

"There is another solution, Alex."

Alex gave John his full attention, despite his hesitant tone. "Tell me."

"Why don't *you* marry her?"

With a shock, Alex realized he hadn't given the possibility a moment's thought. Should he have? Having such a lady as his wife . . . Despite the appealing image of Lily in his bed every morning and every night, the absurdity of the idea struck him hard, cutting deep into his pride. He hid his pain, instead releasing his frustration in a disbelieving laugh. "Don't be daft, man. I want her safe, not sorry. That's rather the point, isn't it?"

"I don't follow."

"You know as well as I do that I'm hardly a suitable match for the girl. What do I have to offer her, except a dubious reputation?"

"Nonsense. You're a great success at the Foreign Office. You've had important assignments with the diplomatic corps in a dozen countries now—"

"Seven."

"Seven, then. You have a stellar future in government. You've even built up a goodly fortune. You have more to your name than a lot of us destitute aristocrats."

"I'm a workingman, John. There's not a lord or lady anywhere in my past, as far as I know. You know how aristocrats look down on people who actually *work* for their daily bread."

John frowned. "I say, you're painting us all with the same tainted brush."

"I'm sorry. But you know it's true. I'm certain Lily's parents didn't send her all this way from New York to marry a nobody. She could more easily have stayed in America and wed a banker, or a merchant's son." *Like me,* he silently added. "Besides, that's not the real problem, and you know it."

"Then what is?"

He threw out his hands. Was John blind? *"Me,* of course! I'm not cut out for marriage. What would I possibly need with a wife?" In truth, since sharing his life with Sikara, he had often fantasized about settling down. Yet he refused to take any step that would upset his career ambitions. Not only would the burden of a wife and family severely limit his options. His role as secret liaison to the Crown would become impossible to fulfill. And that dangerous yet lucrative position was the only reason he could afford to satisfy his expensive tastes and mingle with the fashionable set.

John had other concerns. "An even bigger problem in wooing Lily is infuriating the prince."

"Well, there is that not insignificant concern, as well."

"It's quite significant," John said. "If I truly pursued a suit—"

"Come now. You're a marquess. The prince wouldn't touch her if she were yours. To do so would cause a terrible scandal. Besides, you have your family influence, your position in the House of Lords. Bertie couldn't ruin you with a single stroke of a pen." As he could Alex. He could assign him to some remote region and forget about him. He could dismiss him from the Foreign Service altogether. He could destroy him in any number of ways.

Virtually all of the high-level positions in the Foreign Office were occupied by noblemen and aristocrats. Through sheer grit and determination, Alex had made himself a place among their ranks, taking the dangerous, risky assignments others shied away from. But he remained an outsider. Should he falter, should he anger those born to power, his life would be destroyed.

John seemed to be considering his arguments. Alex had to act fast, before his friend thought up more objections. He sat beside him on the sofa and spoke with sincere urgency. "Listen, John. Please reconsider. Every time I think of Lily trapped in marriage to the duke, or turned into a plaything of the prince's, it makes my blood boil." His hand clenched on his thigh.

"I admit it's not a pretty picture, but I'm not sure I'm the right fellow—"

Alex clapped him on the shoulder. "You can win her! I'm certain of it. You're a marquess, you have a clean reputation. You meet every one of her requirements, and those of her family. I'm sure you can win her. You know she's worth the trouble."

He shrugged. "Well, yes, I suppose . . ."

"For heaven's sake, John, even if she wasn't a goddess, as you put it, she's an heiress to millions! Her father is a railroad baron. Think of her dowry. Think of what you could do with it, all the ways you could spend it. You could put a new roof on that dilapidated family seat of yours at Haversham. And weren't you saying the other day that you wanted to invest in some racehorse or other?"

"Gilded Lily, that's her name." His eyes widened. "My God, do you suppose that's a sign?"

Alex would take any coincidence that presented itself, anything that gave John confidence. "Yes, yes, of course it's a sign. Why, you can buy her the horse as a wedding present." Alex was rather proud of that embellishment, especially when John's face lit up as he considered the possibilities her money could buy.

"I certainly would welcome her dowry. Who wouldn't?" His exuberance began to fade once more. He tightened his lips and blew out a breath in frustration. "But it's just so blasted hard to court someone like her. I'm certain she thinks I'm incredibly dull."

Dull? What had Lily said about John? *He's pleasant enough, I suppose.* Alex decided to put his own spin on her statement. It might be stretching the truth, but it was for her own good. "You're wrong, John. She told me she finds you quite pleasant company."

John's expression brightened considerably. "She did?"

"Most assuredly. I'd say she's as enamored of you as you are of her." Surely this would be considered a forgivable lie, even though it was to his best friend. In any event, his ploy seemed to be working. Even now, John appeared more confident, his head lifting, his back straightening. Secure in the "knowledge" that Lily welcomed his attentions, he'd have the fortitude to pursue her. To marry her. To keep her safe.

"She likes me?"

"Definitely."

New enthusiasm entered his voice. "Then I suppose I *might* court her, if—"

Alex didn't give him a chance to voice more objections. "Excellent." He clapped his hands and rubbed them together, then jumped to his feet. "Here's what you must do."

* * *

The carriage had never moved slower. On all sides, other open victorias and broughams filled the lanes in Hyde Park as society's elite took a leisurely turn on Rotten Row on a pleasant Thursday afternoon. Sitting beside Lord John Moseby and across from a chattering Mrs. Digby, Lily felt so restless and bored she wanted to scream.

Every few yards, they paused as Mrs. Digby engaged her friends and acquaintances in discourse. That alone would be enough to tire anyone out. Lily had no idea whom they were gossiping about, the names and titles spinning in her head. Worse, Mrs. Digby had described her various aches and pains at least a dozen times to a dozen different faces. Lily adored her English hostess, but sometimes she longed for more exciting company. Longed for Mr. Drake's company.

Right now, the most exciting person available was Lord Moseby, who had said almost nothing to her. Perhaps if they could be alone for a few minutes, she could finally get to know this man Mr. Drake seemed determined to match her to. And assuage her curiosity about her enigmatic "guardian."

Lily leaned over and tapped Mrs. Digby on the knee, drawing her attention long enough to ask, "Excuse me. Lord Moseby is going to accompany me on a short walk, here along the lane."

Mrs. Digby glanced up from her conversation with a gray-haired lady friend. "Lily, I'm not sure . . ." As usual, Mrs. Digby was concerned that her charge do nothing untoward.

"It's just a stroll to stretch our legs. We'll walk ahead and you can pick us up when the carriage reaches us. Come," she said to Moseby, then unlatched the brougham door.

"Allow me." Moseby exited first, then helped her

to the muddy ground. "Are you quite sure you wouldn't rather ride?"

Hiking her yellow skirt, Lily sidestepped a pile of steaming horse droppings in the muddy track and settled her ruffled parasol on her shoulder. "I wanted to be alone with you, Lord Moseby," she said with a smile.

Moseby began to grow pink, and Lily groaned inwardly. She decided to turn the conversation in a more fruitful direction. She had noticed as many gentlemen as ladies out and about, even thought it was a weekday afternoon. At this time of day, her industrious father would be at the office of his company, Atlantic-Southern Railroads. "Here in England, I've noticed that many gentlemen of stature are also men of leisure," she said. "There are so many men out and about today, for instance. Yet I haven't seen your friend."

"Alex? Oh, he'd laugh if you called him a gentleman of leisure. He's dedicated to his career."

"His career as a spy, you mean?"

"Spy? Oh, goodness." John looked a little surprised by the description. "It's not supposed to be general knowledge."

He added nothing more, so Lily pressed ahead, determined to make the most of her opening. "Have you known Mr. Drake long?"

"Oh, yes. Since Cambridge. He was there on scholarship."

"Really." She gave him her full attention, encouraging him to continue with an avid expression.

"Yes," John nodded vigorously. "He had to work three times as hard because he wasn't from a privileged family. And he was constantly reminded that he was a 'charity case," as the other boys called it. Yet by graduation, he'd won over even the most snobbish of fellows." John had never uttered so much to Lily at one time. He seemed pleased to find a topic he could easily discuss with her.

"I'm not surprised," she commented. Alex possessed charm in abundance, as she well knew.

"He has a gift for languages," John continued. "And intrigue, which is why he's already attained such success with the Foreign Office. I truly admire his achievements. I have no skills more helpful than hunting game or hosting parties."

"I'm sure you have much to offer. You serve in the House of Lords."

"Yes, there is an evening session tonight, in fact."

Lily needed to keep him from going off on a tangent. "You consider Mr. Drake's achievements are more remarkable than those of other men?" she asked carefully. She longed to know more about Alex, yet didn't want to reveal too strong an interest in him.

"Indeed. Alex is a self-made man, the sort you in America most admire. From what I've read of your own father's business dealings, I'd say he's one as well."

Lily nodded. "Yes, he is. My grandfather was a sea captain, not at all interested in business. My father built his fortune on his own drive and sense."

"I can hear the pride in your voice."

Lily smiled. Learning Alex shared characteristics with her beloved father only increased her admiration of him.

"Alex also built his own fortune," Moseby continued. "That is, the Crown pays him handsomely for his unique services."

"Because the work is dangerous."

He gave her a wide-eyed look, as if surprised by her insight. "Precisely."

They reached a particularly rough section of track,

the mud churned up by the wheels of numerous passing carriages. John helped her up a grassy knoll so that they could stroll above the traffic. Tucking his arms behind his back, he continued. "Alex has an incredibly strong drive to succeed in whatever he puts his mind to. Through sheer determination, he's bettering his lot in life. Here in England, we don't hold self-made men in very high esteem, not as you do in America. We put much greater store in station and rank, even if such men are lazy or incompetent. Because of that, I fear in a few years your country will surpass ours as a leader of other nations."

He drifted into a discussion of the countries' relative places in the world. Lily nodded and agreed in the right places, even though she had little idea whether John was right. All she could think about was Alex, and how else she might encourage John to talk about him.

"Yet Mr. Drake does have some time to socialize," she commented.

"Yes, he always jokes that he makes just enough to spend between assignments. He'll probably be returning overseas in a few months."

"He has no plans to settle down, like other men?"

John gave her a curious look, and Lily worried she'd pressed a little too far. Still, he answered her. "Alex has no desire to settle down. Considering his past, he may never settle down."

Now they were getting somewhere. "Why? What happened?"

Moseby pondered a moment, then finally said, "I really ought not to be discussing this with you. I should never have alluded to it. My, what a pretty posies." He gestured to a trim bed of roses.

Lily refused to lose this chance. "You're referring to his foreign mistress, aren't you?" she said boldly.

Young ladies weren't supposed to even know about mistresses, but she didn't care. She had to learn about Alex.

Moseby was so startled, he froze in place. "You know about her?"

She nodded, feigning knowledge she didn't have so that Moseby would feel free to discuss the topic with her. "How did he meet her?"

A smile slid over Moseby's lips, lifting his thick moustache. "That's the most amazing part. He rescued her. He was assigned to negotiate peace treaties between Bedouin tribes in Oman. It was his first truly important assignment for the Crown. We promised the tribes British protection in return for their promise that they would only deal with us, and not other countries. Well, that was all fine and dandy, until Alex discovered that some of the tribes were running a healthy slave trade right under the nose of our Royal Navy."

"Slaves?" Lily's spine tingled. Such an exotic story! And Alex had been in the middle of the trouble, risking his life, his every move crucial, his senses keenly alert. Her own heartbeat accelerated in response. "And, the lady?"

"Sikara was in a slave caravan bound for the coast when Alex stole her, so to speak."

Stole her? He stole a woman? She imagined Alex astride a horse, garbed in desert raiment, charging into the face of danger, sweeping the woman into his arms and carrying her off. What a seductive way to meet! No wonder she became his mistress. "What happened to her then?"

"She had no family, so he kept her with him. She lived with him for two years, until . . ." His voice trailed off. "I really ought not to be discussing such things with a well-bred lady."

"Of course you can. I'm an American girl. We're not as circumspect as your English sisters." If any time called for use of her feminine wiles, this was it. Sliding her hand up his forearm, she gazed pleadingly into his face. "Please, Lord Moseby. Tell me what happened."

"She died in childbirth. It hit Alex hard, that he wasn't able to protect her in the end."

Words failed Lily. She became lost in thought as she walked quietly beside Alex's best friend, pondering what Moseby had revealed. How terribly sad, to lose a mother and child both. This must be the source of the shadows she'd sometimes seen in Alex's eyes. Did he think of her often? Did his heart ache still?

And the biggest question of all, Instead of being appalled that Alex had taken a mistress, why did she only long to take his pain away?

Seven

Just as Mrs. Digby had envisioned, Lily sported a stylish hat at the Royal Ascot racecourse in Berkshire. This was Ladies Day, the second day of the four-day event. It was a day to see and be seen, to display fashion as much as watch the Thoroughbreds compete.

Lily looked at the scene before her from under the broadest hat she'd ever worn—a full twenty-eight-inch platter decorated with pale pink roses and cornflowers. A scarf tied in a bow around the crown matched her blue silk dress. She noticed that most of the ladies present wore gowns without bustles. Worth had been right. She'd actually caused a change in London fashion.

"Come, Miss Carrington. Let's take a turn about the pavilion while we wait for the Royal Procession to begin. If you don't mind, Richard." Duchess Walford turned to her son, seated on Lily's other side.

Since being picked up at Mrs. Digby's house in Belgrave Square, Lily had been bookended by the dowager duchess and her son, Richard, the current duke. They'd driven by carriage to Paddington Station, then by hired carriage from the Ascot station to the course. She had anticipated Richard himself asking to stroll with her about the pavilion, rather than his mother. Unlike her other suitors, he had yet to expend any effort seeking time alone with her.

"I don't mind at all," he now said. "Go on. I know how ladies enjoy mingling and gossiping." Lily detected a hint of censure in his tone. His mother seemed oblivious to the undercurrent, probably because he'd accompanied his words with an open smile.

He certainly was a handsome man, more so when he graced her with his too-rare smile. He wore a neatly trimmed moustache on his square face. His oiled black hair glinted in the sun, a thinning patch at the apex of his scalp betraying his maturity. Small lines radiated out from the corners of his brown eyes, and a scar marred his forehead.

Despite these flaws, he looked the very picture of a storybook duke: well spoken, aristocratic, and authoritative.

His mother was susceptible to his charms, that was obvious. She doted on her only son and heir. As for herself, Lily enjoyed the duke's company but still felt she knew next to nothing about his character or his personality. He remained a polite enigma. She wasn't even certain what attracted him to her. Though he'd invited her to accompany him to this prominent event of the Season, they'd engaged in only superficial conversation. He'd given his racing form most of his attention.

Lily rose and followed the duchess as she exited the Walfords' private box. The crimson and purple feathers covering the duchess's hat bobbed above the crowd, signaling her passage as she wended her way along the walkway toward an open-air pavilion. Lily watched how the great lady walked, so regal and serene despite the pressing crowds. Gentlemen paused in their conversation as she passed to tip their top hats; ladies nodded their heads. As her companion, Lily received their curious yet friendly smiles. Occasionally, the duchess acknowledged their deference with a slight nod.

When they reached the open space of the pavilion, the duchess walked beside Lily. "I'm so happy you were able to join us today, Miss Carrington. It's been years since Richard went out of his way to invite a young lady to accompany him at one of the Season's events."

Years? How odd. "Is that so?" Lily asked, unsure what to say to such a remark.

"He's been reluctant to settle down, you see. Now that he's reached his fortieth year, he's finally realizing the logic of what I've been telling him. He can't wait much longer to find a suitable bride. While I had hoped—excuse me, I know you will think this rather rude of me, but you must understand the situation of a great house such as ours—I had hoped he would find a good English lady to wed. But how he has resisted me!"

Wed? Lily tried to hide her shock. She barely knew this woman's son, and his mother seemed ready to announce an engagement!

"Now that I've met you, I can say that perhaps it wasn't so bad that he waited so long."

"Milady, the duke hasn't said anything to me of such intentions. I honestly don't know what to say."

She made a dismissive noise and waved her gloved fingers. "Nonsense. Of course he hasn't, not to you. But he has to me." Her eyes sparked as she revealed her secret. She lowered her voice confidentially. "He told me when he asked me to invite you today that he was quite set on you. Naturally, I was concerned he had settled his attentions on the wrong sort since I hadn't yet laid eyes on you. And you *are* American.

I had, however, heard rumors of your beauty and grace, and of the prominence of your family. Now that we've met, I am satisfied to give the prospect of a union my full support."

Lily fought for a polite reply, not ready to commit, but not wanting to irritate the woman. "Thank you, Your Grace," she finally said.

That seemed to satisfy the duchess. Taking Lily's arm, she strolled with her about the pavilion as if she were already her daughter-in-law.

Is this what I want? Lily asked, her head spinning. Certainly, such a match would thrill her socially conscious mother to no end. Her mother had been engaged in a long-running battle with Mrs. Astor, who ruled New York society. Since her family's fortunes were considered new money, Mrs. Astor had cut the Carringtons from the elite Four Hundred. In retaliation, her mother had vowed to see her daughters make the most splendid matches imaginable. She had sent Hannah and Lily to England to find noble husbands, with plans to send her other three daughters—Pauline, Clara, and Meryl—when they came of age.

Surprisingly enough, Hannah had made such a match instantly, on their first day in Europe. She and Lord Benjamin Ramsey, an earl, had fallen in love at first sight and married within the week. Hannah's easy success had filled their mother with visions of marrying her remaining daughters to dukes and earls and counts.

As for Lily . . . Her mother had frequently said that her socially adept second daughter had the greatest prospects. Everyone in the family knew it. Lily was expected to make a stellar match. Her mother would crow with her success, and rub the Four Hundred's noses in their failure to accept the Carringtons.

Until recently, Lily had secretly enjoyed bearing the

weight of her family's expectations. She'd been thrilled with the attention and the accolades, with being considered a "beauty." What nineteen-year-old girl wouldn't? Everything had seemed so dreamlike and easy. She'd envisioned herself at parties and balls being doted on by ardent suitors. Envisioned herself courted by those dukes and earls and counts. Envisioned having the enviable problem of making a choice among such eligible men.

All of that was coming to pass.

And she was enjoying none of it.

Alexander Drake. It was entirely his fault. She squeezed her fan in her gloved hand, frustrated beyond measure. Not a moment went by that she didn't think of him, of his ironic smile, of his deep silken voice speaking her name, of the shocking, delicious pressure of his mouth on hers. Not a moment.

He'd possessed her. He could ruin her. He could destroy her chances for marriage if she didn't put him out of her mind. Yet every day that passed, she longed for a message from him. He'd agreed to contact her to meet him secretly in his garden, and she'd heard nothing.

Had he forgotten all about her? About their illicit kiss? How could he? How could she have allowed her heart to be so taken with such a scoundrel, when so many proper gentlemen vied for her attention?

His friend Lord Moseby, for one. He was now actively courting her. He'd taken her for rides in Hyde Park and invited her to an evening musicale. Every moment in his company Lily had to force herself not to mention Mr. Drake's name except in passing, not to demand answers, not to quiz him on everything he knew about his friend. Through sheer unladylike brashness, she had learned about his mistress Sikara. Other than that, all she knew was that yes, he was in town, but his social calendar was limited since he was hard at work for the Foreign Office.

And still Lily couldn't get him off her mind. *Forget about him,* she now counseled herself. *You could very well become a duchess. A duchess! That's why you're here in England. That's why you came. Not to have your heart stolen by man who can bring you nothing but heartache.*

She looked at the lady beside her and tried to imagine taking her place. Tried to imagine people deferring to her as she walked past them. What a strange, fantastic life that would be. She would become a great lady overnight. She'd heard that the Walford's holdings were extensive, their family seat historic and immense. What a fairytale life that would be.

Yet, would she be happy?

That depended on her husband. She longed to love her husband and receive his love in return. No title could compete with that.

Then you must make yourself love the duke. A simple solution. She must look upon the duke and see all the positive attributes he had to offer.

If he's determined to marry you, you must fall in love with him. And forget about Mr. Drake—

Just then the crowd parted. As if conjured by her own thoughts out of thin air, she found herself looking at Alexander Drake.

Eight

Lily's heart hitched and her breath jammed in her throat. Though two weeks had passed, Alexander Drake's presence had lost none of its power. He leaned against a support column, perfectly at ease in top hat and tails. His gaze slid to hers, cool, enigmatic, and thoroughly male.

"Oh my," she murmured, just loud enough for the duchess to hear.

"Excuse me, did you say something?" she asked.

"I—It's nothing. Perhaps we should return to our box?" She tried to maneuver the duchess in the other direction, but the duchess remained firm. Lord Moseby, Lily now realized, had been standing beside Drake, and was now advancing toward them, Drake right behind him.

"My lady, it's good to see you. And Miss Carrington," Lord Moseby said, smiling brightly at her.

"Good afternoon, Lord Moseby," the duchess said, nodding at him. "Mr. Drake, is it? My son mentioned you had returned from Ara-bee."

"Yes, milady," He bent over her proffered hand. "Actually, I was last in Persia rather than Arabia."

"Oh, pooh. I can never keep those savage countries straight."

Mr. Drake's gaze turned to Lily, and he nodded in greeting. "Miss Carrington." To her keen disappointment, none of the warm intimacy they'd shared was reflected in his azure eyes. As if uninterested in her, he focused his attention on the duchess.

Lily simmered at his cool dismissal. He'd forgotten their encounter! How unfair. How dare he come into her life, steal such a heated improper kiss, then pretend nothing had happened?

"Are you two coming to our hunting party?" the duchess asked. "I believe the invitations have been extended."

"Oh, yes!" Lord Moseby said instantly. He smiled at Lily, hope shining in his eyes. "I'm looking forward to it very much. Your estate offers the best grouse hunting in three counties."

"And Mr. Drake?"

"I hadn't anticipated attending, unfortunately. I have work—"

"Oh, bother work." The duchess waved her hand dismissively. "What a sorry excuse. Why, I'll speak with the secretary himself and demand that you be freed from your duties. The party would not be the same without your delightful stories of distant lands."

"I would hate to put you out," Drake protested. His smile had completely vanished. Lily knew he had no desire to attend the house party, though she couldn't understand his reticence. He certainly had enjoyed the company of aristocrats before.

"Nonsense," the duchess said. "I'll see to it immediately. Come, Miss Carrington. Richard is no doubt growing anxious for your delightful company." Tucking Lily's arm in hers, she turned her around to lead her back to their box.

Lily risked a glance over her shoulder at the two men. Lord Moseby continued to smile at her. Beside him, Alexander Drake's expression had darkened considerably.

The duchess said, "I do enjoy their company, particularly Mr. Drake's. He's so charming for a commoner. Why, I should have thought of this before!" She halted and turned around. "Mr. Drake? Lord Moseby? If you would like, you may join us in our box. We have room."

Moseby looked at Drake, waiting to take his cue from him. Drake nodded. "We'd be honored."

Lily's pulse quickened, despite her irritation with the man. He would be sitting near her, only a few feet away.

Suddenly, her sophisticated, relaxed outing threatened to turn dangerous.

Alex found it difficult to contain himself as he watched the duke charm Lily. The man had absolutely no honor. He tried to win her with occasional smiles and overblown flattery, yet he paid scant attention to her.

Two tea-size round tables and eight chairs occupied the duchess's box. John and the duke sat on either side of Lily, and Alex had taken the chair directly across from her. He'd hoped giving John the place beside her would encourage the girl to compare her two suitors, and realize the duke was no kind of man compared to the kind-hearted John.

The duchess had invited them because she knew they were her son's friends, part of the Marlborough Set. Alex didn't care why. He was simply glad of the opportunity to see firsthand the progress Duke Walford was making in courting Lily.

And he seemed to have made a great deal of progress, if his mother's acceptance of Miss Carrington was any indication.

Was she truly in danger of marrying the man? Or

did she see him for what he was, a dissolute individual with a preference for opium, gambling, and the company of men?

The immense clock on the bell tower above the grandstands struck one. At that precise moment, the Golden Gates at the far end of the racecourse swung wide, admitting the royal procession. Prince Edward and Princess Alexandra sat in a coach pulled by four, waving to the applauding crowd as they rode around the racetrack.

"Bertie looks simply smashing," the duchess said, peering through her lorgnette. "And the princess—is that amber-colored satin she's wearing? And a matching bonnet! How *darling.*"

"As soon as they take their seats, the races can finally commence," the duke told Lily with a smile. "What do you think, Miss Carrington? Is Jubilee Hour destined to win this year's Gold Cup? Or have I squandered my bet?"

"Let's hope that isn't the case," she replied, her soft lips turning up in a smile. In response, the duke's eyes glittered in pleasure.

A shaft of jealousy cut through Alex and he gripped the wrought-iron armrests of his chair. He resented how the duke looked at her loveliness and saw nothing but pounds. And he resented *her* for being so damned naive that she didn't see the truth.

Time was critical. Engagements had already been announced as a result of the whirlwind of activity surrounding the Season. If John didn't act quickly, Lily could be engaged to the duke any day. He had no idea how often the man had visited her.

He nudged John with his elbow.

John's eyes widened. He silently formed the word. *Now?*

Alex frowned and nodded. Did he have to do everything himself?

John cleared his throat, then turned toward Lily. "Miss Carrington, have you placed a bet for this next race?"

Arching that graceful neck, she partially faced him. "Oh, no, I don't know enough—"

"We're choosing the horses together and betting together," the duke interrupted, drowning out further response. He had the audacity to pat her hand where it rested on the table near her teacup.

Yet after she turned her attention to the field, the duke's smile slid away. He stared at John over her head, his jaw tight, his eyes hot with warning. Under the duke's threatening glare, John seemed to shrink. He leaned slowly back in his seat. Crossing his arms, he looked away, as if he had no interest whatsoever in the lovely female a few feet from him.

Damn. Alex leaned toward John and whispered, "Say something else to her. You've been courting her, haven't you? Hell, you're practically engaged!"

John's Adam's apple bobbed as he swallowed. "He doesn't like it."

"To hell with him."

John sucked in a breath. To his credit, he leaned forward and tried again. "Miss Carrington, that is a most lovely bonnet. I'd say it's the finest here—the only exception being yours, milady," he added for the duchess's benefit. The duchess nodded acknowledgement from her place beside a lady friend at the other tea table.

John glanced at Alex, and he nodded his approval.

"How nice of Moseby to notice your couture, Miss Carrington. He's not known for his fashion sense."

"Isn't he? He has a great interest in art," Lily said. "Is fashion so different from the fine arts?"

Good girl, Lily, Alex secretly rejoiced. She hadn't been so swept away by the duke that she agreed with his every word.

At her defense of John, the duke's smile faded and his eyes darkened. "It is quite different, miss. Requires a different sensibility. A social sensibility, something Moseby is so aptly demonstrating that he lacks."

"That's rather harsh, milord," Lily said.

Alex wanted to kiss her—again.

The duke leaned close and whispered in her ear. Alex strained to pick up a hint of his words but couldn't make anything out. Pulling back, Lily gave John a sharp stare, no doubt wondering if the poison the duke had fed her were true.

Don't believe him, Lily. If it suits him, he has no compulsion against bald-faced lies.

John looked as if he wanted to crawl under the table and hide. Alex's heart went out to his friend. With his open and honest nature, John was ill-suited to court intrigue. He had to bolster his spirits before John began to doubt himself again. He tapped his arm. "Come place a bet with me. It's still five minutes to post and I need your advice."

Without a word, John rose and followed him from the box to the rear of the grandstands and a row of betting windows. They approached one of the windows and Alex spoke briskly to the clerk behind the iron mesh screen. "A quinella on Blessing in Disguise and Randy Deliverer." He slid him his pound notes and received a ticket in return.

Turning around, he found John long-faced, hands in pockets, staring at his shoes. He clapped his friend on the back. "Don't lose heart, John. Today's arrangement makes for a bad situation, but when you have her alone—"

John's entire body stiffened. "Don't say it, Alex. You're only going to make this harder."

"What? I'm making *what* harder?"

Lifting his chin, he stared at him, his gray eyes filled with trepidation. "I can't do this. I simply can't."

Alex's chest clenched. *God, no.* What would he do to protect Lily if he couldn't marry her off to good-hearted John Moseby?

"Go ahead, call me a coward," John said. "That's probably the best word for me right now. But I can't go against the duke. He's too . . . dangerous."

"Dangerous? Don't be silly," Alex scoffed. "He's nothing but a sycophant, a rounder. He takes his orders from the prince without a thought in his own head. He has no more mettle or ambition than a field mouse."

John chuckled, but the sound carried no humor. *"You* may think of him that way. To you, that's probably all he is. But I know in my gut I can't compete with him. I know if I anger him, he'll do something to make my life miserable. I just can't—I can't live like that, worrying about intrigue and plots against me. I can't."

"But what about Lily? You've been getting on so well."

John sighed. "Alex, if I truly thought she had the same esteem for me that I have for her, I might be able to find the courage to ask for her hand, or even suggest we elope. Don't get me wrong. She treats me with every politeness. But I'm certain she's set her heart elsewhere, and it's not on me."

Damn the girl. Was she really falling for the duke? Alex's fists clenched, his chest tightening in dismay. He wished he could shake some sense into her.

Perhaps he could. If he got her alone.

Speaking low, he imbued his words with intensity. "Don't give up yet. Give me until tomorrow. I have a feeling things will change for the better."

At his promise John looked only a little relieved.

The horn sounded, alerting the crowd that the horses were in the gate for the first race. "Now, come. We have a race to watch."

The piece of paper burned in Lily's palm. She slid it into her purse, praying no one had noticed Mr. Drake slipping it to her.

The man certainly enjoyed living dangerously. Here she was, the duke and his mother mere inches away, and he'd chosen now to pass her a note.

They'd all risen to their feet, cheering on the Thoroughbreds as they rounded the final bend during the second race. That's when she'd felt a curious tickling sensation on her palm and found a piece of paper placed there.

She'd turned around to look at Alexander Drake. He glanced at her just long enough to send her a silent warning, then turned his attention back to the race. His horse had just taken the lead, after all.

For the second time that day, his horse won, nosing out the favorite that the duke had bet on.

"Good show, Drake," the duke said, shaking his hand. "Still know your horseflesh, I see."

"I try my humble best," Alex said dryly, accepting the compliment with a nod.

"The man was born under a lucky star, I always say," he told Lily, but spoke loud enough for them all to hear. "Wins at almost everything—cards, horses, women. It's downright annoying. If he didn't have the prince's patronage, I'd see him barred from the club." He glanced pointedly at Alex, then shifted his gaze to John beside him. Alex understood the silent threat.

"Just joking," Walford added to soften his words for the ladies' sakes. "I hold nothing against an honest gambler. As long as he remains loyal to his friends."

Ever since Mr. Drake and Lord Moseby had joined them in the box, Lily had felt the men were talking in code. She struggled to understand their underlying meanings, but could only determine that Moseby in particular had done something to anger the duke. And he was ready to extend his displeasure to Alex.

What had the marquess done?

She longed to talk to Alex. He could explain it to her. He would have to explain it to her. If she could get him alone, she'd make him tell her.

Alone . . . Suddenly she remembered the note he'd given her. Was it an invitation to a private rendezvous, as she hoped? Oh, please, let it be so!

When next she and the duchess visited the WC, she slipped the note from her purse and read the contents. It contained one word, one promising word which made her heart beat fast and her spirit soar.

Tonight.

Nine

Tonight.

Lily knew she had to take the utmost care in keeping her appointment with Alexander Drake. The clock had struck nine by the time the duke and duchess's carriage returned her to Mrs. Digby's. Another two hours passed as Lily worked to satisfy the good lady's curiosity about her day at the most elite of races.

When the clock struck eleven, Lily finally found herself alone.

She said good night to Mrs. Digby on the landing, then entered her room. Lily stood behind the door, listening carefully for Mrs. Digby's footsteps to quiet. After several minutes, when all sound ceased, she cracked open the door. The light under Mrs. Digby's door remained lit for several more minutes. Anxious and impatient, Lily walked back into her room and stared at herself in her bureau mirror. She set her fancy hat on the bureau and fixed her hair. Goodness, the flush of her cheeks would be a telltale sign to anyone that she was anticipating further adventures this evening. She had no intention of letting a soul get that good of a look at her.

She took a charcoal-colored cloak from her armoire, one she had packed for rainy days. She hoped wearing a woolen cloak on this warm summer evening wouldn't draw too much attention. But she had no choice.

Pulling the hood over her head, she again peeked out her door. This time, the crack under Mrs. Digby's door was pitch black. Already she could hear the lady's sonorous snores.

Lily extinguished the light in her own room, then closed her bedroom door with the utmost care. Guided by a single wall sconce in the hall, she tiptoed to the stairs and stepped carefully down, avoiding the spots she knew were squeaky.

A few moments later, her heart in her throat, she was on the street. On this quiet residential lane at this late hour, there were no pedestrians or carriages about. Quickly she walked down Chapel Street to Grosvenor Place, a main thoroughfare. Here carriages bearing late-night partygoers drove up and down the street. Couples and small groups walked by laughing and talking. No other single women were about.

She approached a hansom cab stand and stood there, waiting. She had never caught a cab before, though she had seen it done many times. At this time of night, how long would she have to wait?

Only a few minutes passed before a hackney drew up. "Where to, lady?" the grizzled driver called down to her.

Lily struggled with the handle of the door for a moment before managing to swing it open. "King Street, please. Near Bedford."

"I know King Street. What do ya take me for?"

Before she was properly seated, he shouted to his horses and the carriage jerked to a start, causing her to land hard in the seat.

She was on her own, at night, in a foreign city. She had defied every convention she'd been taught for a well-bred lady. She'd gone out on her own without a chaperon, at night. Someone might see her, someone who knew her and could spread rumors about the wild girl from America. Someone could tell Mrs. Digby, hurting the poor woman's feelings as well as her own reputation. Everyone trusted Lily.

What am I doing? She bit her lip and wondered where this adventuresome spirit had come from. She'd always been a good, well-mannered girl, an example to her sisters of how to behave. A social paragon. Yet tonight, she'd done something she'd never imagined doing. Not only had she gone out without telling a soul, she was going to meet a *man*. Not just any man. A known rake. If the social set got wind of this, her chances of a good match might be ruined forever.

Then why was her heart beating with such anticipation?

At the corner of Bedford and King Streets, the cab pulled over. Lily scrambled out. She dug in her purse for a shilling and gave it to the man. He doffed his hat and rode on, leaving her alone on the gaslit street.

She strolled toward the enclosed garden slowly, as if walking irrevocably toward her fate. She should turn back. It wasn't too late. She still had time to stop this folly, to return to Mrs. Digby's and climb into her safe, cozy bed. To ignore Drake's request for a private rendezvous.

Yet she knew she never would.

You asked to meet him again, she reminded herself, fingering the key he'd given her. Everything had seemed possible that wondrous night. She'd said and done the most outrageous things.

Still, when she reached the locked garden gate, she didn't hesitate. She slid the key he'd given her into the brass lock and swung it open. It creaked loudly in the quiet evening. She looked behind her, afraid that she'd attracted attention. No one was about. Shaking off her fears, she entered the garden.

As if she'd opened the door on a memory, the feelings of that other evening swept through her, filling her with bliss. The sweetness of a summer eve not much different than this. He'd kissed her here. Taken her in his arms and kissed her, right under the spreading limbs of that tree.

She closed the gate behind her and stepped farther into the garden. Moonlight slid through the branches of the oak tree, drawing a lacy pattern on the ground that trembled and shifted with the breeze.

A nightingale cried softly among the branches, startling her. Leaves rustled. Lily stood under the tree, her breath slowing, her ears straining for any sound at all. Only one light glowed at the rear of his house, fifty feet past the hedge bordering the garden. Was he even awake? He'd told her to come here, tonight.

Then where was he? He probably didn't know that she'd arrived since he hadn't specified a time. She knew which house was his, so she followed the gravel path leading to his backyard. She passed a tall hedge and found herself looking through a pair of French doors into a parlor. And there he was.

He sat on a sofa against the wall, his side to her, his elbows on his knees, his hands clasped. My goodness, he wasn't dressed! He wore only a midnight blue dressing gown trimmed with gold. Even his feet were bare.

Lily found herself taking advantage of this rare opportunity to study him. The blue of his robe made his already startling eyes seem an even deeper shade of cobalt. His chestnut hair was mussed, as if he'd been abed. Her gaze slid over the silk robe, pulled taut across his thick biceps. My goodness, he seemed alarmingly powerful. How positively pagan of her to

enjoy the sight. Yet she lacked the inclination to chastise herself. The robe bared half the length of his
calves, which were bunched and tight, as if ready for
him to spring into action. Only then did she realize
he was studying something across the room. But
what?

He nodded. Opened his mouth to speak.

He wasn't alone! Her gaze shifted sideways, but
his companion was beyond her sight. Then she noticed a shadow on the wall, cast by a tight bodice, a
long skirt, a rounded bustle. The shadow of a woman.

*He's entertaining a woman! He invited me here,
and he's entertaining some other lady?* Outrage filled
her. In a flash she spun around, ready to march right
back home and crawl into bed. And wash her hands
of him forever.

Alex sighed, unable to come up with a solution to
help Mrs. Cuthbert. He could hardly think clearly as
it was. He'd spent all evening waiting for Lily to
make an appearance, prayed she'd be willing to come,
prayed she'd find a way to come. But she hadn't. Just
as he was about to give up hope, the doorbell had
rung.

And Mrs. Cuthbert had entered. "You know I can't
go back to him. You know I can't! If he finds out
about us—"

"Why should he? It happened years ago."

"Only two years. Oh, Alex, I don't know what I'm
going to do!"

Damn, why had this happened tonight? He wasn't
in the mood to comfort a former lover, especially a
hysterical one who kept dropping hints about returning to his bed. Damn it all. Not that it mattered. Lily
hadn't shown. He must have gone into the garden a

dozen times hoping to find her. Each time, he'd returned to the house disappointed.

He glanced toward the patio and caught a flicker of movement. Was that—a skirt? Or was his mind playing tricks on him?

It was so late. Would she really be out this late? Would she really be reckless enough to come at all? She must think him a fool to expect her to come.

Then again . . . If it *was* her . . .

"Excuse me, Joanna. I have to—" He swung open the door and stepped onto the patio.

"You have to *what?*" Joanna demanded, her voice sliding into a high, ear-piercing register.

"The neighbor's cat," he tossed back over his shoulder.

Picking up his pace, he hurried over the chill, mossy flagstones and through the hedge. His dressing gown snagged on a stray branch of boxwood. Annoyed, he yanked it free, heedless of the damage to the rich silk. Entering the public garden, he spotted a woman pushing open the iron gate leading onto the street.

He knew immediately it was Lily, despite the shapeless gray cloak covering her delectable form. Recognized her stance, her bearing.

His heart thudded in his chest and desperation spurred him on. She unlatched the gate and began to leave him.

"Lily!" Breaking into a run, he raced toward her.

She froze and looked back at him, her eyes wide, her expression haughty. Then she spun away and pushed the gate wide. It squealed in protest.

"Don't leave." Before she could take another step, he grasped her arm and spun her toward him. "By God, you didn't come all this way in the middle of the night to leave now."

"Let go of me." Lily shoved at him with both hands. In his haste, his robe had pulled open, only loosely held together by the belt at his waist. He sucked in a shocked breath at the erotic feel of her fingers sliding across his bare skin.

She seemed equally shocked by the unexpected intimacy. She yanked her hands from him as if she'd burned them. "I said, let me go."

"No." He locked both hands around her arms and dragged her closer. "I will not. I need to talk to you, damn it."

"Me and how many other women?" She gazed into his face, her eyes sparking hotly. God, she was gorgeous like this, so passionate, so aroused.

He shook his head emphatically. "No others. It's not like that. I didn't expect any women tonight except you."

"No doubt you say that to all the ladies you seduce."

"Damn it, Lily, this is not how it's supposed to be."

"No doubt you prefer more willing females."

"Damn it, Lily, stop it."

"No doubt—" Unable to think of any other way to shut her up, to make her stay, he pulled her close and kissed her full on the mouth.

At first she was too stunned to resist, her soft body folding against his, her lips opening beneath his. How many hours had he spent dreaming of kissing her again? How many times had he recalled how it felt to touch her like this? He'd thought he would never hold her again, but here she was, once more in his embrace.

He'd just begun to relish his good fortune when she gave him a hard shove and tore her mouth away. "Let me go."

He refused to release her for fear she would bolt. "I didn't know she was coming, Lily. You have to believe me."

"Do you often have women showing up in the dead of night?"

"*You* did."

His factual statement created a firestorm. He nearly lost her as she tried to tear herself from his embrace. He tightened his hold to keep her with him. He locked her arms at her sides and, for a blissful moment, had her entirely in his power. But he didn't want her to fear him. Quite the opposite.

"I'm sorry, Lily, please," he said, speaking as soothingly as one would a frightened child. "Please."

He began kissing her cheeks, her forehead, every part of her he could reach. His mouth sealed against hers, coaxing and cajoling a response from her. Keeping one arm tight around her slim waist, he freed her hood with the other and laced his fingers through her silken hair.

His ardent attentions had the desired effect. This time she settled into the embrace with natural enthusiasm, allowing him to cup her cheeks and guide her mouth in the kiss.

Only when she'd submitted did he risk pulling back. Stroking her downy soft cheeks, he breathed soft kisses onto her forehead. She submitted to his tenderness, her breath shallow and ragged. He teased her earlobes with his thumbs, causing a gasp to escape her softly parted lips. He murmured against her skin, "Please. Don't leave. We have to talk."

"Do we?" Her full chest rose and fell with her breaths.

"Oh, yes." He settled his lips on hers once more, pulling her fast against him.

Her hands settled on his chest. This time, instead

of being alarmed at touching his bare skin, she pressed her palms flat on his chest.

Then she did a most shocking thing. She began to touch him. She slid her hands along his chest, then down his rib cage to his waist. Her innocent exploration made his stomach tremble and his groin tighten with desire. Following the contours of his body, she caressed his sides, then her palms drifted up his back. His body took flame at her intoxicating touch. Wearing only the dressing gown and boxer shorts, he feared she would discover the effect she had on him. As a well-bred lady, no doubt she had little idea where her sensuality could lead. Lord help the man who unlocked the full range of her passion. Would that man were he!

"Lily," he moaned against her lips. "Oh, Lily."

"Alex? Alex, what's going on out here? Alex, I—" Joanna's strident voice came closer then abruptly stopped.

Yanking his mouth from Lily's, Alex swung her around, turning her back to Joanna and pulling her hood over her head to protect her identity. "I'll be right there," he called.

"You have a woman out there!" Joanna sounded put out, but not surprised.

"Please, Joanna. Go back inside. I'll be there in a moment."

Joanna spun away and marched back inside. He sighed in irritation. What did she expect, showing up on his doorstep without warning? He gazed down at Lily, saw her forehead gathering. "I don't know . . ."

He cupped her shoulders, his thumbs tracing her collarbones through the wool. "Think, Lily. Do you honestly believe I would have invited you if I'd made another assignation? You must stay, just for a while.

Allow me to deal with Mrs. Cuthbert; then we can talk."

Sucking in a shaky breath, she nodded once. "Very well. I'll stay."

"Excellent. You wait here, and I'll send the lady on her way." He stepped away from her slowly, not wanting to leave her for even a moment. As he slowly increased the distance between them, he kept his gaze on her, worried at any moment she might change her mind and leave. Perhaps he should have locked the garden gate and taken the key to keep her there. He lifted his palm, as if coaxing a wild animal to his bidding. "Please stay."

She smiled at him, moon shadows caressing her face. "I'm considering attempting to leave again, so that you'll shower more kisses on me. Does that make me terribly wanton?"

His heart thundered in his chest, desire warring with common sense. Her hood had fallen back again, revealing mussed hair, tendrils of which curled about her cheeks. He longed to run back to her and sweep her into his arms. He breathed, "Beautifully wanton."

Forcing himself to turn from her, he slipped back through the hedge. On the patio, he paused and took a calming breath, willing his heartbeat to slow and his blood to cool. Willing himself not to think of the delicious woman in the garden.

He readjusted his silk robe, pulling the flaps as close together as possible to completely cover his chest—and his lingering arousal. God forbid Joanna get any ideas about his interest in *her* this night.

"Joanna?" She was no longer in the parlor. He padded on bare feet down the hall toward the front door just as it slammed shut. Thank God.

To be certain she was gone, he looked out the window and saw her stepping into her carriage. He watched until she rode away, then hurried back to the garden and called for Lily to come inside.

Soon she would be in his house. His house. Alone. A vision of his bed popped into his mind, a vision of lifting her in his arms and carrying her to it, of initiating her into the sweet world of sensual love . . .

Keep your head, man. He couldn't allow the girl's charms to seduce his very reason. He couldn't. He'd always been strong and self-determined. The one time he'd allowed a woman into his heart, he'd paid a stiff price. That experience had taught him the wisdom of remaining aloof.

His uncharacteristic weakness just now, in the garden . . . He had to end it, for he'd invited the girl here for quite a different reason.

Shame washed through him as he recalled his purpose. He had to keep his distance from Lily, emotionally and physically. Be rude if necessary. Keep temptation at bay. Convince her that she'd be foolish to assign any romantic notions to his attentions, attentions born purely from lust.

Lust. Certainly nothing more. Anything else was merely a young lady's romantic fancy.

Her heart thundering, her stomach fluttering in anticipation of more lovemaking, Lily slid through the door Alex held wide. For some reason, he seemed much stiffer than earlier, not meeting her eyes even when she stood inches from him. He'd tightened his dressing gown to cover every inch of his chest. She felt a pang of regret that she wouldn't see his firm body, with its tantalizing texture of warm skin and hair, in the amber firelight of the room.

He closed the door and moved away from her, then gestured to the sofa. "Please take a seat."

Before she did so, she unhooked the fastening of her cloak at her neck and slid it off her shoulders, revealing a demure peach-colored day dress. Though it fastened all the way to her neck, Alex's gaze slid down her body as if assessing her curves through the gabardine and lace, making her skin tingle all over.

Yet his interest seemed to last only a moment. His posture stiff and mannerly, he took her cloak and draped it over an ottoman, then took the chair across from her. Lily had expected him to take her in his arms instead of putting so much distance between them. What was wrong?

He looked confused, as if unsure where to begin. She took satisfaction in the thought that their emotional confrontation had scrambled his thoughts. He'd certainly scrambled hers. "I was afraid you weren't coming," he finally said.

"So was I. I can't stay long. No one knows I'm here."

"I've put you in danger asking you to come."

"Nothing I can't handle." Her lips slid into a teasing smile. "I feel deliciously naughty even answering your summons. I'm unaccustomed to such secret assignations."

"And I'm unaccustomed to wasting time on inexperienced debutantes."

His insult dampened her heady spirits. Certainly, she wasn't experienced. But he'd known that before he'd pulled her into his arms and began making love to her.

"Tell me, Lily. Do you care for the duke?"

She cocked her head, refusing to follow where ever he intended to lead. She wanted to talk about *him*. "Tell me why you want to know."

"That should be obvious."

He did care for her! Of course he did. Why else

would he seek to know her feelings for the duke? "Oh, Alex—"

He cut her off. "John is in love with you, you know."

John? Not that again! "Lord Moseby? What does he have to do with this?" He lifted his hands. "He is fervently courting you. Why else would I ask to meet with you? He's concerned you aren't taking his suit seriously."

She shook her head, struggling to understand. After kissing her with such passion, he still had no intention of courting her himself! Yet, if he merely intended to seduce her, why discuss his friend's suit? "You're not still trying to matchmake me with your friend," she said in disbelief.

"Miss Carrington . . ."

He was trying to force a wedge between them by his distant manner. How could he so easily set aside the passion they'd shared moments before? She certainly couldn't. And she wouldn't allow him to, either. Speaking as sweetly, as honestly as she could, she said, "After the attention we've showered on each other, surely we can give each other permission to use our Christian names. *Alex*," she breathed, speaking the name as if it were golden. And to her, it was.

He squeezed his eyes shut and looked away. Lily thrilled to the secret knowledge that she'd touched his heart. A sense of intimacy permeated the room. The fire danced over his mussed hair and she longed to stroke it back into place. She imagined spending every evening in his company, marrying him, living with him openly as his wife by day. As his lover by night.

Her fantasy died a quick death. His gaze shot up, hard as stone. "It would be a mistake to believe that such ill-advised behavior, however mutual, should dictate further intimacy, Miss Carrington. Consider it a brief madness, nothing more."

She blinked back a sudden surge of tears. How could he be so cruel, so cold? Didn't he, even in some small measure, imagine a future with her? Didn't he have any feelings for her at all?

Rising, he began to pace. Lily noticed a few leaves of grass on his bare feet, a lingering reminder—at least to her—of their moonlit lovemaking.

He crossed his arms, stretching the blue silk taut between his shoulders. "Now, as to John. He told me he wants to marry you. When he proposes, you must accept. Then marry him as soon as possible." He stopped and gazed at her, his eyes a shade softer. "If you don't, you'll break his heart."

All he cared about was his friend's heart! He had no concern for hers, despite the way he'd kissed her, the way he'd caressed her. She tried her best to conceal her pain, but her voice cracked when she spoke. "How nice of you to be concerned for your friend's happiness. Perhaps our encounter was ill advised— I've no doubt of that. But, as you say, it was entirely mutual. How can you set aside the very fact that *you* were just making love to me in the garden? Surely John wouldn't approve of *that* if he intends to wed me."

He locked his hands behind his back and stood with feet spread, his demeanor as haughty as a king's. "As I said, that was a mistake."

A mistake. No, never that. While she'd no doubt been foolish to allow him such liberties, she knew he'd intended every warm touch, every heated word. She knew it in the deepest part of her feminine heart. He couldn't honestly want another man to take her from him. He couldn't truly want never to hold her again.

Yet he had no intention of courting her himself. No intention of ever marrying her.

Something else had to be going on in that clever mind of his, some plan, some idea . . .

An explanation struck her, dastardly on the face of it, yet flattering in its own awful way. She nodded slowly, meeting his gaze. "I'm beginning to understand what this is truly about. I see the plot here. I know your reputation with married women."

He shifted uncomfortably, then settled his hands on his hips. "What docs my reputation have to do with anything?"

"It's so obvious, it's a wonder I never thought of it before. You resist the very idea of courting me yourself. You scoff at the idea of marrying yourself, while you frequently occupy the beds of married women."

"While your assessment of me is harsh, it is not ill founded," he said dryly. "But I fail to see—"

She threw up her hand. "It's obvious! You're encouraging me to marry your friend so I'll be easily accessible to *you*. Once I'm legally wed, you intend to turn me into your mistress!"

Ten

Her charge was so outrageous that it heated his blood to an instant boil. Yes, he refused to court her, but for her own damned sake. He knew he'd be unacceptable to her family. He knew she could do much better. And he knew he'd make a terrible husband, at that.

Yet for her to believe he looked on her in the same cold light as the prince did, that *he* could be as manipulative of her tender heart when he'd done everything possible to help her—

"That's—that's an outrageous charge! Simply outrageous!" He hacked the air with the side of his hand as if seeking to cut the very idea from the air of the room. She sat calmly watching him, her wide eyes disbelieving.

He fought to rein in his tempter. Desperate to explain, he pressed his hand to his chest and approached her. "That's not *my* plan, Lily. I'm not the one endangering you. Don't you see? It's the duke and the prince!" He threw out his hand in the vague direction of St. James Palace. "The prince. He wants you for his mistress once you wed the duke."

Her eyes glittered with disbelief. "Oh, that was clever of you," she scoffed. "Turning my charge into a plot against me by the prince! You may think me quite naive, but trying to throw your own sin upon another is a schoolboy's trick. And you, sir, are hardly a schoolboy."

Like sand draining out of an hourglass, he realized he'd missed his chance to reveal the truth to her. If he'd been up front before she accused him of the same damn thing . . . He shoved his hand into his hair and began to pace. "Bloody hell."

Trying to convince her now of the prince's plan would only shove her farther away. So how could he keep her safe? He stopped pacing and faced her. She'd come to her feet, her arms crossed, an imperious expression on her face.

"Miss Carrington, listen. I really am thinking of your happiness. Whether you believe me, I can't help that. But I can honestly say that good-hearted John will make you a wonderful husband. He worships you."

She cocked her head. "What makes you think I want to be worshiped?"

He had no answer to that. But he understood what she was saying nonetheless. She wanted a husband who saw her for the dynamic, sensual being she was. Lovely, yet flawed. Living, breathing, real. She wanted to be treated as *he* treated her, as a woman with desires and ideas of her own.

Given enough time, surely John could learn how to treat her. Whereas the duke—He turned from playing up John's assets to concentrating on the duke's shortcomings. "You don't really care for the duke, do you?"

"Why shouldn't I? He's handsome, he's titled."

"He's been a cold fish to you, hasn't he?"

"How would you know—" She caught herself. "Do you honestly think I expect all my suitors to treat me as you have? Why, I'd be ruined! No, Mr.

Drake, he treats me with the utmost courtesy and deference."

"And that's what you want? We both know that's not true."

She blushed, her gaze darting from his. Yet she didn't deny it. She longed to express her passionate nature as much as he longed to free it.

He stood before her, his blood pulsing through his body, hot and dangerous. Damn, she infuriated him. Aroused him. Made him wild with need. He was on the verge of yanking her once more into his arms. With the greatest effort, he restrained himself. He stepped back to put more distance between them.

Turning, he again began to pace. "This was supposed to be an organized, rational discussion, but it's gotten completely out of hand. Miss Carrington . . . Lily. John is going to ask for your hand. Please consider accepting. That's all I ask. For his sake."

"You really care for your friend, don't you?"

He nodded. "I may be a scoundrel, but I am a loyal scoundrel."

She smiled ruefully. "Very well. I shall consider his proposal, when it comes. Now, I need to return home." She retrieved her cloak and shrugged it on, then turned toward the back door.

He halted her with a hand on her arm. "Lily, let my driver take you home. It's not safe to take a cab at this late hour."

She glanced at his hand, then up to his face, as if considering whether to protest his touch. She remained stiff but didn't shake him off. "Very well."

"And the duke?" he persisted. "What will you say if he proposes?

His eyes searched hers, but he saw no sign she truly understood the danger she was in. "I shall consider his suit as well."

Sighing, he released her arm and called for his driver. He had done all he could tonight—and, despite his best intentions, managed to make the situation worse.

Lily fell into bed exhausted by her adventure—and more confused than ever about her feelings toward Alexander Drake. She thought she was falling in love with him. But how could she love a man who preferred that she marry his friend?

His request made her temper flare every time she thought of it. "How dare he?" she whispered into the silent room. Realizing she'd been crumpling and knotting her Spanish lace–decorated bedsheet, she forced her hold to loosen, her fingers to relax. Still she remained keyed up, her nerves on edge, her senses alive with memory of being with Alex that night.

How dare he make love to her in his garden, only to turn around a moment later and request—no, *demand*—that she wed Moseby? What could possibly be going through the blackguard's mind? Or his heart?

As for his demand . . . Should she seriously consider accepting Lord Moseby's proposal? She had to think it through. Fighting her exhaustion, she focused on that one question.

Her first impulse was to turn Moseby down flat, to prove to Alex that he had no say in her life and no *right* to a say. Oh, how she longed to refuse John merely to see the look on Alex's face when he learned of it!

She sighed, struggling hard to fight such an impulse. She'd come to Europe determined to be smart about her future, to make the right choices. Being petty was hardly a mature approach to her future happiness.

No, to be fair to Moseby, she must disregard her anger toward Alex. She must disregard Alex's advice and his curious interest in her future. She must consider Moseby's proposal on its own merits.

She *did* feel warm toward the gentleman. He was kind, well mannered, and rather interesting. True, he lacked the magnetism of Alexander Drake—but then, every other man on the planet lacked that elusive fire that drew women to him like moths.

"Stop thinking about Alex and think about John Moseby!" she whispered fiercely. *Are my feelings for Moseby strong enough to make a lasting and happy marriage?*

Sighing, she flopped over onto her side and tucked her hands under her cheek. "I don't know. I just don't know."

The painful truth crept through her, a despondent echo of wants and needs that must go unfulfilled. She'd been fighting it for weeks, but she had to face it. In her heart of hearts, she understood her reluctance to consider John, or any other man. For if she married someone else, she would lose all chance of a future with Alex.

She threw herself onto her back and stared at the ceiling, watching the dancing shadows of a tree cast by the streetlight outside her window. Why couldn't Alex be one of her suitors? Yet he refused to even consider himself eligible, much less treat her as a beau would. None of his actions indicated he intended to seek her hand, ever. She must accept that truth. She must do her best to forget the illicit passion he stirred in her with every intense look, with every burning touch, with every heated kiss.

At the memory alone, her body warmed pleasurably. Her breasts tingled, her lower belly felt hot with secret need, and her heart yearned to feel him against her once again. The full measure of her being cried out for a deeper exploration of her sensuality . . . Of *his* sensuality . . .

No.

She tried to shake off the potent, delicious feeling. She must never let him touch her again. She'd been a fool to allow it, had danced on the brink of ruin without a thought in her head. Thank goodness both Lord Moseby and the duke still considered her a virtuous lady. Was she? She ought to feel a terrible crushing shame at having engaged in such intimacies with a scoundrel like Alex. A virtuous lady would never have allowed it, much less enjoyed it. Much less longed for more.

Yet she felt no shame. She had no idea why, or what to make of this realization. Perhaps it meant she was destined for disgrace. Certainly, if she continued playing with the delicious fire Alex offered, she *would* be scalded. She would be utterly disgraced, her reputation in tatters, her family desolate.

Her only salvation from such temptation was to marry as soon as possible. Once she married, she'd be so busy with her new life, she'd be able to forget about Alex. Her new husband's kisses and caresses would obliterate the memory of Alex's touch—or so she longed to believe.

She must wed soon, regardless. She was already in her second Season. Most debutantes were considered successful only if they wed before their third Season, or at least became engaged by then.

Moseby could be asking for her hand any day, perhaps even *this* day. The room's shadows had already begun to transform into muted grays as the morning crept forth. Perhaps this day.

She had to decide what to do. She had to . . .

When she awoke several hours later, hardly rested at all, she discovered she had run out of time.

Eleven

"It was kind of you to see me, Miss Carrington. I hope I haven't come at an inconvenient time."

"Not at all. Tea?" Lily gestured to the teapot in its cozy resting on the tea cart.

When the parlor maid told her who had come to call, a tremor had run through her. She knew exactly why he'd come. With the truth of it staring her in the face, her confusion of the previous night vanished. She understood what she should do.

Then he entered the parlor and, for a long, tense moment, she quailed despite her intention. She exhaled in a rush, and her courage returned along with her conviction. When this man, Lord Jonathan Moseby, proposed, she would accept.

To Lily's surprise, her usually cheerful visitor looked strained and uncomfortable. He wouldn't meet her gaze, and he refused her offer of tea. He kept hold of his bowler rather than relinquishing it to the parlor maid. Now he was twisting the brim out of shape in his nervousness.

He certainly had the demeanor of a man about to pop the question. Lily looked toward Mrs. Digby sitting on the other side of the room by the window. The older lady smiled knowingly, then pointedly turned her attention to her stitching.

"No tea, then?" Lily asked. "Is there something else I can get for you, milord?"

His earnest gaze lifted to meet hers. "Oh, please don't call me that, Miss Carrington. I've never been comfortable with it." He shrugged. "It's a fault of mine. My friends tell me I'm too humble for my own good."

"Nonsense. Humility is a virtue." Yet, if she had the incredible luck of being born with a title, she'd certainly enjoy wearing it. Why not? People made so much of titles. She knew as well that if Alex had a title, he would carry it easily. He was probably one of the friends who teased John about his humility . . .

Stop thinking of Alex. For the thousandth time that day, Lily forced her mind off of him. *This is exactly why you must marry, as soon as possible. You must rid yourself of this unholy, ruinous obsession.* Alex said this sweet, attentive man adored her. He said this was what she ought to do. While she hated the idea of letting him win, a dark side she hadn't known she possessed longed to cry out, "Very well, than you shall have it, and suffer the consequences!" For, once wed, she would never, ever betray her husband. Alex would never, ever have her.

She gazed at Moseby, wondering how long it would take her to love him with her whole heart, how long it would take before his ardent attentions obliterated all thought of *him.*

Moseby seemed more strained than she'd ever seen him. Rarely did he completely let his guard down in her presence—as *he* always did. But this morning, Moseby displayed more than his usual gentlemanly reticence.

She had to do something to relieve his stress, or he would never propose. "Would you like to take a turn in the garden?" she finally asked.

Mrs. Digby glanced up and smiled, then gave her a nod of permission. She trusted her charge not to engage in any inappropriate activity with her noble guest. Certainly Moseby wasn't the type of man to attempt to have his way with her. He could barely look her in the eye!

He assented, and together they stepped out into Mrs. Digby's small yet neat backyard garden. A stone wall bordering it on three sides enclosed a figure-eight gravel walkway with a gurgling fountain at its center. Other than that, there wasn't much garden to take a turn in, but by walking very slowly toward the arbor on the rear wall, Lily managed to settle into a stroll with the gentleman by her side.

"Lovely weather we're having," she remarked, feeling false and silly. She didn't give two hoots about the weather. She wanted to know what was on Moseby's mind, or rather, his heart. Hoped and prayed that when he finally confessed his feelings, her own would grow strong, so strong she'd never again think of *him*.

"Perhaps we should sit," he finally said.

Lily let him lead her to the stone bench. He kept his eyes forward and toyed with his hat between his knees.

"You seem to have something on your mind," she prompted.

He nodded. Finally, after several long minutes, he began. "Lily, over the past few weeks, I've enjoyed nothing more than visiting you, and courting you. You must believe that. I hope someday to . . . That is . . . Men have dreams, and I'm no exception. I would have liked—" He sighed and looked away again. "I wish this were easier."

Not feeling nearly as timid, Lily decided to help him along. Sliding her hand over his, she pulled it until his fingers dropped from his hat. She cradled his hand in both of hers. "Please, go on. I have a feeling you'll be very glad you did."

Finally, he met her gaze. "Miss Carrington . . . Lily . . . I can't see you anymore. Not as a suitor. I'm sorry."

"Oh." Lily released his hand, stunned beyond measure. Suddenly she felt as foolish as a girl fresh from the schoolroom. She had thought . . . He had given her every indication he cared . . .

He worships you. . . . He'll make you a wonderful husband . . . When he proposes, you must accept.

Alex had misled her, cruelly and without remorse! Just last night he had insisted John wanted her as a wife. Yet nothing could be further from the truth.

Had Alex lied? Why? Or was Alex truly mistaken in his friend's interest? Or had Moseby's feelings changed in such a short time? Her head spun with confusion. "I don't know what to say. I'm sorry. I thought you felt some regard for me."

His face grew pale and she rushed to console him. "But I understand. Things happen. I hope we may still be friends?"

He sighed in relief. "I would like that very much."

"Good." She nodded, feeling as if a great weight had been lifted. She'd been prepared to accept this gentleman's proposal. Yet now that she knew he wouldn't ask her, she had to fight to keep her relief from showing on her face. She could never hurt him in that way.

"Well," she said, for once at a loss for words.

"I should go. I'm deeply sorry if I have hurt you. That was never my desire. I fully intended . . . That is, in the beginning . . ."

Which meant he *had* been courting her with marriage in mind.

Lily began to wonder, a sick, queer feeling twisting in her stomach. What had happened to change his mind about her? He was close to Alex, closer than any of his other acquaintances. She had rarely seen them apart, except when Alex was alone with her.

Did Moseby suspect that she and Alex had secretly met? Secretly kissed?

Did he *know?*

Lily felt suddenly ill. Perhaps worldly men like Moseby and Drake could see it on a girl's face, sense the awakened desire, know she dreamed of expressing her passion with a man . . .

"Miss Carrington, are you well? You look pale."

Now he was comforting her, his gray eyes filled with concern. Reaching inside his pocket he extracted a linen handkerchief and pressed it into her hand. "I'm so sorry if I've hurt you. I had no idea—that is, you're so lovely, and have so many beaux, I never imagined . . . I ought to go now." He rose and placed his bowler on his head.

He thought he'd broken her heart, and here she sat worrying about her reputation! This man was too good for her by far. He deserved a woman who loved him without reservation.

Sucking in a breath, she rose and gave him a gentle smile. "I'm fine, John, if I may call you that."

He smiled in response.

She continued, "I truly appreciate your honesty, and that you took the trouble to see me in person rather than sending a brief note as other men would have done. You're quite a gentleman, and will some-day make a wonderful catch for some lucky woman."

Just not me.

As she walked John to the garden gate and saw him off, the mystery continued to plague her.

Was she now a fallen woman?

* * *

"Alex, I must speak with you."

At the sound of his friend's voice, Alex's heart sped up and his hands moistened. He continued to play it cool, however, until the hand of cards concluded. "In a moment, Moseby. Stand."

The dealer nodded. Alex flipped over a card to reveal the ace of hearts. He set the card beside the king of spades he'd just been dealt. *"Vingt-et-un."*

"Again?" Colonel Trimble pushed back in his chair. "Go on, Drake, visit with Moseby. You're too damned lucky for me. I'll have to call it a night."

Alex rose and retrieved a stack of pound notes from the center of the table, then pocketed them. Nodding to the colonel, the dealer, and the other two gentlemen at the table, he turned to follow John.

His friend led him to a private alcove off the large gaming room of the Marlborough Club. There, they settled into a pair of burgundy leather chairs.

A uniformed waiter immediately appeared and took their order for drinks. "This one's on me, John. Have to spend my winnings sometime." Alex instructed the waiter to put the drinks on his tab.

Once the waiter left, he turned to John and took a good look at him. He wore a frown under his moustache. He certainly didn't look like a man who'd just won the hand of a lovely heiress. Despite his efforts on his friend's behalf, Lily must have turned John down.

Alex's fingers tightened on the arm of his chair. How dare she? How could she? *She wanted to defy me, that's all it is. John will have to ask her again— after I get hold of her and give her a good spanking.*

He imagined pulling Lily over his knee and ruching

up her skirt, revealing her garters, her bloomers, her sleek thighs—

Lord, not now. The image sent a jolt of desire through him so fierce, it threatened to publicly embarrass him. He shifted and crossed his legs, then focused on his friend. "I haven't seen you in days. You've asked her, I take it."

"Actually, no."

So, she didn't defy him. He tried not to feel delighted by that realization. "Then why the long face?"

John swallowed hard. "I broke with her, Alex," he announced. "I thought it was best."

Alex squeezed his eyes shut. John broke with her. He cut her loose.

He ought to feel anger. He ought to be worried. He ought to demand an explanation. Soon enough, he would.

Yet, at this moment, his overwhelming feeling was relief.

Lily—his Lily—remained unattached. She wouldn't become the wife of his best friend. She wouldn't.

Then, what? He opened his eyes and stared at John. "I assume you have your reasons. Let me guess. The duke?"

John considered a moment, then shook his head. "I suppose so, but that was just an excuse. His threats worried me, definitely. But it's . . . something else."

Alex sat forward, his elbows on his knees. "Well, what, man? Out with it."

"I didn't fancy having as my wife a woman whom . . ." he hesitated.

Alex grew impatient. "Who *what?*"

John's clear gaze met his, and his voice softened a notch. "Who you can't tear your eyes from."

Alex felt suddenly naked, his weakness, his emotions exposed like the underbelly of a landed shark.

To cover his discomfort, he barked out a laugh. Keeping a smile of disbelief on his face, he leaned back in the chair. "I have no idea what you're talking about. It's utter nonsense."

"Alex, I've seen how you look at her, like she's a delicious marzipan you can't wait to taste. No, more than taste. *Consume,* like a man who is starving and must have her, or die." He exhaled in a rush. "Deny it if you like, but I know you well enough to see that glint in your eye for what it is."

Hearing John define his secret, inner obsession with the girl sent a bolt of terror through Alex. He couldn't be that transparent, could he? When had he grown so foolish as to allow his feelings to show? "Granted, she is attractive, but . . ."

"It's more than that. *All* men find her lovely. But you . . . Admit it, Alex. You want to bed the girl yourself."

Again Alex laughed, though he feared it sounded forced. "So, I'm a randy scoundrel. No reason not to marry the girl."

"Perhaps that alone wouldn't deter me. But she looks at you in the very same way. I noticed it at Ascot. The air between you reminded me of the time I put my finger in one of those new electrical sockets—and made me feel about the same, too," he added wryly. "There's a curiously alive, almost visible power between you. I know it's best not to interfere with whatever you two feel for each other."

Alex stiffened, fury and desperation filling him. "By God, that's utter nonsense! Electric lights and candy. Where do you come up with such rubbish? We feel nothing for each other, damn it, absolutely *nothing.*" He hacked the air decisively.

"Yet you worry about her so." John's quiet observation rang louder than all of Alex's protests.

Alex tried to cajole sense into him, "Come, John. You know I can't bear to see a woman in trouble. Like Sikara—"

"Who became your mistress after you rescued her."

Damn, that was a bad example. "I have no intention of becoming personally involved this time." His friend's understanding gaze told him he didn't have to elaborate. John was well aware Alex hated to feel vulnerable, as he had when he'd loved, then lost, Sikara.

Yet, knowing there was no way Lily could ever be his, he felt oddly inclined to dance close to the fire, and John was calling him on it. He decided to remind John—and himself—why he became involved in the first place.

"I feel partly responsible for suggesting the prince's mad plan. Naturally I desire to keep her out of trouble. That's all it is. That's all it will ever be." Again he hacked the air.

His emphatic response did no good. John's expression—almost one of pity—showed that his friend remained unconvinced. Well, he'd drag the two of them to the altar personally, if that's what it took to convince him.

To think John imagined some involvement between him and Lily—something powerful enough to threaten a marriage! Yes, he wanted her. Of course he did. He'd tasted her lips, held her in his arms. But he was gentleman enough to control such impulses once she became another man's wife. He could extinguish them when the time came. How dare John think otherwise? He lowered his voice. "I would never cuckold you, John. It hurts me to think you'd believe that."

John sighed. "One can't talk oneself out of love, Alex. You ought to know that."

"Love? Oh, now I *love* the girl," he said sarcastically. "Utter nonsense." He settled back and crossed his arms, battling his discomfort with John's words. Of course he didn't love the girl. He was nowhere *near* loving her. Yes, he found her company exhilerating, her smile intoxicating, her touch as powerful as a Persian aphrodisiac. Those animal responses had nothing to do with love. Logically, he knew she was no different under her corset than any other woman.

Yet, for some reason, John's words had pushed him to the brink of unreasoning panic. Desperately, he tried to find another explanation, a reason for his friend's allegation. "I know what this is about, Moseby. This is simply a sad excuse not to wed the girl. It can't be the real reason. Why, it's no reason at all! The duke convinced you to stop pursuing her, didn't he?" He glanced around the room, looking for the man who was really at fault.

"No, Alex, truly—"

"I've a mind to share a few words with him." Alex lurched to his feet and strode from the alcove, intent on ending this awkward conversation as much as seeking out Walford.

Alex found Walford in the prince's private room. Bertie was absent, but the duke wasn't alone. A young redheaded man with a slim build shared his chaise, and his pipe. The air reeked of opium smoke.

"Drake, come join us." Walford slung his arm around the young man and his eyes glinted suggestively. "I'm sure David won't mind."

Alex gritted his teeth. "No, thank you. What did you say to Moseby?"

"Moseby? Hmm . . . Why should I talk to him?"

"Quit feigning ignorance," Alex said harshly. "You know what I'm talking about."

Walford took a long pull on his pipe, then exhaled a perfect ring of smoke. "This conversation bores me. Please leave us."

Infuriated at being dismissed, Alex stepped forward and snatched the mouthpiece of the hookah pipe from Walford's hand, then tossed it aside. "What did you say to him? How did you threaten him?"

"Watch yourself, Drake." Despite his warning, Alex's violent move brought a shadow of fear to Walford's face. "It wasn't necessary to tell the man anything. He knows what's good for him. As should you."

Alex narrowed his eyes. If society at large knew just how dissolute this man was, it would destroy his reputation. He'd be barred from every parlor in town. Just last summer, Lord Arthur Somerset, third son of the duke of Beaufort, was driven from polite society—and fled the country—when it came out that he'd patronized a male brothel on Cleveland Street. Walford would fare no better. "I'm not afraid of you, Walford. I know your weaknesses, and I won't hesitate to use them if necessary."

Walford's dark countenance turned a shade paler. Rather than challenge Alex's statement, he changed the subject. "You're much more vulnerable than I, Drake. Much more vulnerable. Besides, I don't see where your interest in the matter lies. You have no claim on the girl, nor are you likely to, considering your lack of breeding."

"This isn't about me. Damn it, Walford, she's a young, inexperienced girl, and she has no idea that marrying you means becoming the prince's mistress."

"Of course she doesn't. That's part of the plan."

Alex decided to reason with him. "Why should you go along with this? It's ridiculous. You know the prince will lose interest in her after awhile, and you'll be stuck with her as your wife!"

"Why should I go along? Besides the fact she's rolling in it, you mean?" He arched a slim brow, then again studied his tobacco-stained nails. "Bertie is providing me with special compensation for my trouble, for having to put up with a shrieking female who will no doubt make a scene."

"What do you mean?"

"Once I reject her, Bertie has visions of consoling her, of dabbing her tear-stained cheeks as she cries on his shoulder, then seducing her *oh*-so-gently." He tapped his chin. "I'm not yet certain of the timing. Bertie is so damned impatient. Would the honeymoon be too soon for her to learn the sad truth about her new husband? Yes, I think it might, since I have to bed the chit myself. Though I might be tempted to introduce her to the fleshly delights in another fashion."

His casual words sickened Alex. He had to bite back the words he longed to say. He'd already shown an inordinate lack of caution toward this powerful man. "The prince wants her for his own. How can you forget that and so blithely threaten to use her?"

He shrugged. "Bertie well knows I need to consummate the marriage, else she may seek an annulment. I can't allow that." He sighed. "I shall have to take her at least once, to prevent that. Then, the fun can begin." He spread his hands like a conductor on stage. "I confess, I've spent a good deal of time imagining the dramatic scene unfolding. Me, with David—" he caressed David's hair and the young man smiled, "or someone equally appealing."

David's expression turned desolate, and Alex knew the youth was in love with the duke. To the duke, he was merely a passing fancy. The man had no love in his heart to give.

"There we are, my lover and I, locked in passionate embrace upon our hallowed wedding bed. She enters; she gasps in shock! Why, her mother never told her such a thing was possible! Her husband and his lover sharing a rollicking, joyous union. Whatever will she make of it? Will she bury her face in her hands and weep? Or scream? Or faint dead away?"

The duke gave Alex a tight smile, his suggestive leer goading a reaction from him, as if he knew how much it hurt Alex to hear Lily discussed in such a way. John had seen his weakness for Lily. Did this man suspect it, too? He had to keep his head, to disregard the man's words. Still, his hands tightened into fists.

Walford crossed his legs and tossed his head. "Perhaps I shall convince her to join us. She does seem to have a voluptuous nature. I wouldn't mind watching one of my lovers enjoy her. A few puffs on my opium pipe, and she'll submit."

"You reprehensible piece of " Alex's temper snapped. Caution be damned! Closing the distance in one long stride, he slammed his fist into the duke's face.

Twelve

The duke flew backward off the chaise. His head slammed into the marble hearth and he went limp.

"Don't hurt me." The duke's lover, his round eyes filling with tears, pressed his hands to his mouth and began backing away from Alex.

Alex looked at David in annoyance. "Don't worry, I'm not going to touch you. Now, get out of here."

The fellow edged past him toward the door, but Alex had second thoughts. Snatching a handful of David's jacket, he yanked him close and glared into his wide, terrified eyes. He spoke in his grittiest, most threatening voice. "Don't say a word, or I *will* come after you."

"N-N-Never," David stuttered through trembling lips.

Satisfied he'd been understood, Alex shoved the fellow away. David scurried from the room like a rat seeking its hole.

Alex stepped around the chaise. He stared down at the duke, disgusted by his violent reaction as much as the duke's abhorrent remarks. Kneeling, he checked the man's breathing and color.

At Alex's touch, Walford groaned and stirred. "David?" he mumbled. Alex knew then he'd recover, though he'd no doubt suffer a deservedly wicked headache.

Alex rose and strode from the room. In the hall outside, he addressed a servant standing at the ready to meet any of the guests' needs. "The gentleman in that room needs attention. He passed out from too much smoke." The servant nodded and hurried into the room.

Passed out. A handy explanation. Of course, the duke would have a different story. *Too bad the fall didn't kill him.*

The thought brought Alex up short. When had he become so self-destructive? He'd always put his own interests first, always sought to cultivate the favor of those in power, to keep their goodwill. Yet he'd just struck the duke. Even imagined the pleasure of seeing him dead.

All for Lily Carrington, a girl to whom he owed absolutely nothing. Why couldn't he simply turn his back and forget about her?

Filled with frustration, he pounded down the stairs into the club's foyer. Anticipating him, a footman in a red coat and white breeches swung open the heavily gilt front door. Alex strode onto the street and flagged a hansom cab.

As the cab trundled down the Strand and toward his home, Alex fought the tight pain in his chest, fought to even his breathing. He replayed the scene in the club over and over, from the lecherous image the duke had painted to his own furious, regrettable reaction.

Which was stronger? His disgust, or his regret?

Did it matter? He'd shown his hand tonight, shown he intended to concern himself with Lily's future. He was in too deep to back out now. He repeated that rationale over and over until he almost believed it. Naturally he'd do his best to repair any damage his impulsive action had caused to his career. That's all that really mattered.

Yet it wasn't his career that he dwelled on. Over and over, he recalled the duke's threats, his plan to draw sweet Lily into his darkly erotic games. A shaft of bile rose in his throat, nearly choking him. He couldn't allow it. He refused to allow Lily to be forced into such a wicked, duplicitous life. He couldn't stand to see her innocence corrupted, her heart broken in such a vile, uncaring manner.

He had to do something. He'd tried to find her a suitable husband. That had failed. Too late, he'd attempted to explain the danger she was in. That had also failed.

What could he do? What would make a debutante turn down a duke's proposal? Why would any girl think such a life unappealing? Lily was such a sparkling, lively woman. If she were the duchess, she'd be hosting parties and balls . . . wearing a tiara, going to court.

For a few days of the year. The rest of the time, she'd be living at Inderby Hall with the dowager duchess.

An image sprang to mind of Baroness De Veaux, a lovely woman he'd been intimate with five years ago, shortly after he arrived in London. She was American, too. She knew the price a girl paid for a title.

Yes, the baroness might talk sense into Lily. If he could engineer a way for Lily and her to meet.

Fox Croft Estate—family seat of earls of Henshaw since 1643—appeared through the beech trees as their carriage jounced and swayed up the serpentine lane.

Lily tightened her grip on the door handle. They had almost arrived.

Lily's fear that her reputation had somehow become damaged, causing John to break with her, had been immediately put to rest. The invitations kept coming, and the duke had intensified his courtship of her. He'd invited her to travel with his mother and him to the exclusive weekend house party.

So once again she found herself rubbing shoulders with the highest ranks of nobility, with a duchess as her chaperon. She should be congratulating herself on her social coup. Any other debutante—especially an American—would envy her position.

Yet instead of thinking about the Walfords' generosity, Lily's thoughts remained on a commoner.

The invitation to the earl's weekend house party had arrived soon after the Royal Ascot, no doubt because the dowager duchess had requested that she be included. The invitation had sent Mrs. Digby into a tizzy. The good lady never failed to be impressed by titles and the most celebrated events of the London season.

For Lily, the events themselves had started running together in a blur of dancing and eating and idle chit-chat. The moments that truly stood out for her, like brightly painted oils in a sepia-toned background, were the few she spent in the company of Alexander Drake. Every event she attended, she looked for him. Every time she knew he wasn't coming—which was nearly always—she fought against her irrational disappointment.

The man had been nothing but trouble for her. Still she sought him out. Like a drunkard, she'd become addicted to the sweet intrigue, the potent attentions he'd showered on her.

This time, she wouldn't seek in vain. John and she

had been cordial since he had stopped courting her. He'd become more at ease with her. And, he'd revealed that Alex was attending the Henshaws' party.

Lily hadn't spoken to Alex since their meeting two weeks ago in his garden. She'd been torn between deciding that was for the best, and an abiding longing to see him. Torn between fury at his interference in her life, and frustration that he hadn't interfered even more. Hadn't tried to court her. Perhaps Alex wanted nothing more to do with her. Perhaps their romance had truly ended.

After this weekend, she would know for certain.

"Mr. Drake, I'm so pleased you were able to make it."

Helen Charmichael, countess of Henshaw, swept toward Alex, her short, rotund form gowned in green velvet. Her blond hair bore traces of gray, yet her skin remained relatively smooth despite nearing fifty years.

Since it was past seven, Alex had immediately been shown his room, where he changed into formal dinner attire, a black tuxedo with a white cummerbund. Though he'd made a small fortune during his career through wise investments, he limited the number of aristocratic parties he attended. Every event required expenditures on suits and carriage rides and train tickets.

"After the last train arrived in Berkshire without you, I thought you'd accepted another engagement, despite your R.S.V.P.," the countess gently chided him as she guided him farther into the parquet-floored gallery. There, fifty handpicked guests mingled awaiting the dinner bell, accepting champagne and port from circulating butlers bearing trays.

Alex gave her a smile designed to charm her. "I could never miss an opportunity to see *you* again, Lady Charmichael."

"Oh, my," she said, fluttering her rose-painted fan. "You are a rogue. You lend such an air of danger to my gathering. I must say, I'd almost forgotten the power of your devilish smile, you've been so absent from the social scene this season."

Leaning close, she whispered confidentially, "I'm compelled to invite some of these fine folk," she said, her eyes on a black-garbed spinster with a pinched face and dour countenance that Alex recognized as her sister-in-law. "But you, I made an effort to procure. I simply hate a dull time."

He chuckled. "Why, thank you. Nothing delights me more than satisfying a beautiful lady."

Her eyes filled with secret mirth. "Watch yourself, Alex, dear." She gazed up at him speculatively, as if she'd heard stories about him that urged her to be cautious. "Just behave yourself, is all I ask."

He executed a small bow. "I would never do anything to cause you to regret extending me your kind hospitality."

She smiled coyly and patted his arm. "I'm so pleased. I need you, you see, or my dinner is ruined. I would have one lady too many, and that would simply not do." Turning, they strolled together through the gallery toward a glass-enclosed conservatory filled with tropical trees and plants. As they passed groups of guests, Alex acknowledged greetings from those he knew, but he kept his eyes out for Lily—the only reason he'd come.

As if reading his mind, Helen said, "She's an American, but not in the least gauche, as so many of those Colonists can be."

"Excuse me?" He realized the countess had been speaking to him, and he hadn't been listening.

"Goodness, Alex, you seem a thousand miles away."

"I'm a little fatigued from the journey, but I'll be myself soon," he assured her. "You were saying something about an American?"

"Yes. She's the most delightful young lady, a find of Duchess Walford's. Word is she's caught the eye of her recalcitrant son as no woman has yet."

"Indeed," Alex said dryly, biting back a scathing remark about the duke's true fleshly interests.

The countess continued, "Once I introduce you, she will be your dinner partner this evening. I'm counting on you to make her feel welcome."

Alex nodded, unable to believe his luck. He'd planned to be as circumspect as possible in meeting with Lily this weekend. Now he was being asked to spend time with her, as if it might be a chore!

The crowd near the conservatory door parted. Though her back was turned, Alex easily recognized her—the line of her slender back, the posture of her shoulders, the red tones captured in her sleek black hair upswept with strands of diamonds. Given this excuse to gaze at her, he thrilled to the sight of her swanlike neck and that tender spot at the base of her hairline. He'd stroked her there, felt her tremble in response. God, how he longed for that pleasure again.

The countess's eyes lit up and she gestured toward Lily. "There she is. Isn't she a lovely young thing? Oh, Miss Carrington!" She waved with her gloved hand.

Lily turned toward them, her lilac gown floating up to reveal matching kid boots. Lilac boots! Alex had never seen anything like them. Only a woman with Lily's sense of style could pull off something so outlandish. More than once he'd heard women remark on Lily's clothing, French fashions that pushed the boundaries, yet which she carried off with great flair. No doubt by the end of the season, every fashion-inclined woman would be wearing a pair of lilac boots.

Her eyes met his and a wide smile spread over her face, drawing him to her like a magnet. As he and the countess came closer, her smile lessened, as though she strained to contain her natural reaction to him.

He understood because he felt the same. His heart thudded at the sight of her, his palms tingling with the memory of touching her face, her neck. Every time he met her, he was more moved than the first time, despite all his logic.

When would this boyish infatuation cease? Of course, he had made things worse by tasting her lips and holding her lithe body against his. Now he was struck not only by her beauty, but by the comprehending glint in her eye as she smiled up at him. They had engaged in scandalous acts, and this secret knowledge bound them together as nothing else could.

The countess began to make the introductions. "Miss Carrington, this is Mr. Alexander Drake."

"We've already met," Lily said. Indeed, her sparkling eyes seemed to say, *We have most definitely met.*

"Wonderful!" the countess clapped her hands. "I'll leave you in Mr. Drake's care, then."

A trace of alarm slid across Lily's gaze. "His care?"

"He is your dinner partner," the countess said. "Now, if you'll excuse me." She spotted another guest who needed tending to and darted away through the gathering.

"I hope you'll do the honor of walking with me, Miss Carrington."

She nodded and fell into a slow stroll beside him.

"Lovely party the countess is hosting, wouldn't you say?" Alex feigned interest in making small talk as they entered the conservatory. Humid air washed over him, redolent with the rich scents of frangipani and gardenia. In the center of the room. water splashed in a marble fountain topped by a statue of naked Aphrodite on a half shell. The atmosphere reminded him of the East, and briefly he thought of Sikara. As always when he thought of her, his chest tightened with regret. But now, with Lily beside him, his life with Sikara seemed so distant as to have been a dream.

"You're somewhere else."

"Excuse me?"

"You were here; then you were gone. Where?"

Her perceptiveness stunned him. He realized he wanted to talk to her, about Sikara, about everything. Yet he hadn't come here to share himself with her. "It's not important."

"Liar."

He stared down at her, irritated yet intrigued by her bluntness. He longed to speak to her alone, but had to be careful, had to resist showing any sign that he knew her much more intimately than anyone around them guessed. A couple already in the conservatory lingered thirty feet away on the other side of the room, admiring orchids on the branches of a moss-draped tree. They nodded in greeting and resumed their conversation.

Alex paused before a thick vine dotted with white and purple star-shaped flowers "This is passionfruit. I believe it's from Peru. It climbs using those curling tendrils, as you can see."

"Fascinating," Lily said dryly. Keeping her eyes on

the vine, she leaned slightly toward him and whispered, "But I'd rather learn more about you. You've told me so little about yourself. You seem to prefer discussing other men's interest in me," she added wryly.

"Knowing about me isn't important. My," he said louder, "look at that giant fern."

"Simply lovely." Again she dropped her voice. "I won't allow you to put me off any longer. The last time we met—"

"We became distracted, or don't you remember?" he said, his voice rich with suggestion.

A soft blush tinged her cheeks, but didn't sway her from speaking truthfully about their last encounter. "That's not all. You spent the time trying to convince me to accept John's proposal!"

Alex was relieved that the Aphrodite fountain nearby muted her emphatic whisper. "For your own good, as I explained."

"You mean that silly story about the duke and Prince Edward. Well, despite that nonsense, you still didn't get your way. No doubt you're quite aware that your friend has broken with me." She added loud enough for her voice to carry over the fountain's gurgle. "Why, how fascinating. Is that a fig tree?"

"I believe so, Miss Carrington." Again he dropped his voice. "You must have said something that caused John to lose heart."

"Me!" Her emotional exclamation caused him to glance around in alarm. The lady nearby was studying them with a speculative gaze. Damn, they'd attracted attention, exactly what he didn't want.

He adopted his most reserved demeanor. "Have you seen the orchid collection? It's quite amazing."

Slowly they strolled to the other side of the room,

where delicate, brightly petaled flowers clustered on the moist branches of a lime tree.

The woman grew tired of eavesdropping and followed her companion to the planting bed nearest the second set of doors, so he again risked speaking. "I apologize if John broke your heart. I had assumed I knew his intentions, but apparently I was wrong."

"Broke my heart? Alex, you know I wasn't in love with him—much as you wanted me to be."

Alex told himself not to ask the question on his mind, the question that had plagued him for weeks. He heard himself voicing it anyway. "If John had proposed, what would you have said?" He tried to make the question sound casual.

"Does it matter now?"

"Indulge my curiosity."

Her brilliant eyes sparked like rich obsidian. "I would have accepted, just to spite you."

He gazed at her in consternation. *"Spite* me! I *wanted* you to marry him."

A confident smile slid along her lips. "Perhaps, in part. But I know your heart feels otherwise."

"This is stuff and nonsense," he scoffed.

She didn't answer, merely continued smiling at him as if knowing something about him that even he refused to acknowledge. It disconcerted him that she might be able to fathom the confusion in his heart. "You're ascribing to me feelings I don't have."

"If you're so disinterested, then you won't be concerned that the duke has become my most determined suitor."

Alex's stomach tightened several notches and his chest burned. Oh, he was concerned, all right. As the Season progressed, bringing her closer and closer to her fate, he could think of little else. And he was increasingly powerless to prevent it.

A group of five guests entered the conservatory, laughing and chatting. Alex led Lily back the way they'd come, aware that time was short, and opportunities few. If he waited any longer, he might lose his chance. He could hardly arrange an assignation with her at dinner with fifty people. He fantasized about visiting her room later in secret, but the danger was far too great. Not only might he be seen entering or leaving her room, but once he was there, alone with her and a bed, would he be able to resist seducing her? His desire proved he was no better than the prince, but he was damned if he'd allow it to take control.

Again he remarked on the plants before them in an effort to keep anyone within earshot from knowing the true nature of their encounter. "Tell me, Miss Carrington, which of these lovely blossoms is your favorite? That violet one matches your gown, I'd say."

Before she could reply, he murmured urgently, "We have to talk. Tomorrow morning, the guests are gathering at the south entrance for a hunt. Meet me at the west entrance. I'll have a carriage waiting and no one will see us."

"Don't be silly. It's too dangerous," she shot back. Her eyes sparked with alarm—and, he believed, anticipation. "Do you plan to thoroughly ruin me? I suspected this is why John broke with me."

"Ruin you!" he gasped, annoyed she could think such a thing, despite his common sense. What else should she think, considering how he'd manhandled her at every opportunity? *"I'm trying to save you."*

She arched a brow. "I don't know what to make of you. You're determined to be my knight in shining armor, yet . . ."

Her eyes glistened, and in the next instant, they were once again in his garden, where he'd kissed her, caressed her. His body ached with the need to hold her again. Without conscious awareness, he leaned close to her, bringing his lips within a breath of her delicate ear. "Promise me you'll be there. There's someone you must meet."

"Another suitor?" Despite her mocking tone, she didn't move away. Her own breath teased his neck, they stood so close.

He ignored her jibe. "Being alone with me may seem risky, but trust me. You're in more danger if you continue on the path you seem determined to take."

"Your distaste for the duke baffles me," she murmured, "especially as you refuse to share with me your own interest in this matter."

He was about to protest when she jerked away, her attention on a man approaching behind him.

"Lord Walford," she said, her gaze intent on the duke. Alex stiffened, his entire body overtaken by simmering rage as he turned to face his adversary.

Thirteen

"Good evening, Miss Carrington," the duke said, nodding to Lily.

His gaze turned decidedly frosty when he looked at Alex. "Drake. I had thought you would be otherwise occupied tonight. Yet I find I am not surprised at how you are spending your time."

Lily found his statement odd, as if Alex ought not to be there with her. Had he overheard some of their conversation regarding him? Regarding them? She prayed not. She understood the need for circumspection, worried as much as Alex that their mutual attraction might be apparent to others.

Alex retorted, "If you mean spending my time in the fine company provided by the earl and countess, I see no reason to be surprised."

The duke's gaze shifted to Lily. "I meant in the company of this lovely young lady." He gave her a regal bow, his deference surprising considering her lack of station.

When he straightened, Lily noticed a fading, purplish bruise around his right eye, which he'd attempted unsuccessfully to mask with face powder. "What happened, my lord? Were you in an accident?"

The duke stiffened, his polite smile vanishing and his eyes sliding toward Alex. A dark tension simmered between the two men, and Lily longed to know the source.

The duke lifted her hand and patted it. "Nothing to be concerned about. A minor fall from my horse. All is well." He gave her a smile filled with reassurance and charm.

"I'm glad to hear that." Lily smiled in response, then risked a glance at Alex. His cold expression would have frozen Hades itself. Oh, he could insist he had no emotional involvement in her fate, but she knew with a woman's sure intuition how wrong he was. Now, if she could only get him to admit it!

"Will you be taking part in the quail hunt tomorrow?" she asked the duke.

"Most definitely. A rousing hunt is a most exhilerating way to spend one's time." He slid his body between them in an attempt to cut Alex out of the conversation. He lowered his voice to an intimate murmur, a tone he had never used with her. Lily took it as another sign of the seriousness of his suit. "I was looking forward to seeing you tonight, Miss Carrington. Very much."

"I'm glad, Lord Walford."

"My mother as well. She finds your conversation most entertaining—especially your American colloquialisms."

"I'm certain your mother is being too kind," she said, not sure she wasn't being insulted. No, she decided, the duke's expression was warm, his manner nothing but respectful. "My conversational skills are merely adequate."

"Nonsense. I have no doubt you are talented in many ways we have yet to discover." For some reason, the duke glanced at Alex when he said this, as if the statement contained a secret meaning.

In response, Alex's expression stiffened still further,

his cobalt eyes burning with anger, his hands fisted at his sides. Lily felt his intense emotion pour off him in waves.

"It occurs to me, my lord," he finally said, his commanding tone impossible for the duke to ignore. "You ought to be very careful if you plan to take part in the hunt. You could very well take another spill, perhaps one even more perilous."

His brash comment stunned Lily and filled her with anxiety. He was threatening the duke!

"That would be most unwise," the duke said stiffly. Not even a hint of good humor remained in his demeanor. He held Alex's gaze, the seconds drawing out as the men sized each other up. Alex's fierce look put Lily in mind of a savage warrior determined to defend his land—or his lady. Fear swept through her at the risk he was taking, a risk she hardly understood. All she knew was it involved her. In a panic, she grasped his arm. "Alex?"

His attention snapped back to her, and his tense posture began to ease. Though his anger seemed to fade, his brow creased in concern. Lily knew the reason. Despite her better sense, she'd risked using his Christian name in front of the duke.

An odd look of satisfaction crossed the duke's face. He hadn't missed the slip, a sign of intimacy that had no business existing between her and Alexander Drake. Lily sighed, a sense of fatality filling her. So be it. If the duke decided her reputation had been compromised, he would stop courting her. With Walford out of the picture, Alex would be free to acknowledge his own feelings for her.

Or, he would lose interest in her entirely.

Lily's heart spasmed in pain at the possibility. She compared the two men causing such confusion in her life. The duke carried the stamp of nobility, his proud, sure carriage the product of generations of aristocratic breeding. He needed a wife, and she had been sent here to marry a title.

What could be simpler?

Alex was born common, but there was nothing common about him. His strong, well-built physique put princes to shame. He navigated the top stratum of society as if he were born to it. His spirit fascinated her and his touch tantalized her. And his motives confused and exasperated her.

Her feelings for Alexander Drake weren't simple in the least.

The dinner bell rang. Ignoring Alex, Walford nodded only to her. Then he departed to take his place at the head of the countess's party as her highest-ranking guest.

Alone again with Lily, Alex gave her a look filled with significance. "Tomorrow."

Lily's heart picked up its pace, a deep longing filling her for time alone with him. Yes, she would take the risk. Just as Alex knew she would.

Her arm tucked in his, Alex led Lily toward the lines forming to enter the dining room. As men turned to watch the goddess in their midst, pride filled Alex that he was her partner, even though it was the luck of the draw.

Lily murmured, "You arranged this, too, to be my dinner partner."

"Not at all. It was a fortuitous coincidence."

"I find that impossible to believe."

"Look around you." He nodded toward the people ahead of them, gentlemen paired with ladies to lead them into dinner according to rank. At English dinner parties, rank mattered above age and even common sense. Following the rigid order of precedence, the duke entered the dining room with Countess Helen Charmichael on his arm, while her husband, the earl, escorted a marchioness. Ahead, a fifteen-year-old count fresh from the schoolroom was matched with an earl's sister old enough to be his grandmother.

At the tail of the procession, Alex and Lily were the last to make their way through the gallery, across the vast hall, and into the elaborate oak-paneled dining room where a massive table stretched before them. Overhead, three gas-lit chandeliers dripped with crystal, while on the walls hung ten-foot-high paintings by the masters. One depicted a gory scene that Alex recognized as the Battle of Waterloo. Odd, what some people considered proper decor for a dining hall.

Alex explained to Lily, "Neither of us has any rank to speak of, so it seems we're suitable partners. For dinner," he rushed to add.

She lifted her chin and arched her delicious neck, her eyes narrowing with a hot glint. "I can't imagine being your partner in any other way."

The quiet, ladylike way she communicated her anger fascinated him. Instead of engaging in a fit of piqué as other debutantes might do, she deftly put him in his place with a toss of her head and a few well chosen words.

And, because of that, he found himself more fascinated than ever with his American heiress. Already the hours until their morning rendezvous stretched interminably.

All through dinner, his anticipation increased. During the first course, he engaged her in light conversation. Despite talking of nothing more interesting than the weather and the differences between American and English food, their every word was fraught with tension. When he reached for his wineglass, his hand accidentally brushed hers where it rested on the table. She started at his touch, while a wave of warmth swept through him.

Unfortunately, during the second course, he was obliged by custom to entertain the woman on his left, a bone-thin spinster with a scowl even his charm couldn't melt. In turn, Lily was engaged by Colonel Rothswell Taylor, a retired army man who regaled her with tales of his adventures as a young man in the Crimean War, to which she responded with suitably interested comments and clever turns of phrase.

Alex noticed that her lively beauty attracted the notice of everyone at their end of the long table, men and women alike. No one was immune to her sparkling personality and lively spirit. He listened to their conversation with one ear as he pretended to be interested in the spinster's complaints about her hired help and the unseasonable chill she imagined in the air.

He resented the social niceties that restrained him from talking to the one woman whose company he treasured, hoarding each shared moment like a collection of priceless jewels. Though angled away from Lily, his keen awareness of her presence beside him made it difficult to focus on idle chitchat. True, the spinster was a dull companion. But usually he enjoyed socializing with the upper crust, establishing connections that would further his career.

Tonight was different.

Every time he heard Lily's voice, he had to restrain himself from gazing at her. If he wasn't careful in doling out his attentions to her, his fascination would become apparent to everyone.

Damn. He prided himself on his ability to keep his thoughts and feelings hidden. He'd negotiated delicate peace treaties, for God's sake, infiltrated enemy camps. He refused to appear vulnerable to the charms of an unattainable woman.

A white-gloved, uniformed servant at his elbow removed his untouched sweetbread au jus and replaced it with a dressed Cornish game hen. Despite the delicious repast, his appetite failed him.

Lily's light laugh filled the air, joined by a chuckle from Colonel Taylor. A shaft of jealousy cut through Alex at the knowledge that Colonel Taylor had drawn that joyous sound from her. Though pushing fifty years, the man was distinguished with his neatly trimmed moustache and beard touched in gray. He'd kept his trim shape and a sparkle in his eye told Alex that he was well aware of the delights of female company. Thank goodness, the man was already married. He may be charming Lily, but it would lead nowhere.

The thought brought Alex up short. Shouldn't he be regretting that circumstance? A man like the colonel could make Lily a decent match. Irritated at his thoughts, Alex stabbed at his game hen and tore off a sizable chunk. His ferocity drew a reproving look from the spinster, but he paid her no heed. He fiercely reminded himself that he was through playing matchmaker, even for Lily Carrington. Especially for Lily Carrington. He had another plan, one that couldn't fail to turn her from the duke, freeing her to marry whichever suitable swain caught her fancy.

Damn his idiocy for thinking this might be easy.

"I still can't believe I agreed to your mad plan," Lily said as soon as the carriage began trundling down the lane. "If anyone saw us leaving together, they are sure to think the worst."

Alex had waited inside the carriage, counting the long minutes, impatient for Lily to appear. At least an hour ticked by as the hunting party gathered at the far corner of the mansion. Finally, amid a flurry of activity, the hunters had departed. Hounds yipped and barked, horns blared, and men shouted to each other out of sheer exhileration that the hunting season had begun.

Alex had no interest in cornering any game but the lovely Lily Carrington. Finally, she'd appeared, at the most opportune time. With the house's attention on the excitement of the hunting party, no one but he noticed the gray-cloaked woman slip from a narrow side door and into the waiting carriage.

He reached out and tugged down her hood, revealing a blowsy chignon. He resisted the urge to rearrange her locks—or free them to spill down her shoulders. "Your timing was impeccable. You have a gift for intrigue."

She sighed and sat back against the black leather seat. "I did my best. I have much to lose if gossip circulates about me, as you well know."

"If I had the smallest doubt that the risk was worth it, I would never have insisted you join me."

Her forehead creased and her full lips turned down. "Perhaps if you were honest with me about your concerns regarding the duke, I would be able to decide for myself whether the risk was worth taking."

Damn, why did she have to be so reasonable? Sometimes, despite her overwhelming femininity, she thought like a man, assessing benefits and risks, trying to strike deals. But such a mind-set could play in his favor. Today, he would convince her—using pure logic—why she would be a fool to consider any proposal the duke might make.

"You needn't worry. We won't be out after dark,

which would surely compromise you. Accompanying me on a ride is not so great a risk to your reputation."

"Nor is it completely safe." As she gazed out the window at the muted and misty dawn, she nervously toyed with the buttons on her cloak.

"Then why did you come?" he asked softy.

"Perhaps I'm curious." Turning from the window, Lily studied him, her dark eyes glinting beneath seductively lowered lids. "Perhaps I enjoy being with you, more fool me."

A shiver of desire swept through him at her admission. He chastised himself for his body's uncontrolled reaction. Of course she enjoyed his company. Every time they were alone together, he began to seduce her, showering her with attention, setting her on fire as surely as she did him. Sensual being that she was, naturally she responded with enthusiasm.

Today would be different. He would keep his physical and emotional distance and focus on the business at hand.

"Fool, indeed," he responded coolly. "I am not the object of this morning's excursion, as you will soon see."

His curt reply didn't stop her teasing smile. "Always mysterious. And never, ever dull."

Again he fought his attraction to her. She continued to flirt with him, and he continued to relish it. "Sit back and behave yourself," he said. Rather than stern, he sounded indulgent.

"Yes, sir," she replied, laughter behind her words.

Alex fought the urge to smile at her. Fought the urge to slide closer to her on the seat and take her into his arms. With focused concentration, he stared out the carriage window at the gradually brightening landscape.

* * *

After a two-hour carriage ride, during which Alex had pretended to sleep and Lily had stared at him to her heart's content, they came to a stop. Outside the window rose a large country house of red brick and stone named Rosebank Hall.

As grand as Fox Croft was, Lily preferred this Queen Anne–style mansion, though it was only half the size. The setting filled her with a sense of peace. From where the house rested atop a gentle rise, residents could enjoy the vista of a small lake backed by verdant rolling hills.

A footman helped her from the carriage, then a hatchet-faced butler led them inside to a light, airy parlor. A slender woman waited for them in the impeccably decorated room. Her blond hair was swept above a face that would be very pretty, if not for dark circles under her eyes and a sad expression that contrasted sharply with the welcoming surroundings. Though Lily knew nothing about this woman, her melancholy air tugged at Lily's heart.

Stepping forward, the lady grasped Alex's hands and kissed his cheek. When she spoke, Lily was surprised to find she had an American accent that matched her own.

"Alex, it's been so long." She ran her fingers along his jacket lapel. "You look so dashing, even more than I remember." She gazed into his face, her eyes wide with desperation as she drank her fill of him.

They've been intimate. A spurt of jealousy coursed through Lily. She wasn't certain of all the ways men and women could be intimate. But obviously these two had shared more than a passing—or appropriate—acquaintance. No doubt he'd kissed this woman, held her and said sweet words to her. *Just as he did to me.*

And this woman adored him still. Lily looked at Alex askance. Why would he want her to meet a former lover? To hurt her? Convince her of his lack of regard?

Alex gave the woman's hands a squeeze, then released them and put a more socially suitable distance between them, thank goodness. "Julia, you're looking well."

Julia smiled, but her expression held little happiness. "You always were a good liar."

Alex stepped beside Lily and touched her arm. "May I introduce Miss Lily Carrington. As I wrote you, she's also from America."

The lady finally pulled her gaze from Alex long enough to focus on her other guest. To Lily's relief and secret embarrassment, Julia didn't seem annoyed at seeing Alex with another female—as she herself had been. Julia seemed to lack the energy to feel jealous, or any strong emotions. Her brief flash of enthusiasm at seeing Alex had already faded, her spirit retreating.

Alex supplied the introductions, and Lily discovered she was meeting the Baroness de Veaux, formerly Julia Williams from Boston.

"Is this why you were so anxious for us to meet?" she asked Alex. She smiled brightly at Julia in an effort to lighten the doleful atmosphere in the room. "I'm thrilled to be meeting another American lady. You'll have to tell me all about how you came to live here."

"Being American is only one of the things you have in common," Alex said. His expression remained somber, as did Julia's.

"Miss Carrington. Please sit." Julia extended her

hand in a graceful arc, indicating the sofa. Lily took a seat beside Alex.

Julia clasped her hands in her lap and gazed from Alex to Lily with her large, sad eyes. "Alex told me you wanted to talk to me."

Lily glanced at Alex. "Did he?"

Alex shifted. "Actually, I want you to talk to her. About your life."

Julia gazed at her lap a moment, then lifted her head and glanced around. Though she was in her own home, she appeared lost. "Tea? I can't think without tea. The English—they so adore their tea."

She lifted a bell from a side table and rang it. A gray-haired maid with a severe expression appeared in the parlor door and curtsied. Her hawk-eyed gaze took in both Alex and Lily and her lips turned down in what Lily would interpret as disapproval. Julia seemed not to notice. She requested tea and scones and the maid silently departed.

"That was Baxter. *He* insists she remain in our service, though he knows how I detest her. No doubt she'll report to him everything about our meeting today."

Lily froze. Julia hadn't lowered her voice a single notch to make her blatant comment. The maid, or another member of the staff, might hear.

Julia smiled thinly. "You think I speak too bluntly, Miss Carrington? The maids are perfectly aware of my feelings. Most of them hate me in turn, so my words come as no surprise."

"I—I think that's dreadful. Not you. *Them.* Why would you allow—"

"Allow? What choice do I have? My husband has the final say over who we keep in service. And in virtually every other area of my life."

A chill swept through Lily as the nature of this

meeting began to come clear. She shot a look at Alex and found his eyes assessing her. "Alex, tell me what this is about."

Alex cleared his throat. "Julia, Miss Carrington is being wooed by several members of the 'set.' Some of the gentlemen in question would be hard-pressed to provide her with the sort of . . . companionship I know that she craves. I thought perhaps—"

"You would like me to tell her my story of woe. Very well." Her eyes sparkled, but not with joy. Pain was reflected in their depths, the pain of dreams destroyed and a life wasted. As the baroness began to speak, Lily knew her impression was correct.

Like herself, Julia had arrived in London a young debutante determined to make the best match possible. "A baron began to court me. I decided he was handsome, though not as handsome as a man *can* be." Her eyes were on Alex as she said this. "Other men lacked his polish, his ancestry, and most of all, his title. When he first brought me here, I was overwhelmed by the age and glory of this place. I was a silly naive girl, and silly naive girls imagine silly things. My head was filled with romantic notions, images of me sweeping down the staircase in my glorious gowns, greeting my guests and our tenants. I actually fancied how romantic my life would be as mistress of this—this—*prison*."

Her voice broke with such intense bitterness, it brought tears to Lily's eyes. She longed to reach out and comfort her, but she took her cue from Alex and remained quiet and still for her story.

Julia paused when the maid reappeared, rolling in a cart laden with teapot, cups, biscuits, scones, jellies, clotted cream, and butter. To Lily, the typically warm and inviting tradition of English tea had never seemed so out of place. Yet she accepted when the baroness passed her a cup of the steaming liquid.

The maid departed. After sipping her tea, Julia regained her demure composure and resumed her tale. "I found it so easy to convince myself I cared for the baron. In truth, I was more in love with the *idea* of him than the man himself. So, my father accepted his proposal on my behalf, with my full agreement."

She set down her cup and saucer and studied Lily. "How much do you know of the relations between husbands and wives?"

Lily's face began to heat. She felt Alex's gaze on her, but didn't dare look in his direction. "I'm not sure . . ."

Julia threw back her head and laughed. "Not sure! What young lady is? Let me try to explain something to you, without shocking your delicate sensibilities. Odd, isn't it, that those sensibilities are allowed to be ravaged on our wedding night? Why is sex an inappropriate topic of discussion before the wedding, when we must submit without question after?"

Lily wanted to run. She also wanted to demand Julia tell her everything she knew. And she didn't want Alex to be in the room when she did so.

He seemed to sense her discomfort. "Your gardens. Are they still as renowned as they've always been? I think I shall take a look." Rising, he set his teacup on the cart and left the room.

"Such a gentleman," Julia murmured, her sorrowful gaze following him out. "Even if we had met before my marriage, my family would never have allowed us to marry. Simply not enough advantage to be had marrying a government official." She sighed and her narrow shoulders sagged. "One mustn't cry over impossible dreams, must one?"

"But shouldn't a lady try to make a happy life for herself?" Lily asked.

"What is happiness? I confess I don't know anymore, only that I lack it. There was a brief time some months after my marriage and before the baron learned the truth, when I was happy. But it was merely a stolen fantasy, as insubstantial as smoke."

Was she referring to Alex? Lily longed to ask, but held her tongue, hoping Julia would reveal the truth in time.

She wasn't disappointed. But the trip there took them on a surprising, even scandalous detour.

With a gentle smile, the baroness asked, "What do you know about what happens between husbands and wives?"

Fourteen

Lily hesitated, toying with the teaspoon on her saucer. She had long wondered about the secret intimacies that occurred between men and women. Would this lady really tell her the facts? Or would she cloak her words in so many euphemisms that Lily would remain as ignorant as she already felt?

"Well?" the baroness prompted. "Tell me what you know. Then I will know where to start."

Lily finally found the nerve to put into words her modicum of knowledge. "I know a man joins a woman in her bed at night. He touches her. Supposedly men like this touching more than women do, but I gather some women enjoy it." Some, like her! She hoped the baroness couldn't tell that she'd relished a man's caresses.

"Go on."

"Well, the man touches the woman in a special way that causes her to become with child. But not always. Some women are barren, after all, like it says in the Bible. Beyond that, I'm not entirely sure . . ."

Julia nodded her approval. "You know more than most girls at your age. Much more than I did."

Lily thought of Hannah, who had tackled the question of men and women as she had Greek or chemistry. "My older sister is very inquisitive. She found out a few things before her own marriage and shared them with me."

Julia nodded. "Very well. Now I will tell you the rest. Do you know about men's bodies?"

"You're referring to their"—she cleared her throat—"their male part?"

The baroness lifted her eyebrows and gave her a curious smile. "I'm glad you know that part is important. Some girls can't even figure that out. A lucky few have brothers who are willing to tell them things."

"I have no brothers, but I took an art class at my girls' school where I saw pictures of nudes. My classmates giggled in corners about . . . that part, calling it a man's 'willy.' That sounds so silly, a willy. A silly willy," she said lamely, her nerves making her sound silly herself. But they were conversing bluntly about topics well-bred ladies were never supposed to *think* about, much less discuss over tea.

The baroness smiled in genuine enjoyment for the first time. "A silly willy! I'm not surprised Alex has taken a fancy to you. You're positively delightful. Now then. The man's"—she smiled—"willy. It looked small in the paintings of the great masters that you saw. Yet when a man becomes filled with desire for a woman, it grows several times larger, and becomes stiff." Lifting two ladyfingers from the plate of biscuits, she placed them end to end and held them in the air. "It grows about this long and twice as thick."

Lily watched the display in fascination. As the baroness described the mystery, she found herself imagining Alex, picturing him nude and his "willy" stiff. The image seemed ludicrous and naughty, yet strangely tantalizing. Thank goodness, the baroness couldn't read her mind!

Julia continued, "When it's stiff like that, he is able to slide it inside a woman, into the canal through which your monthlies flow. Usually this is accomplished lying down, in bed. Though more creative lovers can make love anywhere."

Creative lovers . . . like Alex. Lily struggled to stop imagining him. She asked, "But if it grows as big as you say, that must hurt the woman."

"If the man is at all good at making love to a woman, he has made her as desirous of the union as he is. That makes the passage much easier. So." She placed the ladyfingers back on the platter. "This is, essentially, how men and women mate."

Lily knew without asking that Alex would be good at making a woman crave him. He had certainly made her desire him, though she hadn't realized until now what her body had been longing for. That fluttering ache between her legs that she had felt when he kissed her with such passion . . . That was her female desire to mate with Alex.

"And this causes babies to grow in a woman?" she asked.

The baroness nodded. "Certainly not every time. But men have a . . . a liquid. When they reach the height of their pleasure, this liquid is implanted in a woman's womb and begins a baby."

"Where does this liquid come from?"

"The end of the man's willy, silly."

At the wordplay, Lily began to giggle, and the baroness joined in.

"It does sound ridiculous, though," Lily said, catching her breath. "Yet I imagine it must feel good, otherwise ladies wouldn't be in such danger of being compromised." Having experienced Alex's passionate embraces, she herself had felt that burning desire to continue, to do *more*.

Julia nodded. "Exactly. You're a very clever young thing, aren't you?"

Lily stared at her curiously. "Somehow I didn't expect to be brought here to learn about this."

"Yes, well, that discussion was merely a side tour on the way to telling my story. But I couldn't resist. It infuriates me how naive I was, how utterly stupid about men, about life. As if keeping me from knowledge was a way to protect me! Nothing could be further from the truth."

She continued her tale. To Lily's horror, she learned that as a result of her ignorance, Julia had been forced to comply on her wedding night. Her "canal" had not been ready, causing her great pain. Her husband had visited her every night and forced himself upon her numerous times. She had ached for weeks afterward, even finding it difficult to walk.

Lily shuddered and squeezed her thighs together under her dress. How could a man be so inconsiderate, so cruel? "Didn't you tell him to stop?"

Julia shrugged. "He didn't care what I thought, what I said. He wanted me to bear an heir, and he enjoyed taking me regardless of what I thought or felt. Very soon I grew to hate him. I would have hated all men, if not for Alex. Almost as much as I hate this house, and this horrid, dreary country."

Lily wanted to hear more about Alex, but Julia began telling her how lonely she had been when she'd come to live here at Rosebank Hall. Used to the lively balls and parties she'd attended as a debutante, she found herself upon her marriage isolated in the country. Her husband had no interest in society, leaving her alone except for her "neighbors," the closest of which was at Fox Croft Estate. Lily knew how far that was.

"Even when I did visit them, which was rare, they

were less than friendly. The country gentry view me as an interloper. They wish one of their daughters had married the baron. And the other aristocrats consider me a low-born American beneath their interest."

"But the earl and countess—they aren't so bad," Lily said, thinking of the pleasant Lady Charmichael who had invited her to her weekend party. Then again, how much of their acceptance was due to the duchess's patronage?

"I found out later that much of their disdain was due to their dislike of the baron—my husband," Julia said. "As his wife, I was painted with the same brush. I became an extension of him and lost myself entirely. Abandoned here while the baron left on frequent trips, I soon discovered how ill-equipped I was to run a country house. The servants are cold toward me, but I lack the power to dismiss them or discipline them in any way. My husband controls all our funds. He rarely gives me more than a token allowance. I'm trapped. I can do nothing without his permission. Simply put, living here is hell on earth."

"I'm so sorry."

"I believe this is why Alex wanted me to talk to you. I expect he fears you will stumble into the same sort of life." Leaning forward, she grasped Lily's hand and spoke emphatically. "I tell you now, Lily. If it had been up to me, I would have run from here, run from that title, as far and as fast as I could."

Lily nodded, trying to determine what Alex imagined might happen to her. Assuming the duke even proposed—and that was hardly a sure thing—what flaws did he see in the duke's character that made him so concerned for her well-being? What caused Alex to care so much in the first place?

She studied Julia, wondering if the lady might shed

light on the man they shared in common. "How did you meet Alex?"

"I became sick, and because of my inability to conceive—despite the baron's visits to my bed—he sent me to Bath. That is where I met him. That is where I learned how wonderful a man's lovemaking can be."

Lily felt warm all over imagining Alex, and his lovemaking. No more could she bring herself to feel jealous of this woman, not after the pain and loneliness she'd suffered. "I'm so glad he was able to make you happy."

The baroness' eyes grew shadowed. "For a brief time. A very brief time. Until *he* learned of the affair." The baron had heard from her maid that she'd been seeing a man. Furious, he had dragged his wayward wife home and locked her in her room for more than a month. "I was given bread and water to eat, but nothing else. I grew so thin, I could count my ribs. Not that anyone noticed. I wasn't allowed to see anyone. Finally, his anger cooled and his lust grew, and he let me out."

"But your parents—couldn't your father have rescued you?" Divorce, while frowned upon, was not unheard of. If Julia had been that abused, why hadn't she left her husband?

"My father is a rigid, tyrannical man. His response was to write me a stern letter demanding I apologize to my husband and beg his forgiveness on my knees. As far as he's concerned, my husband is the wronged party and a saint for not disowning me."

Lily's heart ached for Julia. This, at last, was where their stories differed. She would never be abandoned by her large, loving family. Her father adored her, her mother cherished her, and her four sisters remained close and dear. "I wish there was something I could do to ease your pain."

"There is," she said, her intense gaze on Lily. "Don't make the same mistake I did. Know your husband before you take those irrevocable vows."

Lily nodded. This, then, was the message Alex had wanted this good lady to impart to her. Alex . . . Why didn't *he* rescue this lady? "Did Alex not even try—"

"My dear, of course he did. You know better than that. His life was threatened, and he was told he would be put up on criminal charges, unless he left the country. Which, as is usual with men, he turned to advantage by taking up a post with the Foreign Office and beginning his career. Since then, as is the way with clever, attractive young men, he has carved out a successful life for himself. I wish him only the best."

"But if he loved you—"

She shook her head. "Nor I him. What we had wasn't meant to last, Lily. We each took what we needed from it. He brought my feelings back to life, my sense of self-worth. In turn, I fed his need to be needed." Lowering her voice, she patted Lily's hand conspiratorially. "But don't tell him that. He refuses to recognize it."

Lily already knew he carried such a need. Ever since she'd met him, he'd been trying to "save" her from her own folly. "He has an amazingly tender heart," Lily conceded. "Considering he's such a rascal."

Julia's laughter sparked Lily's own, their girlish giggles filling the house.

"I hope you're not laughing at my expense," Alex appeared in the doorway and leaned on the lintel. "Are you two ladies finished? Lily and I need to be getting back."

"I believe so," Julia said. She looked at Lily. "We've had a nice little chat, haven't we, dear?"

Lily studied Alex's strong physique framed in the doorway. Despite her best intentions, her gaze slid to his hips, to that place where—inside his trousers—his "willy" lay snuggled in his drawers, She bit back a smile.

As she lifted her eyes, his gaze snared hers, sending a jolt straight through her heart. His frown caused her face to burn, and she had the strong feeling he knew her thoughts. Snapping her attention back to Julia, she rose and clasped her hostess's hands. "Thank you," she murmured. "Thank you so much for opening your heart and your home to me."

"Anything for an old friend," she said, glancing at Alex behind her. "And a new friend."

At the door, Alex had already gone ahead to talk to the carriage driver when Julia pulled her aside for one last word. "Follow your heart, Lily, never listen to others. Not about love. Life is too short for mistakes you will regret the rest of your life."

Lily left the baroness with shared smiles and good wishes, and a promise to visit again.

But after their carriage was underway, a sense of melancholy descended on Lily. Speaking so honestly with the baroness had left her shaken and worried about making the right choices in her own life.

After traveling a mile, Alex spoke. "You seem pensive." Beside her, he leaned back and extended his arm across the seat back as if settling in for a heart-to-heart chat.

"Last night, after you told me to meet you . . ." Lily shook her head. "This is not what I expected. I'm overwhelmed by what she told me."

"I had hoped you would find her story of value."

"I've never seen the truth as clearly before. Young

ladies aren't taught to consider our lives beyond the wedding day. Our primary goal is to make the best match possible. That is where we focus our energies. We think of our husband-to-be in the vaguest of terms—will he be handsome, will he be rich . . ."

"Will he be titled." His penetrating gaze threatened her composure.

She bit her lip and shifted her gaze from his. "I've assumed finding the 'right man,' whatever that means, would guarantee my happiness. I've been such a naive fool."

"Nonsense. You were raised not to think too hard about these things."

"How could a man be so wicked to his own wife! It infuriates me."

She fisted her hands on her lap. "She made a bad match, unfortunately. Something you won't do, after today."

She met his gaze. "You really believe I face a similar fate?"

"You may, if you don't let titles and status sway you from what your heart tells you."

Her heart longed for this man, and no other. The baroness's words echoed through her. *Listen to your heart.*

She met his purposeful gaze. Was he trying to declare himself to her? If so, he was doing it in a frustratingly oblique way. She knew he cared about her, cared about her fate. Else why take her to meet the baroness? She knew he enjoyed kissing her. But for such a worldly man, was that the extent of it? Was his heart involved, too?

"Did you love the baroness? You were her lover."

He exhaled a soft laugh. "You deduced that, did you?"

"From the first. She looked as if she wanted to feast on you."

He chuckled, then his smile began to fade. He studied Lily. "No, I didn't love her, nor she me. If I'd known how her husband would punish her, I would never have bedded her. She was so sad and beautiful then, like a tragic heroine in a Russian novel. I longed to bring a smile to her face—which I succeeded in doing, but at a terrible cost to her."

"No, Alex." She grasped his hand and cradled it against her chest, drawing a startled gaze from him. "You're too hard on yourself. The baron would have been cruel regardless—that's why she was so sad to begin with. At least you gave her a few hours of happiness to treasure."

"You put a pretty spin on things, Lily, but that doesn't change the facts. I'm a rake, as you well know. We've had our moments, after all."

"What does that really mean, being a rake? You're still a gentleman when it counts."

"Damn, you can be naive, Lily. I would have thought you'd heard the rumors about me by now. They've been circulating for quite some time."

"You mean about your foreign mistress. I had heard, yes. Mrs. Digby insisted this made you entirely unsuitable for me."

"Of course it does. As does the number of married women I've seduced, the amount of pounds I've stolen from the wealthy by my frequent gambling, and my late nights wasted at private clubs and opium dens."

"None of that makes you a bad man, not like the baron."

He pulled his hand from hers. "Bad? What do you think my disregard for convention has done to these women?"

"And I fail to see how the color of your mistress's skin matters in the least. You showed her love and affection and tenderness."

His brows lowered in a dark frown. "What would you know about it?"

Though she didn't answer, he guessed the truth easily enough. "John—he told you, didn't he?"

"Don't blame him, Alex. I insisted he tell me, and I'm so glad he did, for I doubt you would have shared the story with me. You rescued Sikara from a fate worse than death."

"And turned her into my mistress."

"You didn't force her, I'm certain of that. Maybe you even loved her." Had he? Had he already loved and lost his one love, leaving no room for her?

"Yes," he said matter-of-factly. She couldn't decide whether to revel in her relief that she'd been right about him, or ponder the painful truth that he may never be able to love again.

"Yes," he continued, gazing out the carriage window. "I loved her. Not the flowery, swept-off-your-feet love of a fairy-tale, but we shared a strong, practical bond. I would never have left her, I can tell you that."

"You loved her, then. But you weren't *in love* with her."

He shrugged as if the distinction made little difference. "I suppose that's one way to put it. I doubt that I *can* be in love. I'm not certain anyone truly ever is."

Lily was certain, and she knew she was falling head over heels for this man, regardless of whether he believed such love was possible. Again, she was torn in two. She was relieved he wasn't living in the past, still pining for Sikara. Yet it saddened her that he felt such a deep love impossible for himself.

Yet he *had* loved Sikara. "You must have been devastated when she died," she said softly, recalling that she'd died trying to give birth to his child. "When both of them died."

"Damn it, Lily. Let's not discuss this. It's in the past." She'd pushed him too far. His eyes glittered and his sharp tone cut her like a knife.

Still she persisted. She had never seen him open up, not like this, and refused to relinquish her small advantage. Laying her hand on his arm, she said quietly, "God decided to take her life, for whatever mysterious reason. That was no fault of yours, Alex."

He kept his eyes turned toward the window, but Lily saw a glint of moisture in their blue depths. "I said I don't want to discuss it." His voice came out raspy with emotion. "As I've explained many times, I am no gentleman. Nothing more need be said."

Moisture pressed against Lily's eyelids at his refusal to forgive himself. Ignoring his words, she slid beside him. Gently, as if taming a wild animal, she touched her fingertips to the back of his head, stroking his hair with a tender caress. He remained unresponsive and still, as if trying to pretend she wasn't there, touching him, reaching inside to a place he kept locked tight.

"You keep your pain deep inside, thinking no one can see it." Bringing her lips almost against his ear, she whispered, "But *I* see it. It's in your eyes, in your attitude every time you talk about yourself. As if you've committed unforgivable acts. But nothing you've told me, nothing I've heard about you, bears this out! *Nothing*."

With the utmost tenderness, she skimmed her fingers along the soft hair at his temple, smoothing the chestnut strands in place behind his ear. "You're a wonderful man—kind, caring, and especially good to women"—she fiercely blinked back a surge of tears—"especially women lucky enough to love you."

For a long moment, he remained frozen. Then he seemed to sag, his defenses blown. He pulled in a deep, shuddering breath. Finally, he focused on her face. A tremor ran through Lily at the stark emotion on his rugged features. He had never looked so vulnerable. "Damn it, woman," he rasped.

Without warning, he grasped her waist and lifted her onto his lap. He pressed her close, chest to chest, locking his arms tightly around her, as if afraid she might escape. In this brief sliver of time, Lily could believe she was the most precious thing in the world to him.

Burying his head in the crook of her neck, he rocked her softly. "You weren't supposed to discuss such things," he said, his voice thick with tears.

"You needed to hear it," she said, her heart filled with elation. She had never felt closer to a living soul.

He stroked her hair and murmured sweet words to her, words her ears couldn't decipher, but which her heart fully understood. His mouth swept along the column of her neck, then slid over her own. "Why do you make me feel this way?" he murmured against her skin.

Lily closed her eyes and reveled in his sensual caresses. "What way?"

"Like a goddamned hero."

The baroness's remark about Alex, that he needed to be needed, returned to Lily. Though she didn't understand why, Lily knew she fed Alex's need to rescue ladies in distress. As Sikara had. As the baroness had. But she meant more than that to him, she was certain of it. Pulling away, she cupped his dear face in her hands and caught his heated gaze with her own.

"You are a hero." Grasping his face, she kissed him tenderly on the mouth. "My hero."

As if he'd been waiting for her advance, he reacted with swift desire. He pressed his palms to her head and seared his lips to hers in a molten kiss. His tongue deftly conquered her mouth, taking total command as he led her in the kiss. Lily submitted willingly, kissing him back with an enthusiasm as heated as his own.

Her heart filled with an almost painful need to be close to him, in every way. She caressed his back, dragged her fingers through his hair, tried to bring him even closer to her. She felt the leather carriage seat against her back, and realized he'd lowered her there. He lay atop her, hard, determined, and incredibly strong. Heat built inside Lily, focused on the secret region between her thighs and spreading outward in delicious, tantalizing waves. His hips pressed hard against hers, and she arched her head back and moaned in delight at the heavenly sensations washing over her.

"Oh, God, Lily, I want you as I've never wanted another woman."

His breath rasped hot and heavy in her ear, his hands touching not only her waist and back, but sliding in front to cup her breasts through her bodice. The intimate touch of his palms stole her breath along with her sense. "I like that," she said, wishing she could feel his touch on her bare skin. "Don't stop."

He danced his thumbs across the tips of her breasts in small circling motions, and she gasped at the sharp pleasure that shafted through her.

"I want to kiss you here. Everywhere. You're the most sensual creature," he said, his voice filled with wonder. "You love me to touch you, and I adore touching you."

Oh, yes . . . The feelings he elicited in her body were like nothing else on earth. She reveled in them. Such wonders . . . What must consummation feel like? Her frank discussion with the baroness came to mind. Burning with curiosity, she slid her hand between their bodies, to his hips. Pressing her palm between his legs, she learned that what the baroness had described had come to pass. He felt positively huge through his trousers, and remarkably hard.

He pressed up on his palms and stared down at her. "Lily, my God." Squeezing his eyes shut, he remained frozen while she continued exploring the length and breadth of him.

He sucked in a harsh breath. To her dismay he shoved her hand away and sat up. "You mustn't do that."

"But why?" She dragged herself to a sitting position, striving to catch her breath. "The baroness explained how men change when they desire a woman. I wanted to see if you desired me."

"As if there was any question!" He collapsed back on the seat and raked his hand through his hair. "I can't believe I allowed this to happen. It's gotten way out of hand. You're a respectable young lady, we're in a carriage; and it's broad daylight!"

She slid close to him. "Does it matter where or how one shows one's affection? As long as it's honest. And what I feel for you is honest."

"Lily, stop talking this way. It's too dangerous. Somehow you've found my Achilles' heel," he said with a grim smile. "Please try to show mercy and not exploit your discovery."

"Exploit? Alex, I don't want to hurt you." She covered his hand where it rested on his knee.

He gently returned her hand to her lap. "Nor I you. We must never have a repeat of today. Now that you know not to marry foolishly, our business together is finished."

Finished? Lily stared at him aghast. How could he say that? Mere moments ago, he'd been cradling her and murmuring love words to her! "Alex, you aren't making any sense! You and I both want to be . . . be intimate. And we could be. We could be free to show our affection without censure, without guilt, with nothing holding us back."

"That's ridiculous, Lily." He shook his head, his lips turned up in a wry smile. "There's no way—"

"Yes, there is. All you have to do is marry me."

Fifteen

Marry her?

Her proposal hit Alex like a bucket of freezing water, common sense returning as bitter shame churned in his stomach. He'd nearly seduced the woman he'd been trying to protect!

He studied her, his groin continuing to throb with each beat of his heart. She looked positively decadent, her hair mussed and her lips swollen from his kisses. He battled the urge to pull her again into his arms, to finish his raw seduction of her.

"Scoot back to your side of the seat and pull yourself together," he said gruffly. Though she ignored him, he attempted to adjust himself within his trousers, then smoothed down his hair, hoping a return to "normalcy" would cause their mutual passion to abate.

The respite also gave him a chance to gather his thoughts.

She wanted to marry him? He knew she had affection for him, of course. Suspected, even, that she'd developed romantic fantasies about him.

But now that she'd actually voiced her thoughts, he had to accept that he'd been fooling himself. He'd been indulging his pleasure without a moment's thought to her heart. He'd wanted to believe their pleasurable dalliances would leave her unscathed.

He'd imagined she would view their flirtation with the worldliness that experienced women possessed.

Yes, she was savvy and bright, more so than any debutante he'd ever met. Yes, she burned with the sensuality of mature womanhood. She was, nevertheless, an inexperienced girl, one he'd been taking terrible advantage of.

And she actually believed him to be heroic! In that, she was most certainly naive.

"You haven't answered me," she said, her determined gaze probing his.

"I—Lily, *no.* The answer is no." Grasping her hands, he pressed them close, praying she would see sense and not pursue the matter, allow them both to retreat from a subject he never wanted to discuss with her.

He wasn't so lucky.

Lily yanked her hands away, her eyes glittering with anger. "Simply *no?* That's all you have to say?"

His stomach tightened further, a hard knot of frustration pressing against his breastbone. "Your parents would hardly approve."

"Why not? They know nothing about you or your reputation."

"They would hear soon enough. By God, woman, look at what just happened! I almost ruined you, without concern for your happiness."

"I will never believe you're not concerned for my happiness," she shot back, her intensity equaled only by her ingenuous faith in him. "You've gone out of your way to involve yourself in my life in an effort to *protect* my happiness. That proves you care for me."

With fierce determination, he ignored the unfamiliar yearning that now plagued his heart. "Nonsense. You've been a—a project, nothing more."

"A project?"

"Exactly. Something to while away the time while I wait for my next assignment from the Foreign Office." Forcing his posture to relax, he crossed his ankle over his knee and stretched his arm along the back of the seat. His mocking gaze on her, he spoke in a scoffing tone designed to embarrass her. "Show some sense, girl. You've shown little so far this afternoon, allowing me to kidnap you from the party, allowing me indecent liberties with your delectable person. What more must happen to convince you I'm a heartless cad?"

Her heart remained in her eyes as she gazed at him. "You will never convince me you're heartless, Alex, despite your reputation as a rake. You brought me on this excursion to help me, and you have."

"Hah!" he laughed coldly. "After which I tried to seduce you. In case you're too naive to realize it, that's what rakes *do*. We accost tender young things and lead them into ruin to satisfy our own base lusts."

She scowled, her eyes sparking. "You make it sound as if I had nothing to do with our encounter. As if I lay here in a daze while you ravished me! We were *both* involved, not you alone."

Of course she was right, but he intended to convince her otherwise. "You're an untried female. *I* am the man here, the despoiler. I am—need I point out— a good deal more experienced in these matters than you."

"What does that matter? Obviously I want you just as much as you want me."

His stomach tightened at her words. He gripped the seat back in an attempt to remain grounded in reality. *She wanted him.* She was acknowledging her desire for him as bluntly as an experienced woman would. The thought of her voluptuous nature centering its potent feminine energies on him, and him alone, was enough to make him throw caution to the wind and finish what they started.

He couldn't. Of course he couldn't. But the temptation was damned near impossible to resist.

"Let me get this straight," she continued, her brow furrowed, her eyes sparking with disdain. "We want each other, deeply, heatedly. In a way that can only be satisfied with . . . with each other."

Oh, God, yes, his heart yearned to answer, but he stifled it. Remaining still, he allowed her to finish, prayed she'd finish soon, before he lost control again.

"You acknowledge that you should not bed me unless we are married, which is the attitude of a true gentleman, is it not? In every way that counts, you've shown yourself a gentleman, except when it comes to our mutual . . . *want.* Yet, because of your reputation, you think you are unsuited to be my husband."

"I know so."

She threw up her hands. "It makes no sense! Why should I care a flying fig about your reputation or your past? If you care for me as I care for you . . ."

He had to shoot down her girlish notions, *now.* Before she said another compelling word. Before she pushed past his defenses and saw exactly how weak he could be. Adopting a chilly tone, he retorted, "I have never professed my love to you."

She opened her mouth to respond, but as his words sank in, she gradually closed it, her expression showing confusion and hurt.

Pushing his advantage, Alex leaned close and grit his teeth. "Perhaps now you are beginning to see the sort of man I am."

"Alex," she swallowed, then began again. "Why have you been leading me on, if you don't want me?"

He gripped her shoulders and dragged her close,

his mouth just above hers. Under his palms, he felt her tremble. *Good. Let her fear him. Let her run from him.* Yet her gaze remained steady and sure.

"Of course I *want* you! You're throwing yourself at me," he said, his words filled with bitterness. Desperate to shock sense into her, he gave her a hard shove, then relaxed back in the seat as if her feelings, her very presence, meant nothing to him.

Though she rubbed her shoulders where he'd grasped her, she didn't flinch or protest his treatment of her. He'd never met a more self-possessed woman. It made him admire her, *yearn* for her, more than ever. *You can't have her, fool,* he reminded himself, struggling to breathe through the sharp pain that cut through his chest.

With heavy irony, he said, *"Wanting* you is a far cry from *love,* darling, especially for men. As for marriage, that state has even less to do with love."

Despite his effort to shatter her romantic notions, she didn't cry or throw a fit as other ladies might. Her calm gaze remained fastened on him, as if she could read beyond his words, see deeper than the front he showed to the world. It was positively unnerving.

"If marriage has little to do with love," she asked stiffly, keeping her chin high, "why do you concern yourself with whom I shall marry?"

It was his turn to pause with mouth open, searching for an appropriate response.

She continued, "You are determined to dictate my choice of a husband, yet—despite *wanting* me, as you say—you have no intention of ever marrying me yourself."

He smiled in cold victory. "Finally, you understand. If anything has happened today, I hope you've learned the truth about me. You see, Lily," he said, once again moving close to her. He slid his hand along the back of her head and dragged her mouth to within a breath of his. He murmured, "I am the man to turn to only if you want to be thoroughly and completely ruined."

He pressed his lips on hers to sear the truth into her heart.

Lily allowed his kiss, but only for a moment. She steeled her heart against the burst of desire he stirred within her with his potent attentions. He'd treated her poorly these past few minutes, put a dark stain on their intimate encounter. His callousness infuriated her, but it was his rejection that cut her heart like a knife. He would never marry her, never be hers.

Instead, he mocked her with a sensuous kiss.

She shoved against his chest and broke away, just as Fox Croft appeared through the carriage window. The sun rode high in the late-afternoon sky, and the carriage's arrival would no doubt be seen by numerous guests. Several of them were already boarding carriages which would transport them to the train station for the journey home.

Throwing her hood over her head, Lily scrambled from the carriage, not waiting for the footman to hand her down. She raced the thirty feet to the side door she'd slipped through that morning and into a darkened hall.

Though she could barely see past her feet, she kept her hood up, hoping no one would notice her, no one would ask questions. She wanted only to be left alone until she reached her room. Once there, she could revel in her mortification, indulge her pain, allow her tears to flow.

Alex had devastated her. She tried to keep from believing his scathing words, but the truth could not be ignored. She'd done her best to hide her pain, prayed he would never know how deeply he'd wounded her.

She still could not believe he was a heartless rake. Yet she understood now that he did not return her feelings. She had conjured romantic fantasies about him, had woven tender feelings where none existed. He cared only for her body, cared only about his physical longing to bed her.

Now that she'd experienced such longing herself, she understood it for what it was. Nothing but lust.

She burned with lust in equal measure. But she felt so much more! What had possessed her to reveal her heart? She had actually proposed to him, something no seemly young lady ever did. Oh, the shame of it! And then to be rejected on top of that. Yes, her pride stung. But that wasn't what drove her to tears.

I've lost him. That thought more than any other left her feeling ill and shaken. With her foolish proposal, she'd ruined her friendship with the only man she'd ever truly cared for.

"Miss Carrington, there you are."

The duke's cultured voice brought her to a stumbling halt. She grasped the carved oak molding on the wall for support. Lord Walford had appeared in the hall so suddenly, it made her dizzy.

In an instant, the duke was beside her, supporting her, his face solicitous and concerned. "Miss Carrington, are you quite all right? You look rather peaked. Have you taken sick?"

Sick at heart, a state worse than any illness she had ever suffered. She struggled for composure. As soon as her emotions were relatively controlled, she slipped off her hood and gazed directly at him. "I'm fine. Just a little disoriented, this place is so huge."

"Come, let's get you off your feet." Taking her tenderly by the elbow, he directed her down the hall.

He took her to the blue room, a sitting room on the first floor, and placed her on the empire sofa. "I'll have tea sent right away. Harcourt! Tea for the lady." His valet, who was never far away, responded immediately from his post by the door. He gave the order to a house parlor maid.

Sitting on an ottoman at her feet, the duke pressed her hands between his. "Soon we'll have you feeling right as rain."

Her spirit suffering, her defenses weak, Lily found herself deeply touched by the duke's solicitous gestures. Tears sprang to her eyes as Walford helped her remove her cloak, then retrieved a quilt from a nearby sofa and tenderly tucked it around her.

Lily gazed into his dark soulful eyes. *What a kind man. A true gentleman. He would never lead me into seductive embraces without benefit of marriage.* No, she had never once felt even a hint of lust on his part. Which was as it should be, she hastened to remind herself. Lust should come *after* marriage.

A parlor maid entered pushing a cart laden with steaming tea and biscuits. The duke dismissed the maid and prepared her a cup himself, even adding two cubes of sugar as she preferred. He passed her the cup and she sipped it. She enjoyed the heat of the beverage, but wished she was sipping good strong American coffee instead.

"Better?" Walford asked.

She attempted a smile. "Much."

She passed the cup to him and he set it aside, then said almost too casually, "I missed you on the hunt."

Lily tensed, not wanting to discuss where she'd been, knowing she would have to lie if he pressed her. She tried instead to change the direction of the conversation. "I take it the outing was a success?"

"Yes, I bagged several dozen quail and a few pheasant."

"I thought pheasant hunting wasn't until the fall." Since it was only mid-August, quail season had barely begun.

"Are you always such a stickler for the rules?" He smiled indulgently. "We must relieve you of that attitude. It's quite unsophisticated. It's unfortunate that you elected not to participate in the hunt. Nothing else gets the blood pumping so well. Or does country life not interest a city girl like you?"

"Not really. Does that concern you?"

He shook his head. "Not at all. I prefer the city myself. When I marry, I should hope my wife would want to spend her time with me in London."

Lily bit her lip, knowing he was hinting none-too-subtly that she might fill that role. And he'd addressed one of the concerns she'd identified after talking with the baroness, just like that.

He continued to study her. "Then, how *did* you spend today, if you don't mind my asking?"

"I decided to remain behind with the other women." After all, only about half the women had planned to join the men on the hunt.

He arched a slim brow. "Indeed? My mother commented that she lacked your company this morning. You haven't been seen all day."

Caught in her lie, Lily raced to come up with a reasonable explanation. "I took a walk, the grounds here are so lovely. And—well, I became a little lost. This estate is monumentally huge."

"Not as large as Inderby." He glowed with pride over his own estate. His brow furrowed again, and Lily knew he wasn't going to let it go. "I'm so sorry you became lost. How simply dreadful. But, I'm not sure I understand. I saw you returning in a carriage, rather than on foot."

Had he been watching out for her return? What did he really know? Though she hated deceit, she had to lie or risk being discovered. "Oh, the carriage. As I said, I became lost. When I found the road, a carriage came by. Mr. Drake was in it, and he brought me back here. It's a good thing, too, since I was walking in the wrong direction."

"Drake. I see." A shadow crossed his face, and he rose to his feet, putting distance between them. Assuming a commanding pose, one foot out and his arms crossed, he studied her. Lily felt like a bug under glass. "It's a shame you were found by him, of all people. You shouldn't have been off alone, but it's even worse spending time with such a fellow."

"He behaved as a . . . a perfect gentleman," she protested, nearly choking on the words. Yet she couldn't allow the duke to think otherwise, not when she was just as much at fault for their tryst.

"Surprising, for him," he said dryly.

"Do you dislike him?" she asked.

His eyes narrowed. "I dislike his ways, most definitely. He is a good enough fellow in some respects, except when it comes to the ladies. I have noticed he has a certain . . . *affection* . . . for you, one I must say I don't find particularly seemly."

"You aren't accusing me of an indiscretion, are you?" she asked with a touch of asperity.

"Of course not, Miss Carrington. You are an innocent, and he is a wolf. A strong, dangerous wolf no woman could tame." He turned away, but she thought he mumbled, "No man, either, unfortunately."

A wolf. Yes, he certainly was. Compared to him, Walford was as tame as a trained poodle. All this time Lily had been comparing Walford to Alex and found the duke wanting. True, he lacked Alex's charisma, his presence, his sheer magnetism. He didn't make her yearn for that elusive something that promised to transform her into a fulfilled and complete woman.

But Walford had so many qualities to recommend him! He was considerate, as his treatment of her this very afternoon proved. He was courtly in the old-world style, proper and careful, as any man with such a tremendous family title should be. He would not be cruel like the baron, despite Alex's dire warnings.

Yet she knew so little of this man! Unlike Alex, whom she knew as well as she knew her own hand, even upon their short acquaintance. And the story the baroness told her . . . How could she not think of it? She had to learn all she could of this man before considering a future with him. "Lord Walford, can you answer a question?"

"Of course."

"Why are you courting me?"

He chuckled. "You, the loveliest lady in many a season, needs to ask such a question?"

"So, it's because of my beauty?"

"What man wouldn't want to court you?"

Lily began to grow frustrated. He kept answering her questions with questions of his own. She decided to be blunt, despite knowing it would sound crass. "What about my dowry? I should think that's an incentive."

His good humor dissolved. "I don't care to talk in such particulars. We both know how things work. I say, if I've earned your esteem in even the smallest measure, that's a definite step in the right direction."

"Of course you have." She studied her teacup. "Sometimes I become confused, is all."

"Understandable, for one so young." He resumed his seat on the ottoman at her feet. Leaning close, he removed her cup from her hands and cradled them in his. "Miss Carrington, you must know how highly I regard you. If you don't, it's entirely my fault for not making my feelings plain. I have been thinking more and more about what it would be like should our courtship reach its logical conclusion. And I can most definitely say if you became my wife, it would make me the happiest lord in all the land."

"It would?" Did this mean he loved her? He hadn't said so, but what other conclusion was there?

"Will you say yes?" His eyes sparkled in the firelight. "I know I need to speak to your father first, but please let me know my inquiries won't be met with disappointment."

"I can't—I'm not sure." Shifting in the chair, she asked, "Tell me . . . What expectations do you hold for your wife?"

His smile stiffened a fraction. "What do you mean?"

"That is, I've heard that Inderby is quite large. You realize I'm not accustomed to managing a large country manor, though I am adaptable and quick to learn."

"Of course you are. I sense you're worried that I would abandon you to your new life, without recourse to help of any kind. Nothing could be further from the truth. You have forgotten, my dear, about my mother. She adores you, and would be right there to help you learn what it means to be a duchess."

Lily nodded. That made sense. The duchess had welcomed her with open arms. "And after we're married . . . What would our life be like?"

"I can assure you that you will remain most popular in society, including with the prince's own

Marlborough Set. The prince *adores* you. I wouldn't think of isolating you at Inderby Hall."

Lily sighed in relief. Every concern she had, the duke dispelled. Her parents would be thrilled to no end to learn she'd captured the interest of a duke. It would be the talk of two continents, and her mother would delight in rubbing the proud Mrs. Astor's nose in their success. Beyond that, her sisters would benefit greatly from such an association.

True, she hadn't been out in society that long. But should she be out for a dozen years, she could never make a more brilliant match.

And if she lived to be a thousand, she would never feel for another man what she felt for Alex. *Alex, who saw no future with her.*

The agony in her heart made the right answer obvious. There was no longer any reason not to accept the duke's proposal. At least then her marriage would please her family . . . if not herself.

"Very well. My answer is yes."

The duke's smile grew broad. He squeezed her hand again and rose to his feet. "I'll dash off a telegram immediately asking to speak to your father. Thank you, Miss Carrington. We'll have a splendid association, I promise you that."

Spinning on his heel, he left the room. Lily stared after him, fighting down dizziness and confusion. He had never even kissed her. Was it because of his courtly manners that he waited? How was she to know?

Her head spun and her thoughts assailed her. Too much had happened in a few short hours, making it nearly impossible for her to know what to feel, what to think. Had she just made a wise decision, or one she would forever regret?

Sixteen

Sit down, Drake. I have an important matter to discuss with you."

Alex took the green leather chair across from the desk of Sir Woolsey Harrison. Though Alex directed sent his reports to the Queen's Office, Harrison oversaw his contributions from his post here in the Foreign Office

Several years ago, architects had vied for the opportunity to construct this important building. Crafted of Portland stone and colored granite, and topped by an Italianate tower, in every way it proclaimed itself the administrative power behind Britain's far-flung empire.

Alex himself hadn't worked in this building since 1882, when he'd been recruited out of Cambridge because of his fluency in exotic languages. He'd worked here only a matter of months before being sent to serve as an attaché to the ambassador of Kenya. Since then, he'd rarely spent more than a few months in London at a time.

Clasping his hands, he studied the director's solemn countenance. Harrison's long, bejowled face with its drooping mustachios appeared even longer this afternoon. Alex's heart sank. He had a hunch his request for assignment to India was about to be rejected.

"Let's not beat around the bush here, Drake. I'm

a busy man. It's come to my attention that you were involved in a rather unsavory row at the Marlborough Club a few nights back. In fact, it's reported that you struck a very high-ranking member of the peerage."

Damn. Alex wasn't at all surprised that Walford had sent this message through society's grapevine, to the director's attention. Alex hated being at the mercy of men made more powerful through circumstances of birth. Until now, he had used their standing to his advantage, befriending those in high places, even the prince himself. For the first time, he was experiencing the dark side of such associations, the retaliatory power plays of an angry and revenge-minded duke.

"The reports are true," he said coolly. "However, in my defense, I was acting to protect the weaker sex."

Harrison arched his brow. "No women are allowed in the club. I can't see why your confrontation came to blows."

"Only one blow." He smiled stiffly, but Harrison remained impassive. Alex doubted the director appreciated his attempt at humor.

"Alex, let's speak frankly. Regardless of why this happened, we both know it was ill-advised. Very ill-advised. You know I think highly of you. You have a sterling career ahead of you—that is, you did. Now I'm not so certain."

"It was only a single incident, Harry," Alex said, calling him by his nickname.

"With the wrong man," he shot back. "If you had become embroiled in an imbroglio with a—a baronet, or a count, even, the Office would hardly notice. But a duke! You've always put your career above all else. And to jeopardize your years of service over a *woman,* and—rumor has it—and American female at that! What were you possibly thinking?"

"I wasn't," Alex said grimly. He hadn't been thinking clearly since Lily entered his life.

"Well, you had better *start* thinking. I know you put in a request for a permanent post in India, but it's a coveted spot. I'm sorry, Alex. I cannot recommend you for that position. The Crown would prefer you remain its personal messenger in farther flung reaches of the Empire."

Which meant he was getting nowhere. All his work, his planning, his efforts to succeed, and he was in the same position he'd been in five years previously, when he'd discovered Sikara in trouble and risked causing an international incident—not to mention his own life—to save her.

Now he'd risked his future for yet another woman in trouble. And it had gained him nothing but frustration.

Attempting to persuade him, he leaned forward and spoke with the shared confidence of a long-time friend. "Harry, I know you don't have the final say. But you know I've served my time. I've faced danger, nearly had my head shot off, all in service to the Crown. I've earned this appointment." He tapped the desk with his finger.

Harrison sighed. "Alex, let's be honest. You've gotten farther than most men would have, given your lack of family connections. It's admirable, what you've achieved. But there are limits—"

"Limits! That's ridiculous. You know as well as I do that I'm more qualified than most of the men around here." "Please be patient. I'm certain something will turn up. But you cannot continue to engage prominent men of society in altercations and expect to make any kind of name for yourself. I'm sorry, Drake. I must be honest with you. Your chances for

India simply are not good." He shook his head. "Not anymore."

Frustrated, Alex shoved away from the desk and stood up.

With his dreams dissolving into thin air, he had the sudden urge to escape, to get as far away from London—and Lily—as he could. Before he saw her again. Before she tore his heart from his chest.

He flattened both palms on the desk and leaned in. "Damn it, send me somewhere. Anywhere. I don't care anymore. I'm tired to death of London, and I want to leave."Harrison nodded. "You seem rather disconsolate, Drake. Quite unlike your usual self. Perhaps a change of scenery would do you good. I'll look into what we have available and let you know." The director pushed to his feet.

Alex thrust out his hand and clasped Harrison's. "Thank you, Harrison. I appreciate it."

His every nerve on edge, Alex strode from the Foreign Office building to Downing Street and hailed a cab, commanding the driver to take him to the Marlborough Club as fast as the heavy midday traffic would allow.

He badly needed to relax in his favorite men's club, to enjoy the camaraderie of other men of status, to be treated like someone by the diligent staff there. He wanted to sip a whiskey and think about his future, ponder some tactic to regain his footing with the Foreign Office. Ponder something other than Lily, and how she'd thrown his plans so completely offtrack.

He'd been counting on the India assignment more than he realized. When he'd started working secretly for the Crown, he'd found his duties exciting and the exotic locales invigorating. Queen Victoria herself had recruited him to provide her with personal reports on the state of the Empire's holdings. In that capacity, he'd served in Zanzibar, Bechuanaland, Sudan, and Mesopotamia. He'd traveled to the frontiers of the Empire, and to foreign lands not yet under the Crown's sway in an effort to protect British commercial interests. His quick tongue, hardheaded reasoning, and ability to mingle with the natives gave him a special ability to root out information the staid bureaucrats couldn't.

As the years wore on, however, he'd realized he missed his visits to London more and more, longed for civilization and the high life of the city.

India would present the best of both worlds—an exotic, exciting post in the Empire, yet with a strong, ingrained British community.

He had to find a way to reclaim his dreams, his future. He had to shake himself free of this dangerous obsession with Lily Carrington.

The cab pulled up outside the club. Alex stepped out and paid the driver, then strode up the familiar stone steps to the elegant glass-and-chrome front door with its subtle handpainted label that read simply, The Marlborough Club.

A footman opened the door for him and, as usual, he stopped at the desk in the foyer. He began removing his hat and coat, but the servant standing behind the receptionist was slow to respond. He exchanged glances with Kent, the receptionist, who of course knew Alex by sight. Right now, his face looked strained, his usual cheerful greeting not forthcoming.

Alex stood before them, still clutching his own hat. "Well? What is it?"

Kent pushed to his feet. "I'm sorry, sir. I regret being the one to inform you, but you are no longer welcome here."

"What?" Alex stared at him, his stomach burning in indignation, his feet threatening to shift out from under him.

"Your membership has been revoked. I'm sorry, sir."

"Why?" Alex demanded, taking a step closer to Kent, who looked almost as unhappy as Alex felt. Kent started to respond, but Alex cut him off. "Never mind, I know why." He'd challenged one of the most powerful men in the land, and been slapped down hard. Excommunicated from his company of brothers. Thrown out on the street like a ragamuffin begging for scraps. He'd lost all standing with the men whose favor he'd cultivated for years!

After a moment, he realized Kent was speaking. "I am most sorry, sir. I believe I speak for all of the staff when I say we enjoyed serving you."

"Yes, right." Shoving his derby back on his head, Alex whirled back toward the door and stormed through it onto the street.

Barred from his favorite club! Barred from the prince's presence, too, no doubt. Barred.

You're becoming an outcast. And what do you have to show for it? Nothing! You haven't even the experience of bedding the girl, damn it!

He'd been a gentleman, tried to rescue the chit, and what had he gotten for his troubles? Blackballed, that's what!

His only consolation was that his efforts on Lily Carrington's behalf were bound to pay off. She had to know better than to marry the duke, after everything he'd risked—and lost—on her behalf. She had to.

Swearing, Alex shoved his hands in the pockets of his trench coat and marched down the Strand, not paying attention to where he was headed. He had to think of something, had to formulate a plan to save the mess he'd made of his life.

But how, and why?

Unable to think clearly, wanting only to retreat, he began to walk toward King Street, and home. At least there, he would be unassailed.

The drizzle transformed to a heavy rain, and still he plodded on, oblivious to the chill in the air. In his thirty years, his determination had never failed him. Even before he left the cramped apartment above his parents' dry-goods store at age twelve, he had worked to improve his life. He'd earned scholarships, learned to behave like a gentlemen, worked his way into the highest level of society. He'd never had a setback in his career.

Until now.

All because of his ridiculous concerns over Lily Carrington. Thank God, he would never have to see her again.

As soon as he entered his own domain, he began to feel better. Hasim, his Punjabi servant, rushed to meet him and rid him of his soaking wet coat and hat, fussing over him like a mother hen. Alex didn't mind. Right now, he appreciated being cared for

Hasim led him into the parlor, to his favorite over-stuffed chair.

Without asking, Hasim crossed to the whiskey cart and poured out two fingers into a shot glass, then delivered it to Alex. Alex sipped, grateful for the heat as it slid down his throat and warmed his stomach. He closed his eyes and leaned back.

He felt Hasim's presence, and realized his servant hadn't retreated. He cracked his eyes open. "Yes, Hasim?"

"Sir, while you relax, perhaps you would find reading the *Times* a way to pass the time." He gestured to the table beside his chair with his elegant, dark hand.

"I'm not in the mood to read, Hasim. But thank you anyway." Again he closed his eyes, expecting Hasim to take the hint and leave.

But Hasim persisted. "Sir, there is a particular item inside you might want to take note of. I know you are needing rest, sahib. Yet I believe you would want to be seeing this."

Alex cracked open his eyes and looked at the newspaper. Though the paper was folded in thirds, as usual, it had been opened to an inside page. Probably a business item about stocks in which Alex invested. "Hasim, I—"

Hasim ignored his protests. "I have opened the paper to the item in question for your convenience."

Hasim could be stubborn when he felt it was in Alex's best interest. That was why Alex found him such a good servant, and friend. He'd learned long ago the wisdom of listening to Hasim when he had advice to share, even if he chose to ignore it.

Sighing, he retrieved the paper and studied the page. Hasim had turned it to the society section, of all things.

Why in the hell—?

A lead ball formed in his gut. There, in neat black type, was an item he had prayed never to see.

Yet another young lady from America has captured the heart of one of Britain's most eligible bachelors. The heart in question belongs to Lord Richard Walford, duke of Inderby. The lady in question is Miss Lily Carrington, second daughter of Richard and Olympia Carrington of New

York. A captain of industry, Mr. Carrington will no doubt be providing a substantial dowry along with his lovely daughter's hand. Miss Carrington's engagement will cause no small amount of heartbreak to many of Britain's gentlemen, who had enjoyed escorting the vivacious, attractive lady to the most illustrious events of the London Season. An engagement party for friends of the duke and his future duchess is expected to take place at Inderby within the month . . .

The words blurred before Alex's eyes. Time stopped as he struggled to cope with the plain facts presented in the article. Lily planned to marry the man. After all his work, all his concern and worry on her behalf and the damage he'd done to his career, and she was going to marry Walford!

Alex's hands tightened so hard, the edge of the paper tore off in his fist. In a fit of anger, he threw the paper across the room. It struck the fireplace screen and tumbled to the floor.

His intervention had amounted to nothing. He might as well have ignored the chit and saved himself the trouble. His words of warning, his attempts to rescue her had amounted to spitting into the wind!

Because of Lily Carrington's stubbornness, he felt worse than powerless. He felt downright *impotent*. Impotent! How galling. He had actually lost. The duke and prince had pulled out a victory despite his efforts. Lost! He never lost. He never failed in anything he set out to accomplish. Never.

Turn your back on the stubborn chit and forget about her. Don't think of her again.

And accept that he'd been outmaneuvered? Fury

and frustration surged through him, drowning out his internal warning bells.

Engagements can be broken. She has yet to take her vows. Before he quite realized it, he'd begun concocting strategies he could employ to rescue the girl . . .

After all, he reasoned, he had traveled so far down this particular path, taking one more step could hardly cause him additional grief. Deep down, he knew he wouldn't be able to live with himself if he turned his back on her. Even after the trouble she'd caused him.

Not giving himself time to back out, he surged from his chair and strode to his teak writing desk in the corner of the room. Grabbing a sheet of correspondence paper from a neat stack, he scribbled a note, then put it in an envelope. "Hasim!" he shouted. His servant appeared almost instantly. "See that this is delivered as soon as possible."

Hasim bowed. "Yes, sahib. With pleasure." He took the envelope and left the room.

Alex stared after him ruefully. No doubt his servant knew more than he needed to about his involvement with Miss Carrington.

Seventeen

Dearest Mother,

What you have always hoped for me has come to pass. Richard Walford, duke of Inderby, intends to seek my hand in marriage. He will be writing to Father in a separate letter to invite all of you to England for a visit.

Mrs. Digby is beside herself with excitement. I admit I did not expect to become the object of a duke's fancy, but that is how things have transpired. I do hope you and Father are able to visit. Hannah and I miss you all so very much.
Your loving daughter,
Lily

"Mother and Father are taking the next ship to London," Lily announced after she gave Hannah a welcoming hug. They took seats in Mrs. Digby's parlor and Lily poured her sister a cup of tea. "Our sisters, too. They'll be here before the end of the month."

"It will be wonderful to see them all again," Hannah said. Yet her eyes seemed less than happy as she studied Lily.

Lily nodded. "Mother and Father were thrilled by my news and immediately agreed to the marriage, though of course the details will be worked out when they arrive."

"Of course." Hannah continued studying her in that clinical way that made Lily feel as if she were a science experiment.

Lily stirred her tea, seeking comfort in the habitual gesture. "Hannah, everything will be fine. I'm getting married. I've accomplished exactly what Mother and Father hoped. I'm going to be a duchess, Hannah. A duchess!"

"A duchess, yes. I only wish I knew that would make you happy."

"Why shouldn't it make me happy? I'll have privileges we could only have dreamed of as little girls. You know what that's like, marrying a peer of the realm."

"I don't love Benjamin for his title, Lily."

"And you're saying that's why I—I care for Walford?" She couldn't bring herself to say the word *love*, not about Walford.

"Do you love him?"

"I accepted his proposal, didn't I?"

"You're evading the question."

"Hannah, come now. Not everyone is blessed enough to have the kind of union you have with Benjamin. I'll be content, I believe. Besides, there will be other consolations."

Hannah set her cup down and leaned close. She grasped Lily's hand and squeezed it tight. "Darling, nothing in heaven or earth can fill that one particular place in your heart, except for love. You're such a romantic, feeling thing. You know I'm right about that."

Hannah knew her too well. Her pointed comments threatened to destroy Lily's carefully crafted barriers. As the two oldest of five sisters by a gap of three years, they'd always been closest to each other. This time, Lily couldn't bring herself to let Hannah in.

She tore her hand free and stood up. "Stop it, Hannah. You're talking nonsense." She walked to the window and pulled back the drape on the dreary, rainy London afternoon. "I've made my decision, and I no longer want to discuss it. There's no reason to discuss it."

She heard her sister sigh but knew Hannah wouldn't push her again, not today at any rate.

"Excuse me, miss. A message just arrived for you." At the entrance to the parlor, Kate, the parlor maid, curtsied, then held out a vellum envelope toward Lily.

Lily took it. As soon as her eyes landed on the scrawled handwriting on the envelope, her heart began beating double time. She knew that broad, confident scrawl as well as she knew her own handwriting. She had read his first invitation to her over and over, had pasted it carefully into her scrapbook, had wondered about the man who wrote it.

Now she knew. He was a man who refused to love her as she loved him.

Her stomach quivered with tension. A wave of dizziness struck her and she gripped the back of a nearby chair. She knew what had prompted the missive, even without reading it. He must have seen the notice in the *Times*.

Her knees threatening to give way, she slid into the chair across from Hannah.

Hannah didn't miss her odd behavior. "Lily, are you all right? Who is it from?"

Lily cleared her throat and fought to regain her composure. "That gentleman, Mr. Drake. Remember, we had dinner with he and his friend, Lord Moseby."

"I remember."

Trying to appear nonchalant, Lily popped open the

flap of the envelope and extracted the single sheet of paper.

Meet me tomorrow, two o'clock, British Museum.

Hannah continued to watch her carefully. "What does he say?"

"He's wishing me well on my engagement," Lily lied. She hated lying, to Hannah of all people. But she couldn't let even Hannah know that Alex had asked to meet her, now that she was an engaged woman.

How dare Alex ask—no, *demand*—to see her now! Did he think to change her mind about her marriage? The engagement had been announced. Her father was coming to London to meet with Walford regarding her dowry. Nothing could change her future. Not even a clandestine rendezvous with Alexander Drake.

No doubt he wanted to chastise her for accepting the duke's proposal. Still, her pulse accelerated at the idea of seeing him again, at the thought that he hadn't washed his hands of her.

With all her strength, she shoved aside her desire to accept his invitation. She refused to meet with him. In fact, she would do her utmost to avoid him. If he appeared at any social functions, she would be polite but keep her distance. She'd had enough of his high-handed interference in her life.

Nevertheless, not a single minute passed that she didn't yearn for his voice murmuring in her ear, his eyes acknowledging the secret longings in her heart, his hands stroking her as masterfully as an artist wielding his brush . . .

"Lily?"

Lily started and discovered Hannah staring at her, a speculative gleam in her large dark eyes.

"That's all," Lily said, sounding falsely bright. "Just well wishes."

"That's good of Mr. Drake," Hannah said. "He seemed rather . . . interested in your future prospects. As I recall, he was trying to arrange a match between you and his friend John Moseby."

"You saw that?"

Her intelligent eyes glinted. "Yet he seemed more interested in talking with you himself."

"Hannah, stop it."

"Lily, what happened? What's going on between you and Drake? And Moseby. What happened there?"

She shook her head. "Nothing, Hannah. Absolutely nothing."

"Yet you're so pale."

"Stop it, Hannah. I'm perfectly fine." Lily realized she was squeezing Alex's note in her fist and forced her fingers to loosen to a more normal grip. Her sister was too perceptive, by far.

Leaving the sofa, Hannah knelt before her, her dark eyes capturing Lily's. "Lily, listen to me. I know I told you to be careful of listening only to your heart, but perhaps you need to, just a little. To be true to yourself. You're not the sort who can set aside her emotions and be rational about love and marriage. Not if you're to be happy."

Lily couldn't look her sister in the eye anymore. Couldn't see the love and concern Hannah held for her and still maintain her pleasant facade. Instead she concentrated on refolding the note and tucking it back into its envelope. "Everything is fine, Hannah, as I've said." Standing, she retrieved a plate of tea biscuits and scones and held it out to her sister. "Take a cookie and stop worrying so much about me. The Devonshire cream is deliciously rich."

"The English call them biscuits," Hannah said wryly, resuming her seat. She selected a warm oval scone and slathered it with butter and thick clotted cream. "I've been so hungry lately. I don't know what's the matter with me."

"Maybe we should be worrying about *you*," Lily said pointedly. "If you keep eating like that, you'll never fit into your corsets."

"Very well, Lily," she said, her eyes sparkling. "You've won this round. But I'm warning you. I'm going to keep an eye on you. You are my little sister, after all."

Lily grasped an almond tart and bit into it thoughtfully. Hannah had better not watch her too closely. Not when she pined secretly for a man not her fiancé.

Lily kept her resolve not to meet with Alex. She ignored a second summons from him, and a third, though she treasured the messages themselves and speculated endlessly about what he may want to tell her. Did he intend to confess his love? Impossible. If he loved her, he could simply visit her and tell her so.

When she finally saw him again, his appearance took her completely by surprise.

Several weeks had passed since her engagement was announced. Her entire family had arrived in London for a visit, in time for an engagement soirée at the duke's family seat and her future home, Inderby Hall.

With crowds surging around them, the Carrington family debarked the boat train that serviced the Southampton docks. Lily rushed to join them on the station platform, then hugged and kissed them all. With her parents and three sisters encircling her, Lily realized how badly she'd missed each one of them.

"Funny, you don't look like a duchess," her youngest and sassiest sister, Meryl, said. Lily noticed that

Meryl's silky blond hair still hadn't darkened, making her the only Carrington child without their mother's Italian olive coloring.

Sixteen-year-old Pauline supplied a typically pragmatic response. "She isn't going to change overnight. She'll always be our sister."

"She looks *marvelous,*" her mother said after giving her a fierce hug. "She's more beautiful than ever."

Lily had never seen her mother so happy. "Thank you, Mother."

Her mother patted her face. "Oh, my darling Lily, you've accomplished a most amazing thing! Do you realize that? Your wedding will be the talk of two continents!"

Lily doubted she was that important, but her mother continued to speak in this vein while her father arranged for a porter to gather their bags and take them to a hired barouche on the street outside.

Mrs. Carrington kept Lily's arm firmly in her own. "You must tell us all about him. You said nothing about him in your letter, except that he's a duke, of course. Is he well favored?"

"I can't imagine he isn't handsome," Pauline said. "If you're going to bother with a husband, he might as well be easy on the eye."

"Pauline, be good," their mother chastised without turning her attention from Lily.

"He's more handsome than most," Lily finally said. *Though not as handsome as some,* she silently added.

"And his family home. I've heard it's incredibly grand."

"I haven't seen it yet."

"Well, that will be taken care of soon enough, when we all visit. Now, tell me everything about your duke. Don't leave out any details."

"Yes, Mother, I'll tell whatever you want to know."

Lily hoped she didn't sound as dispirited as she felt. Discussing Walford and her ambiguous future only made her feel sad and lonely, despite her attempts to look on the bright side, to be thankful for what she had.

As they rode to the hotel, her practical father voiced his own concerns that the man was a quality fellow. "I'll be able to size him up once I meet him," he said firmly. "He's not getting a cent of my money—or my daughter—until I approve."

"You will, father," Lily said. "He's a perfectly proper English gentleman." *Proper and distant, and still a stranger . . .*

"He's more than a gentleman," her mother said. "He's a peer of the realm! My, how glorious that sounds. I thought Hannah had made an exceptional match, marrying her earl. But I always knew you would make the most brilliant of matches, Lily. I always knew it."

Lily didn't miss the look her three sisters exchanged. Their mother made no secret of the fact she put great store by Lily because of her beauty. Ever since Lily had transformed into a woman, she'd been made aware that her appearance and figure were considered unusually attractive. She'd been told that gentlemen preferred comely women, therefore her value in the marriage market would be quite high.

With Lily marrying exceptionally well, their nouveau riche family would finally achieve unqualified acceptance among the highest ranks of society, both here and back home in New York.

Lily's engagement to the duke had confirmed her mother's instincts.

The attention over her looks embarrassed Lily to no small degree. While she adored fashion and being stylish, she knew in her heart that she had merely been lucky to be born pretty. And her sisters were perfectly lovely, too. Why did her mother insist on overlooking their assets, and constantly remarking on her own?

"Thank goodness she's marrying a duke," Pauline said dryly, tossing back her straight, light-brown hair. "Then *I* won't have to marry anybody."

"No one would want to marry you, anyway," Meryl shot back. She turned to Lily. "Pauline thinks she's going to travel the world and have a grand adventure. She's more likely to fall in a canyon or get eaten by a tiger."

"Be quiet, pest," Pauline shot back, but she was too used to Meryl's sass to be truly angry.

Meryl's eyes suddenly lit up. She leaned forward and grasped Lily's hand. "Oh, Lily, you should have seen Joe's face when I told him you were engaged. He was positively crushed." Joe Hammond was the son of their father's partner in Atlantic-Southern Railroads.

Lily smiled slightly. "Don't be silly. Why should he care?"

"And you thoroughly enjoyed his distress, didn't you, Meryl?" Pauline said. She said to Lily, "Oh, come on, Lily. You must know Joe's smitten with you. It's obvious."

Lily supposed the lad might have been—he had always treated her with deference and politeness, while he took great delight in teasing and terrorizing Meryl.

Pauline continued, "Meryl has been in a snit all summer because Joe is working at the firm, and she's not allowed."

"Well, why should *he* be allowed?" Meryl demanded. "Just because he's a *boy.*"

"He's entering his final year of prep school,

Meryl," her father explained with tired forbearance—and no doubt for the thousandth time. "Then he'll be studying business at Columbia so he can join us in the firm."

"I could do that," Meryl shot back.

Mr. Carrington sighed in exasperation. "You'll do what your mother and I tell you to."

Clara, who had been staring out the window during this latest exchange, suddenly asked their mother, "We *are* going to see the East End while we're in London, aren't we?"

Their mother looked positively horrified. The East End was the polar opposite of the posh West End, where they were now headed. Soot filled the skies from dozens of dirty factories, filth cluttered the streets, and run-down tenements abounded. "We most definitely are *not,*" Mrs. Carrington said.

"But how else can I fully understand the problems faced by the laborers, and the poor street urchins, and the beggars?" Clara said. "I hear it's positively dreadful. Something has to be done."

"Not by *you,* it won't. You will do just as Lily has, find a wonderful man to marry. Preferably one with a title. That goes double for you, Pauline. And you, Meryl," she said with unaccustomed sternness, causing the girls to quiet.

She laid her head back and sighed deeply. "See what I have to put up with, Lily? Pauline thinks she doesn't need a man, Clara wants to save the world, and Meryl—Meryl's just trouble. Thank goodness, I have you. I can't begin to describe how happy you've made me."

Happy . . . Such a simple word. Why couldn't she feel as happy as her mother and her father?

Beside her, Clara whispered, "How do you feel, Lily? You look tired." She had a perceptiveness Lily always admired, an ability to see when people were in distress.

"Nonsense, Clara, I'm fine. It's just the excitement of my engagement, I'm sure."

"Odd. You didn't seem very excited in your letter," she commented.

Lily sighed in exasperation. "I was in a hurry, is all. A hurry to share my wonderful news."

She refused to let her family see any sign of her inner turmoil. She was bound and determined to play the part of the thrilled fiancée. After all, she *should* be thrilled. She had decided she would marry Walford and nothing else mattered. She wouldn't allow anything else to matter.

Lily had seen dozens of lovely country homes during her two months enjoying the whirlwind of events known as the London Season. But nothing prepared her for Inderby.

A shock ran through her when the carriage brought them within sight of it. The mansion dwarfed most country homes. Two immense wings flanked a central core that, on its own, was grander than any manor she had ever seen.

Rows of gabled windows seemed to stretch forever down the several faces of the gray stone building. Crenellated turrets anchored every corner. The mansion was surrounded by immaculately kept grounds. Manicured hedges outlined flower gardens to the left, while on the right lay a sweeping lawn stretching for several acres. Here and there, a copse of ancient spreading beech trees provided shade.

The sight of the imposing residence caused a queer, sick feeling in Lily's stomach. In a matter of months, she would be the mistress of this centuries-old palace, which looked more like a museum than a home.

No one should own a place like this. The thought echoed in her head, growing fiercer the closer their carriage drew. *This is more house than anyone could possibly need!*

Was it her American sense of democracy at work? Or did something much less noble grip her, something more like terror?

A hand grasped hers. Lily turned to find Clara's expressive blue eyes in her pixie-like watching her closely. "You'll do fine. You always do everything very well," she whispered.

"Thank you." Lily squeezed her hand in appreciation, then released it and returned her attention to the manor looming ahead.

The meeting was a rousing success. Sighing in relief, Lily sagged against the wall outside the parlor. Within, her parents were meeting with the dowager duchess and Walford to discuss the dowry and the wedding date. It was considered inappropriate for Lily to be involved in this part of the meeting, so she'd been sent out of the room. She had the feeling the duchess thought all the women ought to remove themselves, but Mrs. Carrington refused, so the duchess remained as well.

Walford had met with her parents' approval. He'd used his suave, sophisticated charm on both her father and mother. The duchess had seemed more reserved but had at least been polite.

Bored with waiting for others to decide her fate, Lily turned and wandered down the hall. The house was so immense, she had almost reached the central gallery before noticing that several of the weekend guests had arrived for the soiree. The staff was busy unloading their carriages and showing them to their rooms. The guests would be spending the next few hours dressing for the dinner and ball that evening, the first public celebration of her engagement.

She hung back, not in the mood to greet those she had recently become familiar with. Which was entirely unlike her usually social nature.

Nothing felt right. In all her imaginings about her social Season, her engagement, she had never expected to feel so displaced, as if she were acting in a play rather than living her true life.

She looked toward the windows along the rear gallery wall, and suddenly everything seemed far too real. Highlighted by the sun pouring through the glass stood a tall, broad-shouldered, and achingly familiar silhouette.

Alex.

Eighteen

Lily remained rooted in place as Alex stepped slowly toward her. The servants' shouts and guests' conversations muted into a meaningless background drone. All she could see was this man who never left her thoughts. All she could feel was her longing to be in his arms. She felt free of time, as if the past few weeks had meant nothing, had merely been a game of pretend. Only this, being near the man she loved, was real.

Then he was before her, gazing down at her. His cobalt eyes pinned hers, instantly filling her with fierce desire. She longed for him to take her, anywhere, far away from here. To wrap her so tightly in his arms, she lost herself completely.

No. This couldn't happen. Not again.

This was the last place she'd ever thought to run into him, here at her own engagement party. She knew of the animosity between the duke and Alex. He'd come at the worst possible time.

Anxiety filled her, snapping her back to reality. "What are you doing here?"

"You know the answer to that." His voice rumbled through her, setting her senses on fire. "This may be my only chance."

His only chance . . . To what? Profess his love for her? Steal her away from her fate as Walford's wife?

Make her his forever? Or merely seduce her and destroy her future?

"Come." After glancing around to make sure no one saw them, he grasped her elbow and tugged.

Lily snatched her arm free. "Are you mad? My family is just down the hall, with the duke and duchess!"

"If you stop wasting time stating the obvious, they won't see us together." This time he succeeded in steering her into a nearby parlor empty of guests.

Once inside, she spun on him, determined to hold fast to her anger and resist his potent charms. "I'm beginning to believe the danger is all that attracts you."

He did not respond to her jibe. Instead, his expression remained serious, with a trace of uncharacteristic despondency darkening his eyes. Despite her resolve Lily's heart hitched, as if recognizing his pain as the twin of her own—a soul-rending yearning never to be fulfilled. Hope sprang to life in her chest.

Yet when he spoke, she heard only stiff determination. "These intrigues we engage in are merely a means to an end. I can think of no other way to talk freely to you without arousing undue suspicion over my interest in you."

"And you have no other interest."

"Of course not."

His stark words shattered her last hope, replacing it with a leaden, lifeless feeling. She had completely misread him. He had no intention of changing his opinion from that day in the carriage. Like a fool, she'd tried to ignore the obvious, ignore what he said. Tried to hope. Now, she had to accept the truth. All he cared about was dictating her future, not making her part of his.

"Did nothing I say to you carry any weight?" he asked, as if chastising a child.

Not again. Lily didn't know if she had the strength to spar with him anymore. She had accepted her fate—why couldn't he? She swallowed and faced him squarely. "I don't know why your words should be given any weight."

The corner of his mouth twitched. "I have always been truthful to you. It's clear a title means so much to you that you chose to ignore every warning I gave."

His words struck her like a slap in the face. Is this what he thought of her? That she cared only for status? Fury coursed through her. "That isn't fair. Walford is a kind man. He's never been cruel to me, not like *some* men."

His jaw tightened. "You hardly know the man. If you knew what I know—"

"So you say! But you never tell me anything specific, do you? That's because there's nothing specific to tell."

The light from the window made his blue eyes shine like ice. "You don't want or need the specifics, Lily. They would sicken you."

His words frightened her more than she would admit. What could be so horrendous that he couldn't speak of it? Yet he gave no explanation, merely caused her undue worry over what should be a happy occasion. If only he hadn't come. Frustrated and upset, she turned toward the door. "I'm tired of this. Tired of you and your strange games. Leave me alone, and leave Walford alone. Leave us both alone!"

"Damn it, Lily—" he began.

"What's going on here?" Walford froze at the entrance to the parlor, his eyes darting from Lily to Alex and back again. "Lily, darling, is this cad bothering you? What in the bloody blazes are you doing here, Drake?"

"Celebrating your engagement, what else?" Alex said dryly.

Seeing Alex so close to Walford forced Lily to compare the two men. Alex always stimulated her. Even if he were silent, she could gaze at him for an eternity and not grow bored. Walford, on the other hand, could sometimes be insufferably arrogant and irritating.

Walford clasped his arms casually behind his back and leaned in close to Alex, giving him a look that would have made a lesser man quail. "Odd. I don't recall sending you an invitation."

Alex took his attack in stride. "I don't recall you ever stooping to deal with correspondence yourself. Your mother issued the invitations, as you well know, and she practically demanded I be here. I would never seek to hurt such a kind woman."

"I don't want you here. Nor does Miss Carrington. Do you, Lily?" Walford looked at her, but she couldn't bring herself to respond.

Alex continued, "If you're thinking of showing me the door, you'll have to explain to your mother why we've had a falling out. Is that your plan? I imagine the truth would shock her utterly."

Walford's fair skin grew a shade paler. "Why, you unconscionable ingrate. How dare you—"

"Might as well make the best of it, then, eh?" Grinning, Alex clapped Walford on the shoulder as if they were the best of friends, then strode out of the room as though he owned the place.

"The nerve!" Walford exclaimed. "Poor breeding certainly shows."

Despite her anger at Alex, Lily was secretly thrilled

by Alex's commanding demeanor. If only she'd understood what they were talking about!

As soon as he was gone, Walford gripped her arm with surprising force, yanking her attention off Alex. "What was he saying to you?"

Lily extricated her arm from his grasp. "You needn't manhandle me," she said tersely. "He said nothing of import."

He glared down at her, his eyes hot with rage. "You expect me to believe that? It's quite apparent to me that he wants you, and badly. But he'll never have you." When she didn't argue, his anger seemed to dissipate. "You're intended for a better man than he. Drake is nothing in comparison."

Perhaps it was expected of her, but Lily couldn't bring herself to agree that her fiancé was a better man than Alex. "Why *did* you have a falling out?"

Walford studied her. "An account of his behavior isn't fit for lady's ears. Suffice it to say his actions resulted in his banishment from the Marlborough Club. Now, I'll speak no more of this—or of him."

Damn men. *All* men, for keeping women in the dark! Instead of pressing for answers she knew she'd never receive, she asked, "Is everything settled between your mother and my family?"

"Yes. Things could not have gone better." He smiled broadly. "Much better than I ever dreamed. I had no idea . . ."

"No idea of what?"

"Your family is incredibly wealthy."

So, he was pleased with her dowry. Good for him. Lily couldn't bring herself to share his enthusiasm.

"Well, now, darling. I promised to give you a tour of your new home, didn't I? This is as good a time as any, I should think. Unless you're tired from the journey?" Once again, he'd become the solicitous, attentive suitor.

Lily tried to feel enthusiastic about seeing this place that felt so alien to her, so unlike the homes she was used to. "Shouldn't you be greeting your guests?"

"That is my mother's duty." Walford tucked her arm in his and led her from the room.

"Along with the correspondence," Lily commented under her breath.

For the next two hours, Lily witnessed Walford's great pride in his noble heritage. And it was impressive, nothing like her own family history. Her mother was the daughter of Italian immigrants; her father the son of a sea captain.

In contrast, Walford's ancestors had the ears of kings, had led troops in battle. Lily began to feel insignificant listening to him recount the role his family had played in Britain's history through the centuries.

She may have feigned her enthusiasm for this marriage, but she was genuinely impressed by the grandeur and history of Inderby. "Just how big is Inderby Hall?"

"To be honest, I'm not certain. There are more than three hundred rooms. And I believe you could fit the entire town of Hillshire inside it."

Lily raised her eyebrows. Hillshire was the closest village, where the land's former tenants had marketed.

"And there is much you won't see, even if you walk these halls for hours."

"What do you mean?"

"My great-great-grandfather equipped Inderby with a network of secret passageways. He was a paranoid fellow, concerned that people were plotting against him."

"You aren't like that," she replied, realizing again how little she knew of this man.

He shook his head. "Not unless I have reason to believe someone is plotting against me. You would never plot against me, would you, Lily darling?" He gave her an assessing gaze that hinted of his wrath should she ever defy him. It sent a chill down her spine.

"Don't be ridiculous," she admonished. "I'm only a nineteen-year-old girl, and a foreigner at that. I wouldn't know the first thing about aristocratic intrigues."

"I believe you are far craftier than you let on. But no matter. As long as you are a proper wife in the world's eyes, I shan't care a whit about what you do privately. As long as you never embarrass me."

What an odd statement! Why wouldn't he care what she did? If he loved her, if she was to be his wife . . . He almost sounded as if he were condoning her being unfaithful. That must mean *he* intended to break their marriage vows.

Lily realized she was more disturbed by the idea of marrying a man who intended to be unfaithful than the thought she might share him with another woman. How could that be? How could his lack of character bother her more than the idea of sharing her own husband? What was wrong with her?

She had always been a romantic at heart. She would never have imagined being happy without her husband's love. Then again, why should she chastise herself? She had agreed to this marriage as a business transaction, rather than a love match. Her heart didn't signify.

He stopped before a tapestry from the previous century showing his grandfather and grandmother astride their horses, their grooms in attendance. "The

Walfords have always been excellent horsemen. And horsewomen. We manage the finest stables in at least three counties, breed some of the finest horseflesh around."

"Yes, I recall your horse running at the Royal Ascot."

"I had two horses entered in the Ascot this year."

"I'm sorry, I didn't realize."

"No. You seemed more interested in the presence of Moseby and Drake in our box," he said with asperity.

Before she could react, his tone changed again, to one of curiosity. Trying to grasp his true feelings seemed an impossible task. "I never thought to ask. You do ride, don't you? All the duchesses of Inderby were accomplished horsewomen, as well as social leaders among the racing set."

Lily recalled the dowager duchess flitting about the Royal Ascot, entirely within her element. An element as foreign to Lily as this place surrounding her. "I can ride a little," she said to reassure him, and perhaps herself.

"Only a little?" He seemed almost irritated.

She gave him a smile. "Growing up in New York provides few opportunities for riding horses."

"Of course, of course," he mused. "We'll have to rectify that."

"We did have friends who managed stables, and we visited their country homes in the summer," she rushed to add, not wanting to sound hopelessly bourgeois.

"Very well. We shall put a small party together and ride on the morrow, after the prince has arrived. He will certainly enjoy riding with you, regardless of your level of . . . experience."

He smiled then, as if at a private joke, and Lily

had the sense she'd missed something important. Still, he seemed pleased well enough, and Lily took comfort in the thought that he wanted to help her fit into her new role as the Duchess of Inderby. Perhaps she, too, would eventually join the ranks of accomplished horsewomen in the Walford family tree.

After a time, she decided, she would find some passion to fill her heart. Some reason to be content.

Alex stroked the neck of the horse a Inderby groom had brought him for this morning's ride. Despite his dislike of the duke, he couldn't deny the family raised excellent horseflesh. Though he'd spent months on horses while serving in Arabia, he'd used sturdy, serviceable mounts, not these fine thoroughbreds with their smooth lines and muscular flanks.

Nearby, two dozen gentlemen and ladies outside Inderby's stables waited as grooms prepared their horses.

"Why, Drake. It's been several weeks since I've seen you. I had begun to think you'd gone back overseas."

Alex turned from adjusting his horse's bridle to face the prince. Bertie seemed surprisingly friendly to him this morning, considering he'd just been blackballed from the prince's private club. "I'm hoping for an assignment very shortly."

"You've grown tired of our company so soon? I no longer see you at the club."

Alex studied him, his mind racing to respond. Apparently, the prince knew nothing about Alex's falling out with the duke. Perhaps he could salvage his future after all.

And, he now understood why Walford hadn't tossed Alex out of his home—a very real possibility. Walford thought he could sweep their conflict under the carpet, that his threatening tactics alone would send Alex a strong enough message to dissuade him from interfering further.

"Walford exerted his influence with the management and had my membership revoked," Alex explained. After all, Bertie was bound to hear some version of the story eventually.

"Did he? Why?"

"A difference of opinion on how he conducts his affairs," he said dryly.

Bertie's eyes darted past Alex, and his eyes widened. Alex felt he'd lost his attention. Turning, Alex saw a feminine vision in red strolling along across the terrace to join the other guests.

"Walford seems to think you fancy his fiancée," Bertie murmured, then gave Alex a sharp look. "But I know you're far too intelligent to embroil yourself in affairs that don't concern you."

His warning given, he smiled and slapped Alex on the back. "Don't worry, Drake. Play your cards right, as you always do, and eventually you may return to the club." He left to intercept Lily as she stepped off the terrace.

Ignoring the prince's warning, Alex again looked toward Lily. Though she stood on the far side of the gathering, his gaze clung to her like a lifeline in a storm. In the past months, she had become such an important part of his reason for doing, for being. Why didn't that frighten him more, make him want to wash his hands of her and run, as the prince none-too-obliquely suggested? Yet he could not get enough of gazing at her, of thinking about her, of worrying about her.

Trying to remain as circumspect as possible, he watched the prince approach Lily and engage her in conversation. While Bertie kept a proper distance, and no doubt discussed nothing untoward with her, Alex imagined the lascivious thoughts going through the man's head.

Who was he to judge the prince's thoughts? He, too, appreciated Lily's delectable appearance on this misty morning. He had no idea what kind of horsewoman she was, but she certainly knew how to dress the part. Her carmine-colored riding habit hugged her generous curves. A white lace ascot tucked within the unbuttoned top made him imagine unbuttoning the rest of the short jacket. The skirt's narrow line accentuated her round hips. A top hat with matching carmine trim sat at a jaunty angle on her upswept ebony hair.

The prince finally left her to converse with other guests. He mounted his steed, a signal to the other riders to prepare to ride out. Alex followed suit, but remained at the rear of the crowd, his eyes on Lily twenty yards ahead. A groom helped her mount her white mare.

As soon as Lily had taken her seat, Alex knew she was an inexperienced rider.

She gripped the reins far too tightly, fighting to juggle the thin leather straps and her riding crop without losing her seat. The other riders passed her as she fought to gain control. Her horse danced several feet forward, then turned around, bringing Alex within her line of sight.

As she gazed at him, her gloved hands tightened even further on her reins. Her chin high, she jerked her gaze away.

Rather than pretend he didn't know her, he lightly tapped his mount's flanks with his heels and drew up beside her. "Are you able to handle her?"

"Of course. My fiancé wouldn't give me an unruly horse to ride."

Her fiancé. Was it his imagination, or was she goading him with that hideous phrase?

"Naturally, since he only wants the best for you."

His droll tone caused her to adopt a haughty demeanor, her dark eyes sparking hotly. She looked every inch the duchess she would soon become. "Can you not have the grace to leave me alone, even for one day?"

She kicked her horse, trying to direct it away from him, but he reached out and gasped the reins, dragging the horse—and her—within two feet of him. "Lily, be careful."

"Release me." Her dark eyes struck his like a hammer, and his heart flipped over. Release her? How could he ever bring himself to do that? Yet hadn't he already released her? He'd pushed her away, told her they had no future. Given her up to Walford. For that is how she must see it.

Alex kicked his horse to a gallop and swept past Lily, fury and confusion tearing through his chest. What else was he supposed to do, agree to marry her? Damn!

The pack of riders began to enter a path that wound through the woods, breaking into a ragged line grouped in twos and threes. Alex, now at the front, steered his horse off the path and under the trees.

He watched the duke's guests ride by. The prince nodded at him. The luscious Lady Hammett gave him an encouraging, flirtatious smile as she rode past. One of his former lovers, she was attending the weekend without her husband, no doubt hoping to make an alliance for the evening. Then the duke rode past, beside Lily. Both of them ignored him, though he was certain they had seen him. After they rode by, he rejoined the tail of the group, the better to keep his eye on Lily.

Not fifteen minutes passed before the duke grew restless with Lily's pace. She wasn't allowing her mount to exceed a slow trot, and still appeared nervous about falling off, especially as the riders began traversing uneven terrain within the heart of the forest.

The duke left her behind, instead riding beside a slender young man that Alex speculated enjoyed the same perverse pleasures as Walford himself.

As Alex expected, Lily was falling farther behind. She was now at the end of the string of riders—except for himself. Still, he could hardly talk openly with her here on the trail.

Her horse slowed to a walk, then stopped altogether to chew on tall grass by the side of the path. Alex laughed to himself at the sight of the perfectly turned out horsewoman who was nothing but. She tugged on the reins and urged her mare to do her bidding, but the beast remained intractable.

This was the opportunity he'd needed, a final chance to talk sense into her—if his plan didn't kill her.

Approaching her horse from behind, he stretched out his riding crop. "Lily, hang on tight."

"What?" Gripping the reins, she glanced around just as he slapped her horse's rump. Startled, the horse shot forward, off the trail and toward an open field.

"Damn you, Alexander Drake!" she screamed, bent forward over her horse's neck, fighting to keep her balance.

Alex's horse caught up with hers in a matter of seconds. He grasped her mare's reins and dragged the nervous beast beside his own. Controlling both horses, he brought them to a stop beside a crumbling millhouse along a creek.

Lily glared at him, fighting to catch her breath, her heart hammering in her chest. She fought down her admiration at his mastery with the horses, at the way he directed his mount with nothing more than a flexing of his thighs and a flick of his wrists. He looked as if he'd been born to ride. His lithe frame in its well-tailored suit gave him a polished and aristocratic air that shamed the ancestors portrayed in the portrait gallery at Inderby.

Her heart yearned for him still. Frustrated by her obsessive weakness for him, she fiercely reminded herself of the grim truth. This man didn't want her. "How dare you! I could have broken my neck!"

"I told you to hold on," he said with infuriating mildness.

She erupted in a fury. "What do you think you're doing, driving me away from the others? What game are you playing this time?"

His smile faded. Swinging his long leg over his horse's back, he dismounted and approached her. Lily wished she could ride with better skill; she would dash off and leave him standing there looking foolish. But she couldn't deny a sharp thrill at the intensity of his gaze as he drew near.

Reaching over, he pried her fingers from the reins, then grasped her by the waist and pulled her off her horse. She fell hard against him.

He caught her up against his chest, his tight hold igniting a inferno of longing inside of her. She had to get away from him. She attempted to wriggle from his hold. She slapped at his hips with her riding crop, but it had no effect on him. "Let go of me."

He released her waist, but grasped her shoulders and pushed her backward a step, against the crumbling facade of the abandoned mill. The moss-laden stones felt cool against her back, a sharp contrast to the fiery presence of the man before her. "You're going to listen to me, damn it!"

"I have no intention of hearing another word out of your mouth."

"I'm going to make you listen, and understand. I had hoped to avoid telling you this, but now I see I have no choice, as distasteful as it is to discuss such a thing with a lady."

She turned her head and looked past him, trying hard to communicate a disinterest she didn't feel. "Whatever it is, I don't want to hear it."

"Of course you do. You're a very curious woman, Lily. You love to hear about people. You love to explore the world, including your own sensuality, as you did with me."

At his outrageous words, she couldn't resist facing him. "That was a *mistake,*" she bit out. "You called it that yourself. One I shall *never* make again."

Did he wince? Lily wasn't sure, he remained so calm. "Very well. That's not the purpose of this discussion anyway. Just hear me out, and I'll be gone from your life for good."

For good? She would never see him again? Lily again looked away, toward the distant hills. As irritating as she found his strange need to interfere in her life, she couldn't imagine never encountering him again. But she would have to face it. That day had arrived.

His tone considerably softer, he gently urged, "Please, Lily. Look at me." He lifted her chin with his finger, compelling her to meet his gaze.

Lily struggled against the heady pleasure of standing so close to him, resisted the urge to fall into his arms and beg him to take her far away from here. Beg him to ravish her. She sighed, feigning disinterest. "Very well. Say your piece; then let's be done with this."

For the longest moment, he said nothing, merely gazed at her as if looking on a treasure he could never possess. His rapt expression bore a trace of melancholy that made her heart ache.

He exhaled deeply, as if every ounce of air were being pulled from his lungs. "It's all so dastardly."

"What is?"

His eyes narrowed. "Their plans for you."

A chill wove up her spine, but she fought it back. "What is this, another story for me? Another plot?"

"So, you *do* remember what I told you before, about the duke and the prince."

He'd thrown out that ridiculous charge the night she visited him in his garden. Told her the duke was marrying her so that the prince could make her his mistress. Such a plot sounded no less outlandish now. "How could I forget such a fatuous lie?"

His lips tightened. "You may scoff now, darling, but they're succeeding. You're now engaged to the duke. Just as they planned."

"Nonsense. You already knew he was courting me. As for the prince being obsessed with me—I've only seen him a half-dozen times, and he has always been respectful."

"And friendly, no doubt."

She hated his suggestive tone. "No more so than with any other debutante," she shot back, though she knew it wasn't quite true. The prince always gave her a special smile, and spent more time conversing with her than with many others seeking his attention.

"Yes, *more so,* and you know it. The prince is a master of proper decorum. But I was there, Lily. There with the both of them. There when his guard was down and he was speaking bluntly, as men will do only with their fellows. The gentlemen in his inner social circle share an understanding, that nothing spoken there will ever be revealed. It's a trust I've now violated, to my detriment."

"You mean being expelled from the Marlborough Club?"

His brows shot up. "Who told you?"

"Don't look so shocked," she said, trying to sound cavalier. "My beloved fiancé shares a lot of things with me. Why should that surprise you? Soon we'll be sharing our lives together."

At her words, his gaze turned thunderous. Lily reveled in finally taking the upper hand. Pushing her advantage, she continued, "The fact my fiancé confides in me is hardly strange. What *is* strange is *you*. You endanger your own prospects on my behalf. Yet you insist I mean nothing to you."

"I merely miscalculated," he said, his lips lifted in an angry smile. Yet a muscle twitched at the corner of his mouth. "Harming my prospects was hardly my goal. Nor am I the topic of this meeting. Once we've finished our business here, I assure you, I will be through with you."

"Nothing would make me happier," she said defiantly. Yet his cold words reopened the wound he'd inflicted that day in the carriage, when he'd first rejected her. She wanted to slap him; she wanted to beg him to take back his words, to hold her, to stroke the pain away. She truly had become a pitiful creature.

Disgusted at herself, she fought back by attacking his own weakness—his pride. "Why must you defame Walford? Is it jealousy over his title, his pedigree? You may deny it, but I know you resent the nobility."

He stiffened, his eyes growing hard. "Flinging insults at me won't change the facts. Your intended husband is a fraud. That is why I summoned you here.

I would do the same for any woman blindly waltzing into such an alliance."

"A fraud," Lily scoffed at such a strong word.

He gripped her arm and shook her lightly. "Damn it, Lily, don't be a fool. You're a sensual creature, as I well know. You must see the truth, you must feel the absence of passion from the man!"

Frustrated, she tightened both fists on her riding crop, and tried to use it to shove him away. He didn't move even an inch to release her. "You keep speaking of truth, but you never say anything! *What* truth? Speak your piece and be done with it!"

"Why do you think Walford has waited so long to marry, despite pressure from his mother, and despite the attentions of hundreds of eligible, wealthy women over the years?" He spoke rapidly, as if determined to make her hear him. "He's finally taking a wife. You. But not for himself. He's doing it for Bertie, and only for Bertie—"

"Marrying *me* for the *prince?* That makes no sense!"

"It makes perfect sense. Walford will gladly hand you over to the prince, with his full blessing."

"Utter nonsense. No man would—"

"The prince wants so badly to bed you, he's concocted a scheme to enable him to have you. He can't be discovered despoiling an innocent female. But once you're wed, Walford will prove to you the sort of man he truly is. And the prince intends to be there to soothe you—and seduce you."

Aghast at such a horrible image, she could hardly force out the words. "But—Walford. *Why . . . ?"*

"Walford *can't* love you, or any woman, as she deserves to be loved. He is a homosexual."

Nineteen

Homosexual. The word sounded strange to Lily. It must deal with sex, that most forbidden of subjects. She had no idea what it meant. "I don't understand—"

"He mates with other men," Alex said, his tone flat, his lips tight. "It's a perverse form of love, never discussed in polite company, and never to a lady. Yet it's more common than you would ever believe."

Lily's mind raced as she tried to grasp the bizarre concept. Men being in love with men? Why? How was it possible? She recalled what the baroness had told her about men, and how, during intimacy, they placed their hardened member inside a woman, thus reaching fulfillment and possibly beginning a new life. "How . . ." No. There was no way. She shook her head vigorously. "No. It's not possible."

"You would be surprised what's possible." His tone was so hard, so unforgiving, it scared her more than any of the shocking words he'd uttered.

Her stomach tightened and she began to feel ill. A wave of dizziness swept through her and she grasped his arms for support, allowed him to hold her waist. "I don't believe you. It's too bizarre. Where is your proof?"

At her charge, Alex remained silent for far too long.

Lily leaped on his reticence like a lifeline. She shoved his arms away. "I knew it. You have no proof, merely horrid rumors." To her surprise, she felt protective of Walford. He wasn't there to defend himself against Alex's nasty accusations. Such scandalous rumors could ruin him and *her* as his future wife!

Alex turned away and exhaled deeply. "I don't know what proof to offer you. I have seen him embracing men, is that enough for you? I have heard him discussing his amorous adventures. Is that enough proof for you? And there's more, much more." He looked at her over his shoulder and crossed his arms. "I had hoped telling you would be sufficient, but you're so damned hardheaded, apparently I was mistaken."

"I don't believe it. You're lying. I don't believe anything you say. I don't," she repeated like a litany, willing it to be so. "Why should I believe you?"

She should not have asked. He took a step toward her, forcing her to press harder against the ancient mill wall. She clutched her riding crop, desperate for support. Sliding her other hand behind her, she grasped the wall, felt the crumbling stones rough against her palm.

A furrow gathered between his eyes. The shadows striking his face made him appear almost ferocious. "Your fiancé is an opium addict," he bit out. *"That* I have seen with my own eyes. I have witnessed him puffing on his hookah pipe, his mind growing soft and numb, his wits deserting him. When he is under the power of that demon drug, he shares *stories,* Lily. Stories of his visits to secret brothels filled with young boys, starving children who give men like Walford the use of their bodies in exchange for a hot meal and a place to sleep. He laughs about it, Lily.

He calls them his *pets*, but he treats them worse than a master would a dog."

Lily felt faint, her stomach so ill she thought she might lose her breakfast. "That's horrible," she said, her voice barely a whisper. "Perhaps that happens in one of those countries you've lived in, but not here. This is a civilized nation!"

"Lies, Lily. Pretty lies told to ladies to keep them happy and content in their place. Well-bred ladies are considered too delicate to know the truth of the world."

"No. No"—she shook her head—"I refuse to believe it. Any of it. It's too outlandish to be true."

"Not only boys fall victim to Walford's perversity. Ask him about a young gentleman named David. He used David mercilessly, until he grew bored. The poor sot is still in love with him, even though Walford would tie him up and force himself on him. That's how some men get their pleasure, by being whipped like horses. God knows why."

Lily felt as if a veil had been lifted, revealing a decadent world she had been shielded from her entire life. She longed to go back, never again think of the obscene images now filling her mind. Yet, as Walford's wife, she would be forced to live within the shadow of such shame and degradation.

"Stop it. You have to stop. I can't bear another word." The pressure of the revelation snapped her temper. Lily swung her riding crop toward his face, desperate to make him stop talking. He caught her forearm, braking the crop just before it struck him.

Through sheer force of will, he pressed her back and drew himself closer. Her head arched back and he brought his face within inches of hers. She was suddenly and completely in his power.

Her arm remained suspended in space, held by his.

After several heartbeats, his expression began to change, his lips relaxing, his deep eyes filling with compassion. With his free hand, he touched her face, tracing her features in a tender caress. When he spoke, his words came haltingly. "I'm so sorry, Lily. I'm so sorry. I never wanted to share what I knew, never wanted you to hear such words, especially not from me. Please forgive me."

Forgive him? Forgive him for hurting her and confusing her? She opened her mouth to protest, but no words came out.

In tandem, their arms lowered, and the riding crop slipped from her frozen fingers. He ran his hand down her arm and clasped her fingers, intertwining them with his own. Lifting her hand between them, he kissed her knuckles and her wrist, then pressed her palm against his chest.

His tender, devoted attention brought tears to her eyes. Her heart thundered in her chest, and a potent longing for his touch swept through her.

"Those men would use you, Lily. Treat you like a sport, designed for their entertainment. By God, Lily, I cannot allow that. You deserve so much more. You deserve to be pampered and coddled. You deserve to be worshiped for everything wonderful that you are."

My protector . . . The power of his magnetism overwhelmed her, making it nearly impossible for her to draw breath. She longed for him so badly, her very being ached. He lowered his face, his nose brushing teasingly against hers. *The prelude to a kiss.* How many hours had she spent dreaming of his embrace, dreaming of being cared for and protected and loved by this man?

Just before his lips touched hers, she recalled how drunk his passion made her—and how utterly foolish. In a flash, the pain of his rejection flared up, hot and humiliating. She'd proposed to him, and he'd refused her. Worse, he'd filled her head with black stories about a man who *did* want her, tarnishing her hopes and dreams. How dare he toy with her like this!

"I've had quite enough of this." She shoved hard at his chest, throwing him off balance enough to slip away from him. She ran to her horse, then passed it by and headed for his. Hiking up her long skirt and petticoats, she tucked her foot in the stirrup and threw her leg over the horse's back.

Alex watched in amazement as she kicked his horse and rode toward the path back to Inderby Hall at a fast trot, her posture sure and confident. She was a much better horsewoman riding astride.

He crossed to her own horse with every intention of mounting and following her. He placed his hand on the pommel—and realized she'd left him a horse equipped with the awkward—and decidedly feminine—sidesaddle.

"Damn!" He turned and stared after her, amused despite his predicament. Despite how he'd shocked her, she refused to allow him to get the best of her.

Ladies were never to know of the things he'd revealed, even those long married. Their cultured, protected minds were considered incapable of conceiving of such perversity. Yet he'd been forced to describe such wretched baseness to sweet Lily.

If only she understood that he had her interests at heart. Instead, he'd managed to push her farther away. No doubt she would think less of him for speaking of such things, let alone conceiving of them.

And time was growing dangerously short.

"Blast!" Lily muttered to herself as she slowed her horse to a walk. She wasn't anxious to go back to

Inderby Hall and face her family's questions about why she'd returned from the outing so early.

She would have to come up with an excuse.

How could she think of an explanation, when she could not get her mind off of Alex's frightening words? *Mates with other men . . . an opium addict . . . visits secret brothels filled with young boys . . .*

It couldn't be true. It was far too awful. But, then, why would Alex shock her in such a way if it wasn't true? Did he hate the duke so much that he would spread false rumors about him? True, the duke had never shown her the type of physical affection that a lover might. That Alex had. But Walford was a well-bred gentleman—he knew the appropriate limits with an unmarried lady. Then again, he had never spoken words filled with passion, or even asked for a simple kiss.

And the prince . . . While never out of line, he was definitely attentive toward her. Did he really long to bed her? She cringed, imagining the old prince embracing her against his corpulent body, kissing her with his tobacco breath.

If she went forward with this marriage, what would become of her? Would she truly be forced into adultery?

Then again, Alex could be lying, or be misled, or . . .

As she came within sight of Inderby Hall, the terror of her predicament struck her full force. A wave of nausea swept over her and she clutched the pommel to keep her balance.

The path she rode took her back toward the stables situated to the right of the mansion. Hannah had arrived at Inderby from London, and was now playing badminton with their three youngest sisters on the sweeping lawn at the back of the house. Hannah was so intelligent. Had she heard anything about the awful things Alex had told her? Did she know about men preferring men to women, or even young boys? But imagining talking to Hannah—or anyone—about it made Lily feel physically sick.

On the broad flagstone terrace that stretched the length of the house, her mother and the duchess reclined in lounge chairs, sipping lemonade and watching her sisters play on the lawn below. The riding path split a few yards up, the branch on the left leading to the stables. If she could ride all the way to the stables, Lily realized, she could enter the manor via the front, and no one would notice she'd returned.

She wasn't that lucky. As soon as she reached the fork in the path, her mother sat up and waved. One of several grooms waiting to attend returning riders rushed over and relieved her of her horse, taking away her excuse to avoid the women.

"Lily!" her mother called, then waved her over. Lily plastered a smile on her face and forced her leaden feet to walk up the steps onto the terrace.

She crossed the flagstones to where they were sitting, trying to appear serene and undisturbed despite the confusion knotting her stomach.

"Hello Mother, Duchess," She nodded to each woman.

"You're back so soon!" her mother said.

"I grew a little fatigued. I'm not used to riding sidesaddle, and there's been so much excitement this weekend. And the dinner and ball are tonight. I thought it would be best if I retired for a few hours."

"It's a little early for your afternoon nap. Are you feeling well?"

"Very well, thank you."

"If you say so, Lily." She grasped her daughter's

hand and looked at the duchess. "Lily is such a social butterfly. I have never known her not to have the energy for parties and entertainments, but then, she's never been a future duchess before, either. I imagine it can be something of a strain."

"I suppose so, if one is not reared to take on such a role," the duchess said. "As she clearly was not. I have never seen a properly bred lady riding astride as she was."

Lily arched her eyebrow, annoyed at being talked about as if she wasn't there, and annoyed with the duchess's slight toward herself and her mother. As if she'd been *improperly* bred!

Her mother did an admirable job of containing her irritation. "That is how Lily learned to ride, but she'll learn sidesaddle, and anything else necessary to fulfill her role as duchess." Still holding Lily's hand, she gave it a pat. "She's always been a model daughter, obedient and responsible. She has never disappointed me. She understands her position."

"Well, if I wasn't certain of that, I would not have approved the marriage to my son," the duchess said.

"Of course, of course," Mrs. Carrington said. "You needn't worry where Lily is concerned. Now, my other daughters—they've often been a trial to me. Hannah, for instance, always had her nose in her books. She didn't care a whit about fashion or feminine pursuits. Thank goodness, her husband, the earl, dabbles in science. And Pauline—she insists she has no need at all for a husband—can you imagine such a thing! She fancies herself quite the adventuress. She prefers sports to men."

"Appalling." The duchess shook her head in dismay. "I hope your children realize that their actions will reflect on our family."

"Of course, of course. Pauline is still young. She'll

grow out of her silly notions. Now, Lily never had silly notions. She always knew her role was to marry well."

Finally, her mother released Lily's hand. Lily immediately excused herself and hurried toward the French doors leading inside. Behind her, her mother continued, "It's so difficult to raise children today, especially daughters. So many women are working for a living, traipsing onto men's territory, trying all sorts of things they oughtn't . . ."

The looming possibility of a twisted, dishonest future haunted Lily. She couldn't bring herself to fully accept what Alex had said. But she couldn't dismiss it, either.

What should she do, what should she say, and to whom? If she told her family she wanted to break her engagement, they would be crushed. She couldn't do such a thing to them without explaining the reasons. But if she told them why, and Alex's charges turned out to be false, she would ruin not only her family's dreams, she'd tarnish both the duke's and Alex's reputations.

She could confront the duke himself, but whether true or not, he would take out his wrath on Alex, she knew that for a fact. As angry as Alex made her, she couldn't stand the thought of seeing him hurt, especially since he'd gone out of his way to protect her. Or was that his true motive?

She had to try. She would speak to someone who had always looked out for her best interests. Her mother.

After gathering her resolve, she found Mrs. Carrington relaxing on a divan in the second floor's blue parlor, having tea. To Lily's relief, her mother was alone.

Lily closed the parlor door. "Mother, I need to talk to you."

"Lily! I thought you were lying down. Come. Have some tea." She gestured her over. When Lily was seated, her mother held a platter of biscuits out to her. "These are so light and delicious. You must try one."

Lily shook her head. "No, thank you, I'm not hungry."

"It's only a cookie. Are you feeling well?"

"In truth? No."

Her mother set the platter aside and gave her daughter her full attention.

Lily sucked in a fortifying breath. "Mother. My upcoming wedding. I'm simply not sure . . ."

Her mother smiled and nodded, as if already knowing what she intended to say. "Oh, darling, all young girls grow nervous at the prospect of marrying. Everything will work out fine. You'll see."

Lily twisted her hands in her lap, desperate to find some way to discuss the possibility of Walford's preference for men. "But, Mother, I don't feel right about it."

"What's not to feel right about?"

"It's Walford," she burst out, praying her mother would ask her questions that might get to the bottom of her fear. Knowing she never would. "I'm not sure he will treat me right."

Her mother arched a brow. "Has he begun to treat you differently than when you accepted his proposal?"

Lily sighed and shook her head. She should have known her mother would want evidence. What could she say? That Alex had described such forbidden things to her? As a young lady, she shouldn't even have been alone with him, much less listening to his talk of *sex*. "It's not that."

"Then, pray tell, what is it? For you're speaking in riddles."

Lily knew her mother was losing patience, and she didn't blame her. "I'm not sure he'll be a good husband to me," she finally said, coming as close to the truth as she dared.

"In what possible way? He's kind enough, isn't he?"

"Yes, but—"

"And well bred."

"I'm not sure. He's—"

"Oh, darling, I know. I know," she said, filled with the certainty of her own experience. Leaning forward, she grasped Lily's hands and gave them a squeeze. "Trust me. All young ladies worry about *that*, if they know anything at all about it. I have been meaning to have that particular talk with you, but I know how you and Hannah share. And *she's* certainly not one to keep certain . . . details . . . secret from her favorite sister."

Lily wanted to scream. Now her mother thought her only worry was losing her virginity! "Mother, *please*. You're not listening to me."

"Walford will surely treat you well. He's a true gentleman, from a long line of gentlemen. He's an aristocrat, darling, with the bluest blood outside of Buckingham Palace itself! You must relax, dear. I know the prospect of becoming a duchess must be daunting, but I have every faith you can handle the role, and with great style. You always were the most socially adept of my daughters. I'm so very proud of you, and so excited about this wedding, as you should be. I'm going to be the mother of a duchess!"

Her mother wouldn't let her forget it, even for a moment. "Yes. Yes, I know."

She accepted the truth. She could not discuss such appalling things with her mother. Standing abruptly, she pressed a hand to her aching forehead. "I think I'll go lie down for a while."

"Very well," her mother said, her spirits still high. "You must rest up for tonight. You're going to be the center of everyone's attention!"

Around four, Lily awoke from a fitful nap filled with bizarre and unsettling images of Walford doing strange, unholy things with other men.

Rising, she crossed to the washbasin and splashed tepid water on her face. She rang for the maid assigned to her by the duchess, and was soon gowned in a yellow day dress.

"You ought to be napping, not dressing," the maid remarked. "Everyone is resting at this hour."

"I have been resting for the past three hours," she said, then excused the maid.

Restless and bewildered, Lily found herself at loose ends. She opened the door to her room but saw no one about. The house had grown somnolent and silent. In the hours from three until eight o'clock, when dinner would be served, the guests usually rested in preparation for the evening's activities. Young ladies in particular were encouraged to nap before the after-dinner ball, which would last until two in the morning.

Alex's revelations continued to pray on Lily. Were they true? What *was* true? Should she have told her mother more? But how could she have, while still protecting her secret friendship with Alex?

She groaned and rubbed her face with her hands.

She had to stop thinking, give her mind a rest. Before Alex came into her life, her biggest worry would have been choosing the right gown. *That's it,* she decided. *Think about selecting a gown for the evening.*

She crossed to the immense cherry-wood wardrobe on the rear wall of her room and swung open the door. She pulled out an emerald-velvet ball gown, one of two she'd packed. If she wore this green gown, she would probably accessorize with her forest green gloves. Except they weren't an exact match for color. And what would she do with her hair?

She could wear the blue gown. Replacing the emerald gown, she retrieved the blue one. It was a light, yet intense blue. A sky blue . . . the color of Alex's eyes when he gazed at her . . . *You deserve to be worshiped* . . .

Stop it!

Irritated at her thoughts, she replaced the blue gown and pushed back the hanger holding the emerald gown so that she could compare the two. That's when she caught sight of a narrow right-angled crevice along the back of the wardrobe, as if the craftsman had patched together the rear panel. Odd, that an otherwise perfectly constructed and expensive wardrobe would have such a flaw in workmanship.

Yet the crevice didn't look like a flaw. Leaning farther in, she traced the crevice with her fingertips, pushing aside the hanging garments to follow it. The garments lay heavy against her arm, impeding her efforts. Giving in to her curiosity, she climbed all the way into the wardrobe. She adjusted the skirt of her yellow day dress and knelt on her knees.

She ran her fingers along the crevice and discovered the shape of a door half as tall as a normal door. A secret door, perhaps? Part of Inderby's network of concealed passages? It had to be. Laying her palms flat on the surface, she pressed at the panel. It gave a bit, so she pushed harder. With a soft creak, it broke free and swung inward. Beyond lay a dark, narrow, and musty-smelling hallway made entirely of the native that which comprised the building itself.

An impulse swept over her to enter the passage and disappear, leaving behind her confusion and pain. To run far away from Inderby, and the duke and duchess, and her mother's expectations, and Alex's terrible revelations.

If Alex's words were true . . .

No, they couldn't be. For if they were . . .

How could she break an engagement that so many people desired? Her mother had never been prouder, her sisters never as excited as they'd been visiting Inderby. Her sisters . . . Their future marriages would be guaranteed once they became the sisters of a duchess.

Yet Alex had painted such a horrible picture of debauchery and wicked indulgence . . .

No. She couldn't allow herself to imagine that Alex's warnings might be true, couldn't give them any weight at all. How dare he frighten and confuse her so deeply? How dare he cast darkness on her engagement party, on her very future?

She realized several minutes had passed while she'd stared into the dark of the passage beyond the door. A secret passage was the sort of thing she would have enjoyed exploring as a little girl, when nothing was complicated and everything was safe. The urge to escape, even temporarily, swept over her.

A moment later, she had crouched low and slipped through the secret door.

The passageway wasn't entirely dark. Narrow skylights high in the far wall let in enough light to enable her to see where she walked.

She'd never been in a house this old, or large, and never in a secret passageway. Not wanting anyone to know where she'd disappeared to, she closed the wardrobe door, then the door to the passageway behind her.

Turning to her right, she began to explore. Her eyes grew accustomed to the murky light, but the air was dank and cloying. She'd traveled about twenty feet when she heard a woman's voice so clear, it made her jump.

She knew that voice! It belonged to Hannah. Had her inquisitive sister also found this passageway? But no, Lily was the only one here.

She remembered that Hannah and Benjamin had been placed in the room next to hers. From here, she could hear them as clearly as if she was standing in their room.

She listened as Hannah said, "If I *knew* that she would be happy . . ."

"She appears quite happy," replied Benjamin. "In her element, even. She'll make a marvelous duchess. I dare say she'll embrace her role with more enthusiasm than you did."

"Or you." The sound of a bed creaking reached her ears. The sounds were so clear, it made goosebumps rise on Lily's arms. High in the wall, she spotted the end of a pipe. The pipe must have been placed into the wall to draw the sound from the room, creating an ideal way to spy on the room's occupants. What a clever and nefarious invention!

"You don't know her like I do, darling. There's something in her eyes . . ."

"Come now. I'm sure everything will be fine. Not everyone is lucky enough to find what we have. Now, kiss me, sweetheart. I've been hungry for you all day."

Her sister giggled. "How hungry?"

"Starving. Famished. This hungry."

What sounded like kissing and heavy breathing reached Lily's ears. She blushed and began to back away, farther down the hall. She didn't realize traveling this passageway would turn her into an eavesdropper. Still, she was in no mood to return to her room.

Her sister's concerns lay heavy on her heart. What did Hannah see in her that made her worry so? Had she done such a poor job of masking her deepest feelings? Yet no one else had seen anything other than a young woman thrilled with the match she had made.

Her pace picked up, voices reaching her as she passed room after room, snatches of conversations giving hints into private lives, and loves. Lily was surprised to discover that what she'd always thought was the most quiet time of day was anything but. Only the very young or naive were actually napping. The air buzzed with gossip and clandestine meetings.

Widowed ladies seeking their own brilliant matches gossiped about the eligible bachelors; Lady Montague complained about the food and poorly trained servants; and Mrs. Sotheby sounded oddly excited to be visiting a man not her husband. Lily recognized her guest as Colonel Taylor, of all people, the dignified gentleman who'd entertained her at the Fox Croft dinner. When their voices gave way to pleasurable moans, Lily hurried on.

This is what people did while the debutantes slept! The passage had opened onto a whole new world, one she'd been oblivious to. Secrets and subterfuge, alliances and affairs . . . Why, she'd been so naive, so in the dark about the world. Intimate rendezvous, afternoon assignations, affairs—

As if on cue, a woman's voice said, "Surely you aren't planning to waste this time actually taking a nap! What happened to the fun-loving fellow I used to know?"

Lily smiled. That had to be Lady Emma Hammett, a lovely blonde who, rumor had it, had long tired of her own husband's attentions.

Lily's steps slowed, and she realized she had reached the end of the passage. She had passed at least a dozen rooms and now faced a normal-size wooden door. Cracking it open, she found a narrow staircase leading down. Sounds of the kitchen drifted up to her, and she quietly closed the door. She had no intention of going down there, of revealing that she'd been spying. Turning around, she began to retrace her steps to her own room.

"Alex, darling . . ."

Lady Hammett's words made Lily freeze. Alex. The irrational thought struck her: Her Alex was behind this door, with some woman! She remembered that Alex had been placed in the room at the end of the hall, as befitted his station—or lack thereof.

"Emma, I'm quite tired. Yes, I do intend to take a nap."

"That's why I came. To help you relax . . ." she coaxed.

"I'm certain your husband will be in the mood to appreciate your abilities in that arena better than I. If you'll excuse me—" She heard a door creak.

The woman sounded quite put out. "Very well, you needn't be rude about it. I swear, Alex, you've turned into quite a drudge since you returned to London. If you don't be careful, you'll turn old before your time. Good day."

The door from Alex's room closed, and Lily prayed that meant the woman had taken her leave. When no further conversation emanated from the pipe in the wall, she turned away and headed back to her own room.

Alex had changed? Dare she hope she had touched his heart after all, despite his protests to the contrary? Or was he merely not in the mood for what the lithe, lovely Emma was offering? If she knew more about physical love, perhaps she would know the answer.

Deep in thought, she continued walking, the conversations passing overhead like the buzz of bees. After a while, she realized she'd traveled past her own door to the opposite end of the passageway. Instead of the short doors cut into the stone wall for the other rooms, here was a full-size door. Within, she could hear the dowager duchess herself.

She hadn't meant to travel so far in the opposite direction. Worry struck her. Could she even find her own door again? After all, she'd closed the door behind her, and all but this one looked identical. What if she picked the wrong door and walked in on someone? How mortifying that would be! Yet she could hardly lurk out here in the passage for the next several hours. She had to locate her own room within these ancient walls and get dressed for dinner.

The duchess's voice came again. "A pretty thing, as I said, but American nonetheless. Thank goodness, it's a fault that money can forgive."

Lily bristled at the duchess's words. She knew that her dowry was her primary value to their family, but she had thought the duchess found value in her beyond her family's wealth.

"They're such a gauche people," a familiar man's voice replied. "The father is intelligent, I'll grant you. But he completely lacks refinement. He is so nouveau riche, the scent of newly minted coin clings to him like cheap perfume on a courtesan. It's a shame we must mingle with their kind merely to maintain our aristocratic way of life."

That voice belonged to Smithson, the duchess's brother. Lily instantly decided she hated him.

"Indeed. Her mother is simply appalling. She actually allowed her daughters to learn horseback riding astride! And the other girls . . . They are as awkward and gauche as the common children of the village. Walford is willing to make the sacrifice, thank goodness. We had to snatch the girl up before some other peer got his hands on her money. Walford is so charming; he knew exactly what to do to win her. It wasn't very difficult, or so he tells me. Makes one wonder about the virtue of Americans, that they can be so easily persuaded."

Lily couldn't bear to hear another one of the woman's degrading statements. She'd insulted the entire Carrington family! Oh, how she longed to give the woman a piece of her mind.

Yet, how could she? She'd given her word to everyone concerned. She was trapped in their careful plan, a plan she herself had understood before agreeing to this marriage. She knew the truth, after all. She had rationalized why this marriage made sense. Only a foolish female would paint such a transcontinental business arrangement in colors of romance and love. She knew better.

She always had, for she loved Walford as little as he loved her.

As if drawn from her own mind, his voice echoed in the passageway, sending a shock through her. "Love me, damn it! Now."

Love him? Had he seen her?

She glanced around, but realized the voice came from the next door over. Heavy panting reached her ears, and the words came again, in an agonized groan.

"Love me." Then came another voice, a man's voice. "Oh, Walls, it's so deep. You're hurting me."

"Take it, damn it. Take it all!"

"I'm trying, Walls. Please. Oh, please, ohpleaseohplease—" The man howled. Lily pressed against the wall, clutching the rough bricks under her hands for support. That horrid sound—a mixture of pain and passion—echoed up and down the corridor, surrounding Lily, pressing into her brain.

She couldn't begin to picture what Walford was doing to the man, but whatever it was, it could not be considered natural.

Alex was right. Walford loved men.

Oh, God. It's true. Lily's denials fell like a house of cards as her mind raced to accept the truth. *It's true. All of it.* Walford's preference for men. His lack of love for her. His dissolute behavior. Even the prince's plan to seduce her. All of it!

Backing away in horror, she slammed against the wall behind her and lost her breath. Gasping, she covered her ears with her hands, desperate to blot out the moans that continued to emanate from the pipe in the wall, taunting her, terrifying her. "No. No, no, no . . ." she whispered.

No one heard her.

She sagged against the cold wall, feeling so utterly alone that her stomach hurt. "Alex. Please. I need you."

Alex . . . From the first he'd tried to warn her, tried to save her—and she had shoved him away. Shame washed through her. She'd wronged him terribly, refused to believe him when he alone had been honest with her.

She had to see him, needed to see him. Needed desperately to talk to him and perhaps find a solution, a way out of the trap she'd fallen into. He alone would give her straight answers.

And, she prayed, reassurance that she hadn't already ruined her hopes for happiness.

She found herself standing before the secret door leading to Alex's room, hardly aware how she'd gotten there. Shivering in the dim hallway, she pressed her palm against the door. On the other side, she heard no voices, only the odd clatter and rustle indicating someone was within. Grasping the small metal handle, she tugged open the door to his bedroom.

Twenty

Lily materialized in his room so unexpectedly, Alex nearly cut his neck with his razor. He dropped it beside the washbasin and stared. She had appeared wraithlike from the depths of his wardrobe. Her face was whiter than he'd ever seen it, her dark eyes huge and scared.

"Where—" he began.

She stumbled and fell against the post of his bed.

"Lily!" Like a shot, Alex dashed to her side and caught her against himself. "What's going on?" he demanded, panic welling in his chest.

She pushed her hands against his chest in a futile effort to appear solid and strong. A moment later, she gave up and collapsed in his arms. He tightened his arms around her, worried for her, but taking deep satisfaction that she was here, seeking solace from him.

"I heard him. And his lover. A man, just as you said. Everything is just as you said. Oh, God, Alex, I've been such a fool!" She pressed her face into his chest, showing no concern that he wasn't properly dressed. She'd stumbled on him wearing only his trousers and an undershirt.

Alex wasn't oblivious. Holding her so intimately set his pulse pounding and filled his heart with a keen sense of need. He pressed her close, rocking her and stroking her back. "Sweetheart. I'm sorry. I'm so sorry." He looked over her head at the wardrobe, and realized she'd come through a hidden entryway. She must have overheard Walford and his lover in the same way.

"I discovered a secret door," she murmured into his chest. "There's a hall outside. So many secrets! Everyone is hiding something. I had no idea. No idea."

He smoothed loose strands against her chignon. "How could you?"

She pushed back and looked in his face. "I should have listened to you, Alex. I should have trusted you. I've been such a fool." Extracting herself from his arms, she began to wander about the room. "I must do something about it. Something . . . I can't—Oh, God, he was hurting the fellow." She sank onto the edge of his bed and buried her face in her hands.

Alex quickly sat beside her and pulled her close. He ached to see her in such a state. He'd grown accustomed to the intrigues and plots of the Marlborough Set only after years of personal experience. He'd discovered what people were capable of and learned to protect himself as best he could. His innocent, romantic-minded Lily had been forced to face the same harsh reality in a single afternoon.

He stroked her hair soothingly. "Oh, Lily. I shouldn't have let it go this far. I should have told you sooner." He had to guide her now, use his wits and experience to lead her out of the morass in which they'd embroiled her. "We'll think of something, I swear it. You will not have to marry that man."

She lurched to her feet, leaving him feeling bereft. "What else am I to do?" she asked, pacing away from him. Turning, she tossed her hands in the air. "I can't even think straight, much less find an answer. Tell me, Alex. What do I do now?"

Heart aching, arms crying out to hold her, he forced himself not to become lost in the desire to comfort her. He had to offer her something more, something of substance. "You need to tell your parents, your mother. Surely she would have your best interests at heart."

"My best interests?"

The scoffing look on her face cut him to the quick. She had changed so much since he first met her, becoming worldly in a matter of hours. He longed to make the two men responsible pay for hurting her, but Lily needed more from him than revenge. She needed answers.

"My mother only sees what she wants to see," she continued. "She has sublimated herself to the duchess's opinions. I have never seen her so . . . so malleable, so agreeable to what another woman has to say. She is so desperate for this match, she has lost herself."

"Still, you ought to try—"

"I *tried* to tell her of my concerns, before I even knew them to be true. I failed, Alex. To her, I am still her perfect, innocent daughter. She would faint dead away if I even admitted I'd heard of such a thing, much less that I knew it to be true about my fiancé. No. No, I cannot bring myself to discuss such intimate details with her."

Yet she could discuss them with *him*. He tried to quash his satisfaction at how comfortable they'd grown with each other, how close. Right now, he needed to focus on her needs, not his own.

Standing, he settled his hands on his hips. "If you cannot tell the real reason, give another reason."

"You mean, tell them I do not love the duke? Or that I am not ready for marriage? Or some other silly girl's reason? No." She shook her head. "No explanation would sway them, not now. My father and the duke have reached an agreement about my dowry. Papers have been signed. If I try to end it now, for any reason, neither party would allow it. Oh, God, it's all so difficult." Sighing, she sank into an armchair by the window. "Why did the prince have to notice me?"

Alex was not at all surprised a woman as unique and perfect as she had become the object of such dastardly intrigue. What hot-blooded male would not long to possess her? His own hunger for her defeated his common sense.

In her place by the window, the late afternoon sun shot fiery highlights through her upswept ebony hair. She appeared both angelic and sensuous, the perfect image of womanhood. Her beauty, accompanied by her underlying vulnerability, made her nearly impossible to resist. Every particle of his being cried out to hold her, to care for her, to make her his in every way.

"I cannot fault the prince for longing to possess you," he rasped. "You're the most beautiful woman to come out into society for years. If not ever."

Her full lips lifted in a skeptical smile. "An opinion no doubt reinforced by my sizable dowry."

"Hardly. For God's sake, Lily, if you were a poor milkmaid, you'd still be irresistible. You're too damned sensual for your own good."

She looked at her lap. "Apparently. Yet I still have no idea how to fight back."

"I know, Lily," he sighed, frustrated that he could think of nothing helpful. "I swear we'll think of something."

"If only I hadn't accepted his proposal," Lily said, sounding like a lost child. "If only he'd never asked. If only I'd stayed in New York." She looked up at him. "But then, I never would have met you."

He looked away, afraid of becoming distracted by her loving words, by her virginal sensuality. "Hell, we could fill a lifetime saying 'if only.' If only you hadn't been so damned innocent and sweet, they never would have imagined using you, nor—"

Her eyes widened. "That's it."

"Excuse me?"

"That will be my downfall," she said with remarkable enthusiasm. She rose to face him. "Of course. It makes perfect sense. My family will be distraught, but my sisters will survive. Hannah is, after all, a countess. And you—everyone knows about you, and your way with women. Why, it's the best possible solution."

Alex could not fathom her sudden change in mood. She appeared almost happy. He crossed his arms. "You're not making sense."

"Of course I am." Settling her hands on his bare forearms, she said, "I want you to ruin me."

Twenty-one

Alex stared down at Lily, at her voluptuous figure limned with delicate highlights by the sunlight falling through the window. He could not possibly have heard her right. "Excuse me? I thought I just heard you say you want me to—"

"Ruin me. Yes." She nodded firmly, her eyes bright with determination.

Alex gazed at her, amazed. She could be discussing a walk in the park for all the concern she exhibited. "Do you have any idea what you're saying?"

She ran her fingers up his arm, sending a tremor through him. "You doubt that I do? Alex, I am a young lady. We are taught from an early age not to allow our honor to be compromised. I understand thoroughly that once this is accomplished, the duke will have to break our engagement to save face. And the prince—he will have to steer clear of me as a ruined woman, at least for a while. If he ever approaches me again, I'll have the knowledge to dissuade him—something I now sorely lack."

"Of course you lack such knowledge!" He hacked the air with the side of his hand, determined to dismiss her arguments. "You're a—a virtuous young lady. You're—"

"Too sensual for my own good. You said it yourself." She pressed her hands to his chest. Her sultry eyes seemed to reflect his own desperate, unspoken desires.

"Lily . . ." he warned, praying she would see sense, praying he would be able to resist her shocking, tempting entreaty.

"It will work, Alex," she urged. "I'll never reveal your name. I'll tell the duke I'm not fit to be his bride anymore, that I've had a liaison . . . And I'll be experienced enough to convince him it's true."

"I'm touched you're worried about my reputation, Lily, but that hardly means—" A shaft of pleasure scattered his thoughts. She'd slid her hand beneath his undershirt and begun running her fingers across his chest.

"Alex, please. Take me to your bed. Keep me safe from the duke. I beg you."

How he wanted to! Alex had thought himself strong, able to say no to women whenever it suited him, in control of his impulses. And he had been—until he met Lily.

She began tracing his face with her fingertips, her gentle yet erotic touch setting his nerve endings on fire. She outlined his forehead, his cheekbones, his lips. Her own lips parted and softened, as if longing for his kiss. Her fingers followed the curves of his muscles as if trying to learn every inch of him.

He didn't have the strength to dissuade her, nor the desire. He reveled in her hungry caresses, in the passion burning fiercely behind her innocent eyes.

"I still want you," she whispered, her gaze hot on his. "I cannot forget how you made me feel, when you held me, and kissed me. Do you want me? Even if you don't love me. I don't expect that."

Did he *want* her? Good Lord. He spent every night in agony longing for her. Here she was, begging him to bed her. And she was right. Her ruination would break the engagement more surely than any argument she might make.

And he was just the man to do it.

Lily held her breath as she awaited Alex's answer. As she continued to touch him, his eyes grew smoky, the muscles in his thick arms tensing and releasing as she stroked them, stroked his face.

Still she waited, wondering whether he would take her to bed, or push her away. Lord, what a risk she was taking! If he rejected her yet again, she didn't know if she'd be able to live with the disappointment.

Let him believe she merely wanted physical intimacy, a way to break her impending engagement. Yet, no matter if she eventually married, no matter what happened to her, she would take this single afternoon in his arms and revel in it for a lifetime. For she had already given him her heart and soul.

Finally, he gave her his answer, without saying a word. Lily's heart pounded as he touched her in turn. He cupped her face and tenderly stroked her cheeks with his thumbs. She expected him to kiss her. Instead, he threaded his fingers into her hair, dislodging her hairpins and freeing the long tresses to fall down her back. With his large, long-fingered hands, he stroked her hair, from her sensitive scalp down her back until he was caressing her hips.

Gripping her there, he snugged her close against him, pressing their chests together. "You had better be ready for this. I warn you, I have been thinking about this for so long, I cannot guarantee I will maintain my control."

"Is that so bad?" she asked.

His lips turned up at one corner, his eyes sparkling with humor. "Kiss me, and let's find out."

Rising on her tiptoes, she twined her arms around his neck and pressed her mouth to his. He opened his lips wide over hers, his tongue immediately sweeping inside and taking possession. He growled deep in his throat. Locking his hands on her bottom, he lifted her in the air. She slid full against him, the movement sending a delicious tingle throughout her body. Still kissing her, he carried her that way, then laid her full-length on his canopy featherbed.

Lily found herself gazing up at a royal blue canopy, touching silken sheets beneath her palms. He gave her scant time to think of his bed, for he had joined her there. Leaning above her, he bracketed her hips with his knees and continued to lay kisses on her mouth, then her face.

"That day in the carriage, I dreamed of doing things to you. Unspeakable, delicious things to make you cry out in delight. I want to do them to you now."

Lily shivered in anticipation, and perhaps a touch of apprehension. She knew only the basics, only what the baroness had told her. How one got from point *A* to point *B* remained a mystery. Yet she trusted Alex, trusted only Alex.

He began by sliding up her skirt and petticoats, then unlacing her shoes and letting them fall to the floor. After that, he lifted her skirts even higher, past her knees. Though her legs were clad in white hose, Lily felt naked before him. She had been taught that a lady's legs must never be shown to a man. Yet Alex was seeing hers now.

Without her realizing it, he had unfastened her silk hose from the straps attached to the bottom of her corset. Crouching between her legs, he began rolling them down, his fingertips tracing paths of fire on her skin. He slid his hands along the tops of her thighs, then along the inside, where she was extremely sensitive. She gasped.

"I wanted to press you back against the seat and touch you like this," he said. "I knew you would feel soft. But this!" Lifting one of her legs, he brought it to his mouth and laid a chain of kisses from her knee to midthigh.

"What else did you want to do that day in the carriage?" she asked, feeling marvelously bold and naughty.

His eyes sparked with humor and shared passion. It thrilled Lily to realize she had given herself over to the power of this skilled and sensual lover. "I wanted to touch you. Here." His hand vanished beneath her skirt and touched *something* there.

Lily jerked in shock at the sudden burst of pleasure shooting through her body. "Alex," she breathed. "How did you do that?"

He gave her a satisfied smile. "That, my dearest, is the center of your pleasure. What makes you a woman. We shall explore it to the full."

"Now?"

He arched teasing eyebrow. "Now?"

"Yes. Do that again, what you just did. Touch me there."

"By God, Lily, you are bold." He lay beside her and propped himself on his elbow but kept his other hand below her skirts. He cupped her through her drawers, his palm settling hot and hard on her. Then his fingers slid through the hidden slit sewn into her drawers and touched her swollen flesh.

Lily writhed underneath his touch, longing for more. For something else. For movement.

His eyes glowed with secret understanding. "You want me to stroke you there, don't you?"

Lily realized he was right. "Yes, that's it. That's what I want."

"Before I take you further, I want you to be completely comfortable. Even though I would not have undressed you in the carriage, I am sure you would breathe easier if we disposed of all this fabric." He held up a handful of her watered silk skirt and petticoats.

Lily breathed in, aware of how her corset was digging into her chest with each breath. She nodded.

Alex expertly flipped her over and began undoing the buttons of her dress. Only a few minutes passed before he had rid her of not only her dress but her two underskirts, her petticoats, and her drawers, leaving her in her gold satin corset and embroidered cambric chemise. At the same time, he had somehow stripped down to his drawers.

"You've had experience doing this," she said.

"As I told you, I am a rake, Lily."

"Good. I need a rake right now." Her voice caught on her next words. "I need *you.*"

Soon, she found herself kneeling at the end of the bed with Alex behind her, his thighs cradling her hips. As he unlaced her ribbon-and-lace-trimmed corset, Lily watched their reflections in the bureau mirror at the foot of the bed.

Alex swept his hands up her chemise, massaging away the impressions left by the corset's whalebone, stroking a delicious pleasure where discomfort had been. "Look at you," he urged, his eyes on her in the mirror. "Your natural body is the shape every woman seeks when she puts on a corset. See?"

Lily nodded, unable to tear her eyes from the reflection of his handsome face, so intent on pleasing her.

His hands locked on the hem of her chemise and

slid it over her hips, then higher and higher, revealing her stomach, then her ribs. "Lift your arms."

Trembling, Lily did as he commanded. Alex slipped the cotton chemise over her head and tossed it aside. Her breasts fell free and full, the dusky nipples distended and aching. Behind her, she felt Alex shiver. He settled his palms on her rib cage, just below her breasts. Slowly, ever so slowly, he slid his hands under her breasts, cupping and lifting them in his palms. His thumbs extended, he teased her nipples, drawing pleasure from her like a conductor making music with his orchestra.

"Oh, Lord." She sucked in a raw breath. The erotic shock of not only feeling such a sensuous touch, but seeing his hands on her, nearly made her faint. Fascinated, her eyes heavy with passion, she gazed at the two of them in the mirror, witnessing his potent seduction of her. His muscled shoulders and tan, hair-flecked arms were a shocking contrast to her own white skin, reminding her this was real, not a heated dream.

Real . . . So real. Every inch of her body burned with fire, threatening to consume her utterly. And how she wanted to be consumed!

He met her gaze in the mirror. Yes, he was an experienced lover. But his expression was one of wonder. "You have the most perfect shape of any woman I have ever seen," he said, sounding positively astounded.

"Or bedded?" She replied in a teasing tone, not wanting him to see how deeply she treasured his every compliment.

"Or bedded," he acknowledged with a wry smile.

His palms replaced his thumbs, sliding over her nipples with agonizing slowness. He began rolling them in his palms, sending bolts of pleasure through her until she sagged against his chest, giving herself up to the sensation, to him. Their images in the mirror blurred, her eyes began to drift closed.

"Look," he commanded.

She opened her eyes as he slid one of his hands down her stomach—and lower. His fingers sliding through her dark curls, he again touched her in that most wondrous of places. Instinctively wanting more contact, Lily opened her thighs wider to give him access.

"Yes, darling, I'll satisfy you," he murmured, laying kisses on her shoulder, her collarbone, her neck. His palm moved in short, delicious strokes, his fingertips dancing over her, sliding and moving, up and around and down, doing marvelous things to her. Lily feared she would float off the bed in a cloud of pleasure. Moaning, she grasped his thighs to keep herself anchored.

Without warning, he slid his finger deep inside her, drawing a gasp from her. Through the mirror, she stared at him in shock.

"This, darling, is your own special place, designed just for pleasure. For sex."

"My birth canal, then."

"If you should have a child, yes, it would be born through here. But most of the time, it's for love."

Our love, she thought, relaxing against him. He continued to explore her, toy with her, his thumb grazing that mysterious nub of pleasure as he plunged his fingers in and out of her. Pressure and sensation had built within her to an unbearable level. She arched her back, her head on his shoulder, her fingers digging into his thighs. "Please," she groaned, desperate for something nameless.

"Yes," he said in her ear, nothing else. Still, she trusted him as he worked his magic.

Her breath came short and fast, her breasts rising and falling as he stroked them each in turn with his free hand. She wanted more of his touch, more pleasure, *more* . . . The need grew so strong, she thought she would die if it wasn't met. If something didn't happen. Something—

Then it came over her. The overpowering need burst into a giant blaze, a fireball that felt as if it were consuming her. She cried out from the depths of her soul, no longer aware of where she was, only aware that Alex had sent her there.

She had no idea how long she spent there. After a timeless moment, she began to float back to earth, her eyes focusing once more on the mirror and the man holding her. He was pressing his face to hers, a satisfied smile on his face.

"Oh, my. Oh, my," she repeated over and over, shocked at her body's response to his caresses.

Alex looked inordinately pleased at what he'd wrought in her. He trailed his fingers down her cheek. *"That* is what I wanted to do to you, that day in the carriage."

"If you had, I would have been unable to walk from the carriage back to the house." Her entire body still buzzed from the effects of her climax. But she knew there was more. After all, he had yet to remove his undershorts, to place his own body inside hers. After she caught her breath, she gave him an innocent look. "That was wonderful, Alex. But surely that's not all you wanted to do to me, that day in the carriage."

A wicked smile spread over his face. "Not quite."

"Then show me the rest."

She was so limp, she was barely aware that he had moved. He carefully laid her back on the bed, then rose and stood beside her. He yanked the tie of his undershorts loose, then shoved them down, revealing his distended manhood, almost on a level with her eyes.

Blushing, Lily stared at him, unable to look away. "It's even bigger than I imagined."

Reaching down, he stroked her hair from her face, his fingers trailing along her neck, her breasts. "That's because you've filled me with such desire. I have never wanted a woman more than I want you."

"To be truthful, it looks rather silly." A silly willy. She bit down a laugh.

"Perhaps you will change your mind, once you feel me inside you."

His blunt reminder of what was about to happen sent a forbidden thrill through her—and a hint of trepidation. She knew it would hurt this first time, but not how much.

"Are you certain of this, Lily? We could stop now. It's not too late to change your mind."

Stop? After going this far? "I cannot imagine that." She lifted her arms in invitation. He slid beside her, his lean body pressing against hers in a delicious symphony of sensation. But more than his touch, she was affected by his expression as he looked in her eyes, as he kissed her. She felt worshiped, adored . . . *Loved*.

No, he had not said he loved her, and she wasn't so foolish as to think these intimate acts would make him love her. But she adored him. She had enough love for both of them.

He gently urged her legs apart, making them a cradle for his hips. His manhood nudged her canal. "Look at me, darling," he murmured, his face appearing strained. "Look at me when we become one."

Her eyes fastened on his, she felt sudden pressure inside her, then a breaking, a giving, and a receiving.

Her body felt stretched, filled, overwhelmed by the feel of him sliding deep, so deep inside her. She gripped his shoulders, taking everything he had to give.

As he slid even deeper, he groaned, his body quivering in her arms. "My God, Lily. I said I may lose control. I can't—"

"Shh, Alex. It's good," she said, uncertain of his concern, but longing to reassure him. *Oh, yes. It felt so right.* She wasn't laughing now. Her body had been made for this, to take him inside her. She arched her hips, encouraging him to slide even deeper, to press hard against her.

"Pain?" he panted, his breath hot on her shoulder. "You?"

"No, *you.*"

She tangled her fingers in his thick hair and lifted his eyes to hers. "No. I'm happy, Alex. Truly happy."

"Oh, Lily." Closing his eyes, he moaned. Then he began to move inside her, thrusting rhythmically. His movements renewed her pleasure, and she arched to receive him.

She gripped his back with her arms and her legs. His muscles flexed against her, and his skin grew hot and damp with sweat. Under his skillful movements, the tension built within her. Once more she was flying toward that amazing peak of ecstasy.

His thrusts came harder and faster, as if frantic to reach that peak with her. *This is what he means by losing control,* she realized, thrilled that she had the power to bring him to such a state.

Then, all thought fled as she once again arrived at that mystical height of ecstasy in Alex's arms.

At the moment of his own release, his eyes were locked on hers. Then he cried her name, once, twice, his body bucking and shuddering. Finally, he sagged in her arms.

Lily shivered, an echo of her climax darting through her body. She knew it was over, knew she had accomplished her goal. Yet she never wanted to rise from this bed.

Nor did Alex seem in any hurry to end their encounter. He continued to hold her and stroke her, his fingers and lips traveling over her stomach and breasts as if memorizing every curve of her body.

"Now, my darling," he murmured, his tongue sweeping over her nipple and sending a fresh shock of desire through her body. "Now you are thoroughly ruined."

Lily didn't feel ruined. She felt reborn. That Alex was an expert lover came as no surprise to Lily. Nevertheless, she had not expected to be transported, to feel so loved.

She had to resist the allure, the false promise in his attentions. She had to keep her feelings for this man separate from their lovemaking. She had to. For he did not love her.

"I must confess I'm embarrassed now that I suggested we marry, simply so that we could . . . do *this*," she said, determined to sound like the worldly woman she'd just become.

"Have sex?" He breathed out softly, his gaze on hers.

"Yes. Sex." The word no longer seemed so forbidden, so darkly mysterious. Yet in her heart, she'd experienced much more than mere sex. She could not imagine being so uninhibited with a man she did not truly, deeply love. And she could not imagine loving a man other than Alex.

She sighed and gazed up at the silk canopy stretching over his bed. She would be an utter and complete fool to assume a sophisticated man like Alex would return her feelings. This was all she would have of him. Once her mother and father learned what she'd done, she would be rushed back to America, she had no doubt of that. Rumors would swirl around her for years. She might never be able to marry a respectable man.

Oddly enough, she didn't care. It had been worth it to make love with Alex. To imagine, even for a moment, that he returned her love.

Twenty-two

Alex considered himself a sophisticated man. He wasn't easily taken in by romantic fantasies. Then why, lying beside this sweetly sensuous woman, did he feel as new and untried as a schoolboy?

Lily had used him. Logically, he accepted that. Other women had certainly done so, and with his blessing. Still, his heart rebelled with a fierce burning frustration.

He could not take his eyes off of her. Propped on one elbow, he studied her oval face, now cleared of all trace of the tension that had furrowed her brow when she'd entered his room. His eyes traced the curve of her cheek, the thick lashes around her dark eyes, the little turn to her adorable nose. He would never grow tired of gazing at her.

He stroked a stray lock off her face and smoothed it back, marveling at the softness of her skin. No other man had ever touched her in the way that he had. A deep possessiveness took hold of him, and he imagined her belonging only to him. To his amazement, he realized he had never felt so close to a woman, so in need of her.

I love her. I have fallen in love with Lily. The realization seemed so natural, so obvious, he was amazed he'd never put it into such words before. Obviously he loved her. John had seen the truth, weeks ago. He'd suggested Alex be the one to marry her. To rescue her.

Marry her . . . Some men weren't meant to marry. He had imagined himself one of them. But he'd been wrong.

How strange that life should surprise him in this way. He had always considered marriage an unnecessary burden to his career serving in the Empire's far-flung outposts.

Sikara had taught him the wonderful benefits of having a companion, but neither of them had ever spoken of love. Theirs had been a union born of convenience. She had known that when he was reassigned, he'd be leaving her behind. After Sikara died trying to give birth to their child, he had realized that despite his protests, he had committed himself to her. He would never have abandoned her. Though several years had gone by, he still thought of his time with Sikara as the happiest of his life. Until now.

For the first time in his life, the prospect of taking a wife—taking *this* woman as a wife—filled him with a deep yearning. He imagined his future without her, year after year, a dark lonely place where he would never again be truly happy.

Lily stretched full-length against him, as lithe as a satisfied cat. Her luscious lips arched into a smile. "Thank you," she murmured. "For agreeing to this."

Thank you . . . He'd done what she wanted. She needed nothing more from him. After the engagement to the duke was broken, her parents would find some other man to marry her to.

He outlined her the gentle arch of her cheek with his fingertips, wanting to imprint this moment on his memory forever. "How could I not? You and I both know we've longed for this, ever since we met."

"Yes. I understand that now." Her smile seemed far

more serene than circumstances demanded. Did she feel the same sense of "rightness" that he felt?

And he had never felt more right or true within himself. He didn't want to let her go. He wanted to keep her here beside him. Which is not at all what she'd asked for. "Lily," he said. "Whatever happens . . . Wherever life takes you . . . You should never be ashamed."

"I would never be ashamed of being with you, Alex." She danced her fingers over his lips. His eyes locked on hers, he saw the invitation there and began lowering his mouth to hers for another kiss.

A knock on the door cut into their privacy. "Who is it?" he demanded.

"Sir, it is Hasim. It is time you are getting ready for the evening."

Damn! Their time was already over. He realized now how long the shadows in the room had grown. It was already early evening. With a sigh, he called out, "Very well, Hasim. Give me fifteen minutes."

He looked down at Lily, wanting to say nothing, wanting to block out the world. He had to force the words out. "It's time. You must leave now."

Lily didn't meet his gaze. "Yes, I suppose I had better." Climbing from the bed, she gathered her underthings from the floor and began slipping them on. She was so calm, as if she'd come from her lover's bed a thousand times. Her composure amazed him.

As he watched her slide back into her drawers and chemise, his heart squeezed as if in a vise. Together, they had created a magical world, a special bond the likes of which he'd never experienced before with a woman. Yet now it was over, just like that. He wanted so much more, wanted some exchange of words, or promises.

He refused to let his weakness for her show. Clearing his throat, he asked coolly, "What is your plan? Simply being here will do you no good, unless others learn of it."

She crossed to his door and cracked it open, then closed it again. Retrieving her corset from the foot of the bed, she slipped it on. Then she stood with her back to him and lifted her hair, waiting for him to lace it for her. As he did so, she explained her plan.

"I must be discovered returning to my room in a disheveled state. Once Walford learns of it, he'll confront me. He'll see in my face that it's true, even if I say nothing. Failing that, I'll describe in detail exactly what I've done." She lifted her gaze to his. "I will never reveal your name, Alex, even if he demands it. I promise you that."

He had no doubt of her resolve, but—he realized to his shock—being fingered as her lover was the least of his concerns, even if it cost him dearly.

She continued, "After such a public embarrassment, he'll have to break with me." She dropped her heavy fall of hair and stooped to retrieve her petticoats.

Anchoring her hips between his knees, Alex helped her tie them in place. Dressing her was almost as erotic as stripping her clothes from her had been. "Yes, that makes perfect sense. I suppose you were thinking of that when—"

She shot him a cool look over her slim, bare shoulder. "Always. It never left my mind."

Her words cut him to the quick. During their lovemaking, she thought only of how it would benefit her?

She slipped her wrinkled dress over her petticoats. She didn't bother to fasten her dress, nor did she pin up her hair. Carrying her shoes, she opened the door and peeked out.

She glanced back at Alex. "The duchess is coming this way. My timing could not be more perfect. After she reaches the end of the hall, I'll leave your room. If I time it right, she won't know which room I've come from, only that I've been ruined."

Alex reached out a hand, longing to stop her, longing to keep her from the firestorm she was about to unleash on herself. "Lily. Wait."

She turned and looked Alex. "Yes?"

"Are you sure? It can never be undone."

"I'm sure." Again she turned around.

"Lily . . ."

"Yes?" she said, not looking at him.

He swung his legs out of bed and reached for his undershorts. "I cannot allow you to do this alone."

She paused then, and gazed at him, her eyes dark and mysterious. "Please, Alex. *No.* You've already done your share. You've tried to protect me, and now you've rescued me. It's time for you to hang up your knight's shield." Her back straightening, she braced herself for the worst confrontation she would ever experience. Then she swung the door wide and stepped into the hall

"To hell with that." He could not allow her face this alone. Without thinking through the ramifications, he snagged up his silk dressing gown. Tossing it on over his undershorts, he followed her out of the room, right into the path of the duchess.

In a remarkably short time, a particular group had been gathered in the blue parlor on the second floor. Lily stood beside Alex and faced a semicircle of inquisitors—her parents, her sister Hannah and her husband Benjamin, her fiancé the duke, his mother the dowager duchess, and even the Prince of Wales himself.

To her shock, Alex had appeared by her side, despite her insistence he needn't be involved. Though warmed by his concern, his continued sacrifice on her behalf frustrated her. She hated to be the instrument of his downfall.

Before she could insist he return to his room, the duchess had seen them—and screamed. The noise had echoed up and down the hall, causing heads to appear from nearly every doorway. Her son—appearing to have dressed rapidly himself—had come running from his own room. Together, they had railed at the both of them, causing quite a ruckus in the hall.

Neither she nor Alex had exhausted themselves offering any defense, not until now, when everyone was gathered before them.

"My daughter was with this man? I cannot believe it," her mother said. "I simply cannot. Not my Lily!"

"It's true, Mother," Lily said.

Mrs. Carrington looked completely bewildered. "But—but why? Lily, how *could* you? How could you ruin your future like this? I simply don't understand. You gave up a duke for *this* fellow? Is he anybody?"

"Alexander Drake is a special agent for the Crown," the prince supplied, "serving in the Foreign Service. He *had* a sterling future. For this outrage, however, he will be blackballed from society and removed from his position." He glared at Alex.

Alex remained cool, his posture tall and unbending. His defiant gaze let them all know how unashamed he felt. Lily took strength from his reaction, for it bolstered her own sense that she'd done nothing to be ashamed of.

"Lily, how *could* you? How could you behave so

abominably?" her mother demanded. "He doesn't even have a title!"

The pain on her features cut Lily to the quick. Perhaps she'd been selfish. But she reminded herself that her mother had also been selfish. "I had to do something to break the engagement," she calmly explained.

"But why would you want to? You would have been a duchess! You were always so well behaved, so obedient. I simply do not understand any of this."

Now came the difficult part. "Because, Mother, Father," she began, looking at each in turn. "I discovered things about Walford's character that meant I could never marry him. Things I couldn't bring myself to speak of, they were so reprehensible."

The duke's cool dissolved. "You dare to insult my character?" he cried, advancing toward her. He looked so furious, veins popped out on his forehead. *"You, who spread your legs for this rogue despite being engaged to me! Why, you whore—"* He raised his palm in the air.

Alex leaped in front of Lily and caught Walford's forearm in a tight grip. "Don't you dare raise your hand to Lily!" He squeezed the duke's arm, digging his fingers between the bones. Walford cried out in pain and sank to his knees.

At Alex's show of strength and protectiveness, Hannah murmured to Benjamin, "I told you he held affection for her."

"Indeed," Benjamin said.

Alex released him, and Walford rose shakily to his feet, cradling his forearm against his chest. He retreated to stand near his mother.

Alex faced the now-silent crowd. "If any one of you says a single cruel word about Lily's character or virtue, I will deal with you. That includes you." He pointed at the servant standing silently in the corner. "I know how servants spread rumors about their employers." The servant bowed his head in acquiescence.

"And you three." Alex turned to Lily's parents and the duchess. "You had better not judge Lily, for your sins are no less. You treated her abominably. You behaved like horse traders, buying and selling her future in a business deal to satisfy your own vanity, your own lust for money and power."

His hawk-like gaze landed on a pale-faced Walford, still cradling his arm. "Then there is you, a man with incalculable vices. I won't enumerate them here, to spare you and your mother the keen embarrassment. You well know what they are. You would have treated Lily like a pawn in a master game for your own ends, and never been a proper husband to her." The duke glared at Alex but kept his tongue.

Finally, Alex turned to the prince. "I cannot speak against you, Your Royal Highness, for I consider myself a loyal subject. However, we both know what has truly transpired here."

"Indeed," the prince said, looking thoughtful. "Indeed."

Everyone remained silent following Alex's condemnation of the prince, and the prince's acceptance of it. No one said a word in their own defense. A surge of love filled Lily's heart at his words. He had defended her expertly. Passionately, even. If only it was a sign of his feelings, rather than what she knew it to be—the result of his own sense of responsibility. He took her side because he'd helped arrange this strange rescue, that's all it was.

Finally, a feminine voice broke the tense silence. "It is clear to me what must be done."

All eyes turned to Lily's older sister. Hannah rose to her feet and smoothed her skirt. "First, we Carringtons must immediately take our leave of the duke and duchess's hospitality. I'm certain they will be happy to see us gone."

The duchess lifted her nose in the air, by that silent gesture expressing agreement.

Hannah continued, "Second, Lily's reputation must be repaired. With none of us speaking of this, no one will ever learn what has transpired. I take it no one will benefit from sharing this?"

Glances were exchanged, and heads began to nod.

"That is the first step," Hannah continued. "And, of course, Mr. Drake and Lily must immediately be married."

Married? Marry Alex? Excitement filled Lily at her sister's suggestion. Valiantly she tried to stifle it. Alex was an unfettered rake. He would never agree.

"By God, yes," her father said, his expression brightening. He stepped forward and gave Alex a thorough once-over, as if analyzing his suitability. "I cannot say I like you. Yet you did well defending Lily just now. And, you have already taken what only a husband should. Because of you, Lily's prospects are so ruined, no truly decent fellow will agree to marry her. Therefore, you shall have my daughter's hand— but nothing else of hers. You shall be granted not a cent of her dowry."

Alex stiffened. "I never sought her dowry. Or her hand, for that matter," he added. Though his brutally honest words came as no surprise, it hurt Lily to hear them.

Her father shrugged. "No matter. That is the end of it. You will be married tomorrow." He began to turn away, assuming the matter had been settled.

Lily braced herself for Alex's protest. Beside her, his body remained stiff, his posture unyielding. Yet he said not a word.

"My most beautiful daughter, married to a—a nobody! This is dreadful. Simply dreadful." Mrs. Carrington sank onto the settee behind her. She extended her finger toward Alex. "I know nothing about that man. Must she marry him?"

"Yes, she must," Mr. Carrington said. He knelt beside his wife and patted her hand. "It will be all right, dear. Hannah made a sterling match. And we still have three other daughters to marry off. They'll think twice before disappointing you."

Unable any longer to witness the devastation she had wrought on her family, Lily began to walk toward the door, fighting down tears. Perhaps she hadn't thought things through. She'd reacted too precipitously, desperate to save only herself. She'd hurt her parents, her sisters—and the man she loved.

By the time she reached the door, she was almost running. She swung it open and hurried down the hall, desperate to return to her room and begin packing, desperate to leave this house forever.

"Lily. Stop."

At the sound of Alex's voice behind her, she increased her pace. She couldn't face him, not now. Couldn't face his resigned, pained expression.

"I said, stop." He grasped her arm and swung her around to face him. "Lily, I'm sorry. I didn't expect this to happen. I should have thought this through, thought ahead. I don't usually take such rash actions. That I did with you . . ." He shook his head, clearly confused and irritated with himself. "Chalk it up to an overabundance of passion on my part. You gave me an excuse to make love to you, something I had longed to do since first setting eyes on you."

"Very well," she said, her words clipped. "It was my idea, too. And I truly thank you for standing beside me as you have done, despite the detriment to your career and social standing. It has meant a great deal to me."

"Darling . . ." He reached out to her, but she took a step back.

"As for this ill-conceived notion of a marriage between us, you needn't listen to my overbearing father. You have my permission to leave at any time. I shall not hold you to plans he made on your behalf."

"Would that be your preference?" His formal tone reflected her own.

"I have no preference. I am merely a pawn, remember? Do not let your sense of honor force you into something you would prefer not to do." Yanking her arm from his grasp, she strode into her bedroom and closed the door.

Twenty-three

Alex stared at her closed door, an unfamiliar yearning filling his heart. In the space of a few hours, his life had irrevocably changed.

He could bolt, as she suggested. But he never would, and not only because of his sense of honor.

She would be his wife! The glorious Lily Carrington, the most beautiful, sensual, wonderful woman he'd ever known, would become his wife. He had no idea what the future held for him, no idea if he even had a career. But he would have Lily. How could he worry when she would be there, by his side, in his bed?

Yet he had never felt lonelier in his life.

She hated the idea of marrying him. She'd made that perfectly clear. Oh, she would go through with it, for the same reasons he would. But she had not wanted this.

He pressed his palm to the door, his chest spasming in agony. Her cool dismissal of him hurt worse than an outright rejection. They'd grown so close, shared a bond deeper than any he'd ever experienced. The pain of losing that intimacy dug deep into his soul, wounding him in places he had never before felt pain.

He would have to ignore his feelings and concentrate on making a life for her. She was taking a tremendous step down in circumstances. While he made a good living, his income was a drop in the bucket compared to her father's situation. He would never be able to provide her with the fashions, the vacations, the houses, and the servants she was accustomed to.

He would work himself to the bone to make the best possible home for her. No matter if they sent him to the farthest corners of the globe.

And he would not force his presence upon her.

Lily looked around at Alex's very male domain, his house on King Street. He had uncovered the rest of his furniture, but little else had changed since the first time she'd been here. The teak paneling and floors and forest green wallpaper, the exotic masks and artifacts on Indian wood tables, the black marble fireplace . . .

So much had transpired since the day Hannah and she had first come here. The day they'd strolled with Alex and John Moseby to the Savoy Hotel for dinner.

And Alex and she had stolen a kiss in his secret garden. Even then, she had been in love with him. Even then.

Now, he was her husband. She was Mrs. Alexander Drake. Yet she felt so distant from him. So miserable. She was never far from tears she constantly fought to hide. Guilt continued to eat at her for forcing him into such a situation. For making him equally miserable.

She watched from the door as he oversaw the cab driver unloading her luggage from the carriage. Alex no longer spoke to her in that dangerously familiar, teasing way. He had stopped flirting with her altogether. Instead, his usual spark of sophisticated humor had been dimmed, his lips tense, his expression implacable.

He hates what I've done to him. He hates that he has a wife. He had never married before, and she knew he had never planned to marry. She knew he considered a family a burden, an impediment to his career. Yet because of her manipulations, her plots, he had been tricked into marrying her.

Trapped. He must feel so horribly trapped.

Did he think she'd planned it this way? Did he have any idea how much she adored him? Did it matter?

They had been married just that morning, in Hannah's drawing room, with a local minister and no one but her family and Alex's friend John Moseby present. John had looked self-satisfied, even gleeful at finding his friend had fallen into such a trap. "I knew it," he kept repeating, as if happy to rub Alex's misfortune in his face. His attitude surprised Lily. She had thought Moseby possessed of a more sensitive character.

Her own sister Hannah was no better. "This is a wonderful day, Lily," she told her, giving her a fierce hug. "You'll see. Things could not have turned out better for you."

"You must be joking," Lily said, trying hard not to cry. "I've ruined everything."

"No, you haven't. Not at all. You did the right thing, in every way."

Her sister had always been considered a strange duck by those who didn't understand her curiously intellectual bent. For the first time, Lily was inclined to agree with them. Hannah seemed to have lost all her common sense.

The ceremony itself was a travesty, nothing like the weddings she'd imagined as a girl. Nothing like the wedding her mother had been planning on. Her mother cried inconsolably and her father looked as though he were attending a funeral. Alex had squeezed her hand in reassurance, but by his expression, her father could have been holding a shotgun to his head. Only when he kissed her, sending a spark of passion through her, did Lily feel even the smallest measure of hope that their marriage might be a success.

At least in the bedroom.

Following the ceremony, she and Alex had come immediately here, to Alex's home. With uncertain prospects, Alex had felt it best not to waste money on a honeymoon trip. And her father was in no mood to help out financially, as he'd already made perfectly clear.

Alex stepped through the door and stood in the foyer. He glanced about as if uncertain what to do next, as if he wasn't in his own home. Because she had invaded it.

"You can look around if you like," he said. "That should take you all of five minutes." He avoided her gaze, and Lily sensed he was embarrassed that this was all he had to offer.

"I've always liked your home, Alex," she said gently. "From the first night I saw it, I was impressed with how well it reflected your own sophisticated, worldly character."

"You may change whatever you like to make it fit your own personality," he said. "This is hardly the sort of home you're used to, I know."

"Nor are you used to sharing your domain."

"I suppose this is merely one of many adjustments we both must make." For a long moment he gazed down at her, as if looking for something from her.

"I suppose so."

"Very well, then." He continued studying her. After a moment, his gaze turned warmer, igniting her own desire. For a moment she forgot the dreadful wedding ceremony, remembered only how they'd been before, in bed together, locked in a passionate, earth-shattering embrace.

He seemed to remember, too. Lifting his hand, he traced her face with his fingers. His voice lowered to a seductive murmur. "You made a lovely bride."

She swallowed hard, wishing she would stop feeling so susceptible to his compliments. "I didn't even have a wedding dress."

A cloud passed over his face. He dropped his hand, and settled both hands on his hips. "I apologize." He began to turn away.

"Alex." She grasped his arm to stop him from leaving, then waited until she had his attention before speaking. "I don't blame you. For anything."

His lips lifted in a wry twist. "That's right. I was merely doing your bidding."

A chill darted down her spine. "You make it sound so very cold."

"Not cold, no. Anything but that." He grasped her arms and dragged her to him.

His sudden commanding touch chased away her chill and replaced it with desire. Yet, at the same time, she sensed a tension in him that hadn't been there when they'd made love. And underlying anger, no doubt. At her. "You still want me," she said, her voice trembling. "In bed, I mean."

"Of course," he said gruffly. "And I know you still want me. *In bed.*"

She didn't deny it. Her palms flat on his chest, anticipation built inside her as she awaited his next move.

She didn't wait long. His hands sliding around her waist, he yanked her hips hard against his so that she could feel his desire. Walking her backward into the parlor, he pressed her against the arm of the sofa until she fell backward onto the cushions. Leaning over her, he bracketed her with his arms and raked his hungry gaze down her body.

His intention shocked and thrilled Lily. He planned to take her right here in his parlor, in the middle of the day!

"You may find bedding a husband less exciting than bedding an illicit lover," he said, his eyes on her breasts swelling above her neckline.

"Not as long as it's you."

Apparently satisfied with her acquiescence, he pressed his mouth to hers.

As his potent attentions chased away her worries, just for the moment, she acknowledged that he was right. "In bed," at least, everything was perfect.

"Come this way, please."

Alex followed the bone-thin palace footman through another hall and into the wing of St. James Palace where the Prince of Wales maintained his offices. The prince's summons that morning had snapped him back to reality. For a full day, he'd been in bed with his bride. She'd been as insatiable as he, her curiosity and passion threatening to exhaust him utterly. Until she smiled in a particular way, or exposed the curve of her hip, and he desired her more than ever.

He'd tried his best to think of his passion for her as purely physical. Yet he'd quickly learned that was impossible. Every time he touched her, he was secretly expressing his love for her. Yet, because he loved her, he could not allow her to suffer because of him.

He paused outside the prince's inner office and gave his jacket a swift tug. Whatever the prince wanted from him, his only goal was to ensure that Lily had as secure a future as he could possibly provide. If that meant groveling— Well then, he would swallow his pride and grovel as he never had before.

To his surprise, the prince looked more rattled than angry. "Drake, you came." He gestured to the chair across the desk from his and dismissed his personal secretary, who closed the door behind him.

Bertie lowered his bulk into the large leather chair behind his desk. It protested under his weight. "Well, Drake. It seems you have me at a disadvantage."

"Sir?"

"You know very well what I'm talking about. You did not reveal everything during that appalling scene at Inderby. If you had, it would have caused a trans-Atlantic scandal the likes of which has seldom been seen. The English prince trying to maneuver his way into the bed of a virginal American heiress! The press would have a field-day."

Alex acknowledged the truth of his words with a nod. Yet surely the prince realized it would not be in his or Lily's best interests to publicly reveal the circumstances surrounding their marriage.

Then again, society women often gossiped, as did men in their clubs. If he or Lily were so inclined, they could start rumors that would make life extremely uncomfortable for the prince. "I suppose so, sir," he finally admitted.

"You suppose right." The prince gave a dry, humorless laugh. "I'm embroiled in enough difficulty as it is, what with this Tranby Croft business rearing its ugly head. I can't take much more. The Queen is furious with me as it is."

"I understand," Alex said. Last week, a simple card game at a house called Tranby Croft had turned ugly when one of the players, Sir William Gordon-

Cummings, was accused of cheating. He'd finally admitted it, and his fellow players—including the prince—had agreed to keep mum about the breach of honor. Of course, as things do, word got out. Angry that the pact had been broken, Gordon-Cummings was now threatening to bring the matter to court to clear his name. And the prince himself would be called as a witness—an embarrassing situation for the royal family.

By God, Alex realized, the prince was a beleaguered man. Alex might have the upper hand after all.

Planting an elbow on the desktop, the prince leaned forward. "Let's cut to the chase. What will it take for you to keep your mouth shut, and ensure your bride does the same?"

Alex sighed and crossed his ankle over his knee. Though he appeared relaxed, his mind was racing a mile a minute. The prince had actually brought him here to make him a deal! He wasn't inclined to let the prince off the hook easily. In fact, if he worked this right, he might be able to restore to Lily everything she lost in marrying him. "Do you promise to leave my wife be?"

Bertie waved his hand in the air. "Of course, of course. I have given up on having her. I confess, in the bright light of day, I am embarrassed that I thought to possess her in such a duplicitous way. It was beneath me. Yet, in my defense, at the time, I thought everyone involved would benefit. She would become a duchess, then be granted the honorable position of mistress to the prince. I did not count the girl falling in love."

In love? Alex fought to hide his irritation at the prince's foolish assumption. "I don't expect she has."

"Indeed? I find it hard to believe a well-bred girl

such as she would bed down with a fellow if her heart weren't involved."

"We're not here to discuss her heart, but her benefit," Alex said stiffly. "Do I have your word, then?"

"Yes, Drake, you have my word." He extended his hand and Alex reached across his desk to clasp it.

Alex leaned back in his chair. "Good. Now that I have that guarantee, I would like to ask you a favor."

The prince gave him a careful gaze, no doubt wondering what Alex's conditions would be. "Go on."

"While Lily may choose to return to New York, she may also choose to remain here in London. If she stays here, I would like you to give her your full support in society, so that she maintains her high and respectable position—as if she had married well. She is quite the social butterfly, as you know. I would hate to see her ostracized in any way."

"Well, no, of course not. But I'm sorry, I'm not sure I understand. What about you?"

Alex pulled in a breath. He was about to take a decisive step in freeing Lily. Without him beside her, there was no telling how far she could climb. "I have spoken with Sir Woolsey Harrison of the Foreign Office about a position in India. Because of the duke, my advancement there was put in jeopardy. I would like that to be amended."

"India . . ." The prince tapped his chin with a pudgy finger. "That's a fair idea, I should say. Get you out of the country for a matter of years, perhaps. I do like that idea, yes. Very well," he linked his fingers. "You shall have whatever position you desire. I must say, I had expected you would use this rare opportunity to request more for yourself. A title, or land, or special consideration—"

Alex stiffened. "I don't believe that would be altogether fair. I'm not a blackmailer."

"I hadn't thought of it as blackmail so much as negotiating, something I'm told you excel at. And you do seem to be an excellent negotiator—for others, if not yourself."

Sensing the interview was nearing an end, Alex lifted a finger. "There is one more thing."

The prince grew more alert, a wary look crossing his face. "There's always a catch. What is it?"

"Lily's father must be made to provide his daughter with her dowry."

Bertie grinned. "Ah! I should have known there would be something more for you."

"Not at all. I don't care if he puts the entire fortune in her name, as long as she isn't denied her inheritance."

"And you think I can have some influence?"

Alex arched his brow. This was the prince, for God's sake. Lily's socially conscious parents would obviously be susceptible to his influence. "I *know* you can."

The prince began to chuckle. "Yes, I believe I can. Upstart American financiers aren't immune to a little old-world flattery and charm. Consider it done."

"Excellent. Thank you." Alex pushed to his feet as the prince came around his desk. Again they shook hands.

At the door, Bertie clapped Alex on the back. "Well done, Alex. I'm not sure I understand your reasoning, but you neither asked for too much, nor too little, considering the favor you will be doing me in keeping mum."

Alex gave him a polite bow, accompanied by a wry smile. "I am happy to be of service, Your Royal Highness."

* * *

Lily started when the front door slammed, every one of her senses on alert. Alex was home. *Her husband* was home.

It was Monday, their first full day as a married couple. She had awakened late that morning after a night of incredible lovemaking, during which Alex had transported her to heights of pleasure she had never dreamed existed.

Yet, despite the way he kissed and caressed her, as if with his whole heart, he remained an enigma. And she remained unsure of his true feelings for her.

As for herself, she knew she would never love another man the way she loved Alex. Every moment she spent in his company, she grew more certain that Hannah was right, that things had turned out for the best. She prayed her love would be enough to sustain them both.

When she'd finally come down to breakfast, he had been on his way out the door, answering a summons to St. James Palace to see the Prince of Wales. All day Lily had wondered and worried about what the prince might want with him.

She heard him in the hall being greeted by Hasim, who unburdened him of his hat and cane. When he entered the parlor, she was standing by the sofa. Anticipation thrummed through her at seeing him again, at the possibility he might open up to her emotionally, even tonight. "Alex. You were gone all day. Were you at the palace all this time?"

Even though he smiled, a shadow dimmed his eyes. "I spent a good deal of time at the Foreign Office."

"Oh. Of course." How silly of her not to remember her husband was a workingman, like her own father! Apparently, this summer she had been spending too much time among the idle rich.

Alex joined her near the sofa. But instead of embracing her as she hoped, he took the chair across from it. "Please sit down, Lily. There is something important I need to discuss with you."

Lily didn't like the dark tone in his voice. Clearly his news wasn't good. She tucked her skirt beneath her and reclaimed her seat on the sofa. "Whatever it is, please tell it to me straight."

He hesitated, looking around the room as if trying to decide where to begin. When his cobalt eyes finally focused on hers, Lily felt as if she were looking at a stranger, he seemed so distant. She knotted her hands in her lap, trying to hide her sudden, irrational terror.

Leaning forward, Alex propped his elbows on his knees. "Can you tell me . . . Would you prefer living here in London or in New York, where you can be near your family?"

What a confusing question! "You have been offered a position in New York?"

He studied his hands a moment before meeting her gaze once more. "Actually, no. In India. I've been granted the position of personal attaché to the Viceroy himself. It's a plum assignment, the sort I've been working toward for years."

"That's wonderful, Alex. But you just asked me . . ." The meaning of his question came clear, obliterating her confusion. She could hardly breathe her question. "You're not planning to take me with you, are you?"

"I hadn't thought so, no," he calmly replied.

Lily couldn't move, not one muscle. Her entire body felt frozen as a flood of pain swept through her, threatening to extinguish her consciousness along with her heart. She accepted that Alex didn't love her. But to learn how badly he wanted to distance himself from her! A black weight descended on her, threatening to steal her breath. She closed her eyes and fought to maintain her equilibrium.

"Lily? Lily, are you well?" Alex's concerned voice penetrated her consciousness, sparking a sudden volcanic fury deep within her. She snapped her eyes open and found him kneeling before her, that face she loved so dearly only inches away. She refused to be vulnerable to him, not one more moment! She shot to her feet to put distance between them, nearly losing her balance in the process.

Alex was instantly standing beside her. He grasped her arm to steady her. "Lily?"

She tore her arm from his grasp and took several steps before turning to face him. "So, you're leaving London for India. When is this happening?" At least her voice sounded controlled. She needed to save face, to keep him from seeing how completely he'd devastated her.

"My ship leaves on Saturday."

"Saturday. This Saturday."

"Yes."

Five days! "I see. Then . . . You have a lot of preparations to make?"

He exhaled. "Exactly. That is why I need to know whether you would prefer to remain here, or live in New York, with your family. I could close up this house if you're leaving, too."

She forced a smile to her lips. "How sensible of you."

"I don't have unlimited funds, Lily," he said, sounding so very reasonable. "If no one is living here, there is no reason for me to keep this place open."

"Of course not. Well, then. I suppose I shall have to decide what to do."

"Yes. Please let me know your decision." He rose

and crossed to the door. For a moment, he paused there, gazing back at her. "Well, then," he murmured under his breath. Then he left her.

Twenty-four

"Lily? Did you hear what I said? You're going to be an aunt."

Lily sat beside Hannah on a stone bench, on the patio of Alex's home. The day was overcast, the first real autumn nip chilling the air. It suited Lily's mood.

Hannah looked so radiant and satisfied, Lily wanted to cry. She wanted to hold her sister and tell her how wonderful this news was. Yet she remained sitting awkwardly, stiffly, afraid if she moved one inch, if she said anything emotional, she would suffer a complete and thorough breakdown.

"This is why I've been so hungry. Benjamin says I'm eating for two," Hannah continued.

Lily knew she had to say something. For Hannah's benefit, she forced a smile to her lips. Truly, she was thrilled for her sister. A baby . . . Yet she found it almost impossible not to cry. So many dreams, so many hopes for the future . . . A life filled with love the likes of which she would never share with her own husband. "That's wonderful, Hannah. Truly. I'm so happy for you."

"I'm actually looking forward to going into confinement," Hannah went on. "It's a great excuse to focus on my laboratory work and avoid those dull social obligations. You know how Benjamin and I prefer each other's company . . ." Hannah's voice trailed off and she stared hard at Lily. "My goodness, I'm being selfish. I'm going on about myself when it's obvious something serious is bothering you. Tell me what's on your mind."

Lily sucked in a ragged breath, desperate to maintain her composure and not ruin this day for Hannah. "It's nothing. Please, go on."

"Lily," Hannah said in a warning voice. She grasped Lily's hand. *"Tell me."*

Lily expelled a breath. She never was good at keeping secrets from Hannah. "He's leaving me." *Leaving me* . . . Her confession obliterated her last emotional barricade and her eyes filled with tears.

"Leaving you! Alex? What do you mean?"

"His ship sails in a matter of hours. I thought I could take it in stride, his desertion. But I—" Her voice cracked, and her next words were barely a whisper. "I simply can't."

"Oh, Lily. No." Hannah enfolded her in her arms and stroked her back.

For several minutes, Lily allowed herself to be comforted. Pushing back, she explained, "We've been married only a few days, yet it's quite clear he would prefer not to have a wife." Feeling suddenly restless, she rose and began pacing, twisting her already damp handkerchief in her hands.

Since Alex's revolation, Lily had spent the week in turmoil, unsure what to say to him, how to behave, feeling only that she was in his way as he closed up the house and made plans to leave London—and her.

Except when night fell. Then, together in the silent dark, his touch alone made her feel treasured and loved.

Last night, she had almost confessed to him, almost uttered those damning words that would show him just how foolish she could be. Almost revealed that she loved him.

In the cold, dreary light of a September morning, she had resolved to stop loving him. Told herself it was for the best. She thought she would be able to talk herself into it until the moment came for him to leave her.

There, on the stoop of his house, he took her in his arms and kissed her good-bye as if he could never get enough of her.

Before she could think what to say, he'd bounded into the waiting carriage and headed for the docks, leaving her bereft.

Lily swallowed down a sob that threatened to burst from her throat. "I don't know what to do. I've already told him I refuse to stay in his London house by myself. But I don't know whether to stay in England or go home to New York. To be truthful, I don't want to go anywhere, not without him. But he doesn't love me as I do him. He wants to rid himself of me."

"I find that hard to believe. Did he explain why he thinks you wouldn't want to accompany him?"

"Probably so that he can take up with some exotic Indian woman. Resume his life as a footloose bachelor. I've heard husbands living overseas frequently live as if they don't have long-suffering wives keeping the home fires burning. He's becoming Odysseus to my Penelope. And Hannah, I do not want to play that role!"

Hannah lifted her hands, as if the answer was obvious. "You must talk to him. You cannot go on like this, not sharing your feelings."

The sheer irony of her situation struck Lily, and she gave Hannah a humorless smile. "Did you know that Father is giving us my dowry after all?"

"No, I didn't know that." Their parents and sisters had set sail the previous day for New York.

"Just the day before yesterday, the prince himself met with Father. After receiving a royal earful, Father decided he'd been too harsh, if you can believe that. I was too stunned to ask why."

Hannah looked just as mystified as Lily felt.

"And Alex—I thought he might want to celebrate with me. He has a small fortune, but he's never been wealthy. Instead, he grew more distant than ever, said something like 'Now your happiness should be assured.' Then he left the room, and that was that." Lily threw up her hands. "I tell you, Hannah, I have never been more confused. I love him so much, but he's simply not the same man I fell in love with. It's like an evil spell has been cast on him."

"Does he know how much you love him?"

Lily pondered her question. Alex *ought* to know! When he touched her, her entire body cried out for pleasure only he could give her. He had to see it! He himself had often advised her not to trust the surface, to look beneath to find reality. Couldn't he then see how she truly felt?

Then again, she had always responded to his sensuous touches, even before she recognized the love in her heart. "I—I don't know. I don't think so. I've done my best to hide it."

Hannah gave her an astounded look. "Hide that you love your husband?"

"I know that sounds silly, but if you could see how distant he's been with me since the wedding—except in bed." She felt heat creep into her cheeks.

Hannah rose and stood before her. "In my experience, that's an excellent place to start."

"Nonsense. You and Benjamin fell in love at first sight."

A trace of embarrassment flitted across Hannah's face. "Actually, I lied about that. Our situation wasn't so different from yours. But I'll save that story for another day. Right now, we need to solve your problem."

Lily stared at her in shock. "Impossible! You two love each other so much—"

Hannah smiled softly. "Yes, we do. Now. Once we each managed to set our pride aside and be honest with each other, love became the most natural thing in the world. Giving up your pride—that is exactly what you must do." Suddenly, she became all business. "Now, when did you say his ship departs?"

"Tonight. Six, I think, on the evening tide."

"My goodness, Lily. It's going on five-thirty now! We must hurry. We have no time to waste."

Try as she might, Lily could not remember the name of Alex's ship, and she had no idea of the shipping company or which dock his ship might be sailing from. Hannah's carriage jounced the two sisters hard as they drove toward the dock as fast as possible. But the closer they drew to the dock, the more crowded the streets became with carriage, cart, and foot traffic.

As each second ticked by, drawing closer to when Alex's ship would lift anchor, panic began to engulf Lily. Why hadn't she told Alex how she felt the night before? She had been so close to crying out her feelings, her love for him. But she'd been terrified of rejection—terrified she would lose him forever.

Yet here she was, as good as losing him despite having said nothing. Oh, what a fool she'd been! Perhaps he didn't love her. He ought, then, to tell her so—not run off and leave her.

"Let's think logically," Hannah said, her calm demeanor helping Lily keep her head. "P&O runs most of the lines traveling to the East."

"P&O?"

"There! That's their headquarters." Hannah banged her parasol on the roof of the carriage. Thrusting her head out the window, she cried to her driver, "Chauncy, pull up here!"

"Yes'm!" The wiry Cockney driver brought the carriage to a halt before a large building. The sign along the front identified it as the Peninsular and Oriental Steam Navigation Company.

"Come on." Without waiting for the footstool, Hannah swung open the door and leaped onto the pavement. Lily gathered her skirts in her hands and followed suit with a bit more care than her eccentric sister had exhibited.

Inside the office, Lily and Hannah found themselves at the end of a long line of customers waiting to talk to clerks behind windows.

Lily groaned. "This will take forever. His ship leaves in fifteen minutes!"

"Let me handle this." Grasping Lily's arm, Hannah dragged her to the front of the line, ignoring the furious looks and comments of those waiting their turn. She shoved Lily in front of the window. "This young lady needs to find which ship her husband is sailing on, this instant!"

The clerk glared at her. "Ma'am, if you will return to the end of the line—"

"I am Countess Hannah Ramsey, and this is an emergency!" she said in her most imperious voice.

Lily watched in amazement as the clerk's manner transformed to one of gratuitous fawning. "Countess, I am so sorry. Excuse us," he told his current customer, a businessman who seemed much less impressed by Hannah's title.

Hannah ignored his glare. "His name is Alexander Drake. He's leaving London for Bombay in a matter of minutes. You must give us the name and dock number of his ship."

The clerk looked confused for a long moment. Lily felt every beat of her heart, the seconds passing relentlessly. Finally, he began to react and not just sit there on his stool. Running his finger down a schedule before him, he muttered, "Let me see . . . Bombay, you say?"

"Yes, India," Lily said.

Hannah added wryly, "You know, the rather large subcontinent in Southeast Asia—"

The clerk shot her an impatient look. "I *know* what India *is,* ma'am," he said coolly. "We run many ships along that course. I am merely trying to determine which it may be. When is the ship departing?"

"Tonight at six."

"Goodness, yes. That would have to be the *Vectis*. The *Vectis* travels from here to Gibraltar, then to Malta, then Alexandria. Then you have a marvelous experience traveling through the Suez Canal, and on to Bombay. Marvelous invention, the canal. Reduced the voyage from three months to three weeks, can you imagine!"

Was the man trying to slow them down intentionally? "Yes, yes," Lily said. "Where is the ship? In which dock?"

"Let me see . . ." Again he dragged his finger down the schedule. He seemed to be reading every word on it, as slowly as a schoolchild.

"Please hurry," Lily said, which prompted the clerk to give her another pointed look—once again drawing his attention from the chart.

"I've lost my place. Let me see. *Vectis* . . . Ah! Here it is. The *Vectis* departs at six—"

"We know that much," Lily muttered.

"—from the Royal Albert Dock. You should find it there."

"Thank you!" Lily said, already turning to run out of the building. Hannah followed.

"You'd best hurry," the clerk called out. "It's ten of six now, and Captain Charmichael is a stickler for keeping to a schedule."

In a matter of seconds, the two ladies had climbed back aboard Hannah's carriage and started down Fenchurch Street toward the Royal Albert Docks. The effort soon became fruitless. Their carriage became jammed behind a cart trying to maneuver across the street, blocking traffic in both directions. Two carriage drivers had already engaged the cart driver in a screaming match, and a bobby on horseback was just now entering the fray.

"I can't wait for this to be resolved," Lily said to Hannah. She swung the door open. Before exiting, she leaned close to her sister and gave her a loving squeeze. "Oh, Hannah, a baby! If things work out—"

"They will," Hannah said with a reassuring smile. "I'll miss you, too. I'll have your things forwarded to you."

"But I don't know that I'm going with him," Lily protested. "He—"

"Just hurry!"

Lily nodded and scrambled out of the carriage. Hiking up her skirts, she ran through the crowd. She slipped around a longshoreman lifting barrels onto a cart, then narrowly dodged a fish flung by a fisherman toward an open warehouse. The overpowering stench of fish guts baking in the sun caused her to gag. She splashed through a puddle of mud combined with God-knew-what refuse, ruining her delicate satin shoes. Still she ran on.

Winded, she finally reached the dock. The commercial hub of the British Empire, the Royal Albert Dock was three-quarters of a mile long. Ships lined up more than three deep waiting for an open slip. With such pressure, Alex's ship was bound to leave on time. Lily scanned the ships in port, a long row stretching along the waterfront, from small schooners with clustered masts resembling a forest, to commercial steamers, their hulls rusty from years of service plying British trade routes.

She ran past two dozen slips before spotting the name *Vectis* painted on the side of a medium-size sloop. From what she could see, there was little activity around the boat, only a uniformed officer walking up the gangway. A loud horn blasted from the ship, probably giving a signal that it was about to sail.

Unconcerned about the stares from dock workers, she hiked her skirts even higher and dashed up the gangway onto the ship's deck behind the officer.

"Miss? Miss!" the officer called after her.

"My husband! I must find him. It's an emergency."

"We are about to sail—"

"Mr. Drake, which cabin is he in?" she demanded. "You must tell me!"

"Sixteen or seventeen, I believe, on Deck C. But you cannot stay aboard without a ticket, miss—"

Ignoring his protests, she ran past him toward the door leading to the passenger hold. According to the signs by the doors, she was on Deck A. She quickly located a stairway and hurried down two flights to Deck C.

Her skirt snagged on the step and she yanked at it until it tore free. She had made it aboard, but still she needed to hurry. If Alex didn't want her—if he truly didn't want her—she couldn't bear staying aboard. She would disembark immediately.

And face the future alone.

Here on Deck C, most of the cabin doors were open as porters delivered luggage to the passengers' rooms. Squeezing past a luggage cart, Lily peeked into Cabin 16.

Her heart began to pound. She had found him.

Inside the narrow second-class cabin, he sat at a cramped secretary's desk attached to the wall. He wasn't writing, but staring trance-like through a port-hole at murky waves and the barnacle-encrusted hull of the neighboring ship.

Lily's gaze traced his rugged features, noting the circles under his eyes and the oddly lost expression on his face. A swell of love filled her. *Yes,* she acknowledged fiercely, privately, *I love him.* Feeling this way, she had no need of pride.

She took a careful tentative step into the cabin. "Don't believe what you see. Isn't that what you advised me?"

Alex started as if poked by a hot brand. He jerked to his feet. "Lily! What the devil are you doing here?" Lily took another step toward him. "I'm amazed how you failed so completely to take your own advice."

"Why are you . . . We already said our farewells."

His stubborn refusal to recognize why she came stirred her ire. "And that is enough for you? Good-bye, forget me, I'm going to the other side of the world," she mocked. "Is that what you mean to do?"

His jaw tightened. "I never said I would forget."

Lily tossed back her head. "Well, I will not allow it, Mr. Drake. I will not allow you to run out on me this way."

"Run out on you!" Now it was his turn to grow angry. "I would never run out on you."

"Hah! You're doing an awfully good imitation of it." She crossed her arms. "This *is* a ship, isn't it? Or am I mistaken that you're about to travel halfway around the world?"

"I've ensured you'll be taken care of," he shot back. "You have your dowry, and I'll always provide for you."

"How sweet of you."

He slammed his fist on the desk. "Damn it, Lily. This isn't easy for me. Can't you see I'm setting you *free?*"

Free? That's what he thought he was doing? "You did not once ask me if I wanted to be free."

"Well, no, I—"

She held up a hand to cut him off, fury roiling inside her. "You presume to know my heart, without even asking me. Did it not occur to you, even once, that I might want to accompany you to India?"

Alex gazed at her, his eyes somber and dark. "Don't be foolish. I *know* you, Lily. I know you would go with your husband because you would think it the right thing to do. You certainly never bargained on marrying *me,* or being dragged to a distant country, one that can be difficult on the hardiest of women."

"You think me that weak?"

"I think you have been cheated," he said flatly. The bitterness in his words shocked her to the core. "I *know* you have. Because of me. I know how much you enjoy the social scene. With me out of the picture, you can have that again. People will remember you are married, of course, but my exact position will become muddled and unimportant as you make friends, host teas, do all those things you're so good at. Without me, you will continue to light up every significant event in London society, just as you did before." His voice turned almost bitter. "You will shine like the jewel you are."

A surge of moisture filled Lily's eyes. He honestly thought this is what she wanted! To be a celebrated member of society, even if it meant being without him.

He cares for me, the realization served to strengthen her courage, enabling her to do more than rail at him. He thought he was leaving her for her own good! Once again, he was trying to save her. Only this time, he had completely miscalculated her feelings. "Damn you, Alexander Drake. Listen to me."

He opened his mouth to respond, but at her fierce gaze, he closed it and crossed his arms, waiting for her to continue.

Lily gathered her courage and found the right place to begin—back at the beginning. "The first day we spoke, you told me not to believe what I see, to look beyond the surface. I nearly failed in doing that, when I became engaged to the duke. But I've learned since then. Unfortunately, you haven't."

"Excuse me?"

"You have never taken your own advice. Look, Alex," she urged, hands outspread. "Look closely, right here. At me. See what is right here before you. See *me.*"

He didn't answer, yet the confusion in his eyes gave her hope she could reach him. Yet he remained still and closed, his arms locked against his chest.

She took a step closer to him, then another, determined to reach him with the truth. *"See* that I love you, Alex. *See* that I want to be by your side, whether you're sent to India, or Africa, or the moon!"

She paused right before him. For a long breathless

moment, he gazed down at her, his eyes searching her face, his expression one of incredulity. "Did you just say you . . . *love* me?"

Lily laid her hands on his crossed arms. "Yes, I love you! I have for a long time. Don't you recall how I proposed to you?"

He barked out a laugh. "I thought that was a young girl's awakened desires talking."

Lily squeezed his arms in frustration. "Don't be daft. Do you think I would have invited you to seduce me if I didn't love you?"

"The prince said the same thing, but I could not believe it," he murmured. He looked positively thunderstruck, and Lily's heart began to soar.

She smiled, feeling surprisingly free. For the first time, she could express her love openly, touch him with the full depth of her heart. She slid her hands along his arms, his shoulders, and cradled the face she so dearly loved. "I wanted you to ruin me, darling, because I wanted *you.* I never expected we'd be forced to wed, at least, I don't think I considered that. No doubt deep down, that is exactly what I hoped would happen. When you became my husband, I thought I was the luckiest girl in the world—until I realized how little you wanted me as your wife."

He grasped her wrists, stilling her hands on his face. "But—you could have had any man, Lily, any man at all. You could have married a man with a title, with—"

She jerked her hands from his. "I don't care about a damned title!"

Her outburst stunned him into silence, freeing her to continue.

"You made me see that I needed to live my own life, not do whatever my parents wanted. Only with your strength was I able to defy them. It made me love you even more, having you stand beside me. I did not expect you to have to pay such a steep price for being so valiant."

"It was easy to be valiant, for you, Lily. I would do it again." Now it was his turn to reach out. To her delight, he caressed her arms, then began pulling her closer.

Lily swallowed hard as she gazed into his forgiving eyes. "I know you don't feel the same way about me. I know you never wanted a wife." She locked her arms around his neck and began to press gentle, loving kisses along the curve of his cheek and the line of his jaw. Bringing her lips to within a breath of his, she murmured, "If you'll give me a chance, I promise I'll be the best wife any man has ever had. I swear it."

"Lily Carrington—I mean, Lily Drake," he said, his voice trembling with passion. "I don't love you."

Lily's heart crashed to her feet. She froze, then began to draw away, mortification filling her.

Suddenly, he grasped her hard against his chest. "I *adore* you." Heated kisses accompanied his loving declaration, his lips tracing paths of fire on her face, her neck, her lips. "I adore the ground you walk on and the air you breathe. I *adore* you. Your face, your laugh, your bright, sparkling spirit. From the first moment I saw you, you've had my heart. I've never felt so—*entranced* before, so bloody out of control of myself."

He gave a self-deprecating laugh and shook his head. "By God, until this moment, I thought I was going crazy, I need you so much. When in truth"—his voice dropped to a gentle murmur, a benediction from the heart—"In truth, the answer is much simpler. I've fallen head over heels in love with you."

Keeping his hands tight on her waist, he stepped

backward to the desk chair and sank into it, pulling her into his lap and locking his arms securely around her. "I swear, Lily, I will make you the best damned husband any woman has ever had. If you'll give me another chance."

Lily felt as if the sun were bursting inside her, she was so happy. She threw her arms around him and gave him a fierce squeeze. Drawing back, she pressed her forehead to his. "The British in India have a society, do they not? With balls and the like? That is what I've heard."

"Yes, they do."

She arched her neck. "Then I shall be a leader among society in British India. And so shall you."

Throwing his head back, he let out a hearty laugh. "You're amazing, Lily Carrington. Simply amazing."

"It's Lily Drake to you, sir. *Mrs.* Lily Drake. For now and always." With that pronouncement, she pressed her mouth on his and sealed the deal.

Epilogue

A punkah fan attached to a rope pulled by a servant gently stirred the humid Bombay air. During the height of the September afternoon, Lily had energy for nothing greater than lifting a cool drink to her lips.

Tonight, after a short nap, she and Alex would host a ball to celebrate the start of the cool weather and launch Bombay's social season. Lily had made the festive gala an annual event.

Alex, now sitting beside her reading correspondence from the home office, enjoyed the opportunity to "showcase his wife and her amazing talents," as he put it. Lily took pride in the fact their circle of friends extended from Bombay to Calcutta and beyond. Already Alex had been promoted and now served as a high-level administrator supervising several district officers—most of them sons of nobility. While he could have stopped working because of her dowry, his career gave him too much satisfaction for him to give it up.

When she thought of their life together over the past two years, it continued to amaze her. She could not imagine what life would have been like had she not pursued Alex aboard that ship.

She'd found the society here much less rigid than that in London, and more in keeping with her freer

American upbringing. Despite rumors about their marriage that followed them from London, she and Alex had been instantly accepted into a British Indian society hungry for new faces.

If Lily had her way, that society would soon be introduced to a new female face.

"My mother is at her wit's end," Lily commented, drawing Alex's attention.

He arched a brow. "What is it this time?"

"Don't be rude," Lily lightly chastised. Yet she was unable to hide a smile. "My sister Pauline refuses to come out into society."

Alex set aside his papers and shot her a curious look. "Is that possible?"

Lily shrugged. "Pauline has no intention of marrying, apparently, so she feels no need to enter the marriage market."

"Well, let's invite her to visit us. If anyone can help her become a success in society, it's you."

Lily leaped to her feet. Leaning over her husband's chair, she gave him a swift, heartfelt embrace. "Thank you! I knew you'd be agreeable. I'll send her an invitation right away."

"Are you sure she wants this? If she's not inclined to marry, she won't be thrilled to join the fishing fleet." British men in India had coined the term *fishing fleet* to describe the single ladies who flocked here during the cool season in search of husbands.

Lily waved away his concern. From her own experience, she couldn't fathom even her high-spirited sister Pauline not wanting to fall in love and marry. "Oh, she's just confused. Besides, she'll be a great help when the baby comes."

Alex looked as if he'd been struck by thunder. "When the—What did you say?"

"Oh, Alex, don't be daft. I said when the baby

comes. You must realize that all that activity in the bedroom would eventually lead to a baby. As Baroness de Veaux explained to me, when a man and a woman—"

Suddenly caught up in her husband's arms, she let out a cry of delight. He swung her around, making her stomach even more unsettled than it had been just that morning.

Alex set her back on her feet and smiled down at her. "You continue to amaze me. I suppose this means I must share you—not with one new person, but two. And that means only one thing."

"Which is?"

Grasping her hand, he led her back inside toward their bedroom. At the door, he gave her a wickedly sensual grin. "Simply that we must make the most of the time we have alone together."

Lily squeezed his hand, delight filling her. She could only agree.

Thrilling Romance from Lisa Jackson